Praise for
New York Times and USA Today Bestselling Author

Diane Capri

"Full of thrills and tension, but smart and human, too."
Lee Child, #1 New York Times Bestselling Author of Jack Reacher Thrillers

"[A] welcome surprise….[W]orks from the first page to 'The End'."
Larry King

"Swift pacing and ongoing suspense are always present…[L]ikable protagonist who uses her political connections for a good cause…Readers should eagerly anticipate the next [book]."
Top Pick, Romantic Times

"…offers tense legal drama with courtroom overtones, twisty plot, and loads of Florida atmosphere. Recommended."
Library Journal

"[A] fast-paced legal thriller…energetic prose…an appealing heroine…clever and capable supporting cast…[that will] keep readers waiting for the next [book]."
Publishers Weekly

"Expertise shines on every page."
Margaret Maron, Edgar, Anthony, Agatha and Macavity Award Winning MWA Past President

NIGHT JUSTICE

by DIANE CAPRI

Published by: AugustBooks
http://www.AugustBooks.com

ISBN: 978-1-940768-00-7

Original cover design by Michelle Preast
Interior layout by Author E.M.S.

Published in the United States of America.

Visit the author website:
http://www.DianeCapri.com

ALSO BY DIANE CAPRI

The Hunt for Justice Series
Due Justice
Twisted Justice
Secret Justice
Wasted Justice
Raw Justice
Mistaken Justice (*novella*)
Cold Justice (*novella*)
False Justice (*novella*)
Fair Justice (*novella*)
True Justice (*novella*)
Night Justice

The Hunt for Jack Reacher Series
(in publication order with Lee Child source books in parentheses)
Don't Know Jack (The Killing Floor)
Jack in a Box (*novella*)
Jack and Kill (*novella*)
Get Back Jack (Bad Luck & Trouble)
Jack in the Green (*novella*)
Jack and Joe (The Enemy)
Deep Cover Jack (Persuader)
Jack the Reaper (The Hard Way)
Black Jack (Running Blind/The Visitor)
Ten Two Jack (The Midnight Line)
Jack of Spades (Past Tense)

The Jess Kimball Thrillers Series
Fatal Enemy (*novella*)
Fatal Distraction
Fatal Demand
Fatal Error
Fatal Fall
Fatal Edge
Fatal Game
Fatal Bond
Fatal Past (*novella*)
Fatal Dawn

The Heir Hunter Series
Blood Trails
Trace Evidence

CAST OF PRIMARY CHARACTERS

Judge Wilhelmina Carson
George Carson

Chief Ben Hathaway
Augustus Ralph
Chief Judge Ozgood Richardson
Kate Austin Columbo

Charles Evan Hayden
Kelly Webb
Tom Bradford
Cindy Allen
Genevieve Rogers
Mitch Rogers

For Aunt Mary

NIGHT JUSTICE

CHAPTER ONE

Tuesday, November 8
10:15 p.m.

TUESDAY NIGHT'S DRIVE HOME began in total exhaustion and ended in tragedy. I was guilty of a moment's inattention, and it changed our lives forever. I'll never forgive myself for that mistake. That's on me.

But what followed wasn't my fault. Not even remotely. It could have happened to anyone.

I'd stopped at a red light on Kennedy Boulevard and glanced through the rain-soaked windshield at the dark November streets. A red-brick building on the corner was colorfully lit for the holidays. A party inside was in full swing. Revelers in business suits and ties were having a good time and toasting liberally. Probably an office party. 'Twas the season.

It was past ten p.m., and I hadn't eaten since breakfast. I was feeling hungry and a bit restless, my thoughts jumbled. Normally during a long trial, my assistant would have laid out a working lunch—tuna, iced tea—giving me time during the midday to breathe a bit.

Didn't happen today, or any day in the last two weeks. Later, I wondered whether a midday respite might have made a difference.

Nothing but a snarl of phone calls and endless stacks of paperwork in the morning was followed by more dreary testimony and bickering lawyers late into the evening. Some were calling the case playing out now in my courtroom "the bank robbery trial of the century."

Given how early we were in the century, that seemed a bit grandiose for my taste. And there were no guns and masks or explosives involved in the thefts. The case did involve stolen millions, and the trial might end with a bunch of high-profile bankers behind bars. I supposed we could hope this *was* the bank robbery of the century, and we wouldn't have a more destructive one to look forward to.

Still, at this point, I simply found the whole thing exhausting.

The weather, of course, hadn't helped. Tampa's nearly perpetual sunshine had vanished. The night was murky and wet and generally foreboding, thanks to a lingering storm system from a late-season hurricane that had fizzled in the Atlantic.

All of which was why I wanted only to get home. I craved a few hours of peace and a good night's sleep before I had to face down the snarling suits across my bench again tomorrow.

As I accelerated through the green light, moving along my usual route toward Bayshore Boulevard, my car seemed to know the way.

I couldn't blame my car for what happened, though. Self-driving cars were still a dream of the future. My hands remained firmly on the wheel, and my foot was the one on the accelerator. No one else was responsible.

Like I said, the mistake was on me. I'd relaxed my vigilance. I shouldn't have.

Vaguely aware of the traffic, my thoughts returned to the case that had consumed my working hours for weeks.

Campbell, et al., v. First Nation's Bank, et al. was the official case name.

Early on, behind the scenes, my clerks began calling it *Big Deal Money Men who lost everything v. Tons of Giant Banks who could pay if they wanted to but would rather not.* When my staff had tired of repeating that mouthful, they'd abbreviated it to *Stingy Dudes Behaving Badly*—which was a pretty accurate description of the conflict. Eventually, the joke became simply *Stingy Dudes*, which was what we'd called the case privately for several months.

My gut said there was plenty of fault to go around in the behavior of all parties. My gut was very reliable. But justice was supposed to be blind, so I made every effort to conceal that these guys, and their lawyers, got on my last nerve.

I wasn't succeeding in my efforts, though. I shrugged. Judges are human, too.

A squad car passed me in the next lane, and my thoughts shifted back to the drive again.

Soon, I would be switching lanes so I could eventually make a left onto the bridge. I eased Greta's accelerator down, going a bit faster despite the weather, loving the purr of her engine around me as I rumbled down the slick roadway. I was traveling at the speed limit, which was still forty, although it was set to change in a couple of months.

We moved into the left lane after we passed the ramp to the Davis Islands Bridge.

Minaret, the house my husband George had inherited from his eccentric Aunt Minnie, reigned on Plant Key, our own private island in Hillsborough Bay. I was pleased to see its twinkling lights welcoming me in the distance.

I'd be home in less than ten minutes, and I was looking forward to getting there.

A weird sense of unease had plagued me all day. Normally, I made the drive home before nightfall and relished the trip. I loved the sparkling turquoise water off the Florida coast and the warm tingle of sunlight on my skin. But the dreary weather, November's shorter daylight hours, and the *Stingy Dudes* case meant I'd seen none of that lately.

My plan was simple. Get home, have a nice hot bath, and enjoy a quiet dinner. My mouth watered and my stomach growled as I pondered my choices. George's Place, my husband's restaurant that occupied the first floor of our house, employed some of the best chefs in the country. Diners traveled from up and down the coast to feast on gourmet dishes to rival any served at a royal table.

The dinner special this Tuesday night was steamed lobster. I'd looked it up online. My stomach gurgled, and I suddenly couldn't wait to sink my teeth into the succulent, buttery seafood drenched in rich and creamy cognac sauce. I could almost taste it, which only made my stomach roar loud enough to be heard two counties away.

I grinned. Maybe I'd even splurge and have a crème brûlée for dessert and—

Suddenly, a shadowed solid something appeared a few feet in front of my car, as if it had materialized from the ether, like spacemen beaming down via one of those transporters in a sci-fi movie.

"What the hell was that?" I said, squinting through the windshield.

A big, shiny, black trash bag?

Everything happened all at once after that, in a micro-second.

CHAPTER TWO

Tuesday, November 8
10:25 p.m.

I SLAMMED ON GRETA'S brakes, and her tires squealed.

Time slowed as I skidded on the wet pavement.

The Mercedes's traction control kicked in, automatically pumping the pedal beneath my foot like a phantom driver.

My fists grabbed the wheel, clenched so tightly they ached.

The skid seemed to go on forever.

My neck and shoulders felt sore from the strain as I prayed fervently to avoid the obstacle, even as I braced for impact.

Then came the sickening *thud.*

Soft flesh meeting hard metal.

The mass tumbled up across my hood, then rolled back down onto the asphalt.

A single loud beep issued from Greta's dashboard before dying away, though the airbags did not deploy.

My seatbelt snapped like a rubber band, jerking me back as my heart pounded, a thundering herd of runaway cattle. My chest ached already from the pounding and the seatbelt and the tension. But I wasn't the one who had absorbed the bulk of the blow.

After we stopped, I sat there, too stunned to move, too shocked to think clearly. An eerie silence enveloped the cabin as I gathered myself together.

I felt like I was moving through viscous air for a long time, even though only a couple of moments passed.

A quick bodily assessment confirmed that I was shaken up but uninjured.

I hoped I could say the same about whatever I'd hit.

Slowly, I turned to squint out the window. Greta had ended up diagonally across both lanes of traffic, her nose mere inches from a huge steel light pole near the curb. Several other cars had stopped nearby.

Some must have witnessed what happened. Others had arrived just shortly after the impact.

A knock on my driver's-side window.

In a daze, I pressed the button to lower it, blinking up into the face of an older gentleman I didn't recognize.

"Ma'am? Are you all right?" he asked, his expression as shocked as I felt.

Adrenaline coursed through my body, causing sweats and tremors and an almost uncontrollable desire to vomit. I closed my lips tightly and tried to breathe.

Numbly, I nodded, unfastened my seatbelt, and fumbled for the door handle with shaking fingers.

What had I hit?

From the size and shape as it crossed the hood, I guessed it was a person. But I desperately wanted to be wrong. The mass had come out of nowhere, almost like it had jumped or been shoved into traffic. I'd tried to stop, but I couldn't and—

I stumbled from the car, ignoring the gawking onlookers as I made my way around the front of the vehicle.

My car's hood ornament had been stolen from the valet parking at one of the posh hotels a few weeks earlier. Which now seemed like a blessing. The metal ornament had projected up from the hood about five inches. It was heavy and substantial enough to have done serious damage to soft tissue. It might have even impaled a human body.

The center of Greta's hood, over the Mercedes logo, was crushed from the impact, and her front bumper was dented. But the damage to my car barely registered as I stared at a foot sticking out in front of the right front tire. A water-logged shoe dangled from sock-clad toes.

A man. On the pavement. Partially under my car.

I had hit a human being with four-thousand pounds of moving vehicle. The damage would be like battering a baby with a baseball bat.

Time sped up then, and things blurred around me. I don't really remember rushing forward or kneeling down, yet the wet pavement was cold and bit into my knees through my black suit.

I felt his neck for a pulse, heart in my throat. My stomach was nothing but a churning black hole of doom. Years and years of legal jargon looped through my head in an endless torrent as I pressed my numb fingers to his carotid artery.

I stifled a sob. *Please don't let him be dead. Please, please, please.*

Then I felt a very faint bump-bump under my fingertips. Was it his pulse or mine? I couldn't tell.

I checked his breathing, found nothing, and began CPR, working on automatic pilot.

Sirens whined in the cold November night, drawing closer, closer.

I kept at it. Obsessively checking his pulse between breaths and chest compressions, alternately afraid he'd die and terrified that I'd already killed him.

He wasn't moving. No normal rise and fall of breathing.

The way he was angled—turned away from the streetlight which cast him in shadows—prevented me from getting a look at his face.

What I could see was the suit he had on, which was tattered and torn, probably due to the impact. The deep-blue silk tie, now wet with rain, glistened beneath the streetlight's glow.

The thing running through my mind was constant repetition of the only prayer that mattered. *Don't let him be dead. Please don't let him be dead.*

While I continued CPR, I noticed more about his clothing. Not only the pricey silk tie. Top-of-the-line Italian wool suit. Shiny, custom-made leather loafers, which now reflected the glare of Greta's headlights.

Almost nonsensically, my brain registered that this guy wasn't a jogger or one of Tampa's population of wandering homeless.

But who was he? Where did he come from?

And why had he jumped into my travel lane like that?

I shuddered in the cold rain and kept up the CPR. I finished another round of breaths and compressions then felt for his pulse again. Another bump-bump. Then another. His pulse. Not mine. Still faint, still weak, but there.

Wasn't it?

He was still alive. He was alive. Alive. Not dead.

At least for now.

Or maybe I was imagining the pulse because I *wanted* it to be there so much. Either way, I kept working.

An ambulance finally screeched to a halt, and two paramedics rushed over to the scene. I moved to the sidelines to let them take over.

Every muscle in my body was achy, twitching.

Thoughts tumbled over themselves. Someone had called the police. Good.

I should've called the police. I'm a United States District Court judge. I know when the cops need to be involved, and they definitely needed to be here.

Yet, I hadn't even called 911. Why not?

You didn't have time.

Where's your phone?

Dizziness overtook me, and my knees threatened to buckle.

Sit down. Before you fall down.

I wandered over to a nearby streetlight and leaned against it for support. Somewhere down the block, the sounds of a lively party echoed into the night, the direct opposite of the horror happening in front of me.

"Ma'am." One of the paramedics came over to me as the other continued to work on the man. He took my arm and shook me slightly to get my attention. "Please, ma'am. Come with me to the ambulance so I can check you out."

CHAPTER THREE

Tuesday, November 8
10:45 p.m.

I STUMBLED AFTER HIM to his rig and sat on the back. He began to examine me, feeling my head, neck, and limbs. Red and blue lights flashed through the darkness, and the wail of sirens grew nearly deafening as responders arrived on scene.

A fire truck had arrived as well. Probably to assist the EMTs. They often worked in tandem during health emergencies.

My logical brain continued to chug along while my emotions were a total mess.

"Do you have pain anywhere?" the EMT asked. "Can you tell me your name and age?"

"N-no, I'm not hurt. My name's Wilhelmina Carson, and I'm thirty-nine," I mumbled through chattering teeth. Along with the shock, the chill in the air seeped deep into my bones and made me shiver.

The EMT grabbed a blanket and wrapped it around my shoulders before palpating my arms and legs for injury. I continued to stare at the man lying on the pavement as a fireman assisted the second EMT. They slipped a neck brace around the man's neck, then together they carefully hoisted him onto a rolling gurney. They covered him with a blanket the same as the one I was desperately clutching in my hands.

"Will he be okay?" I asked, though they likely wouldn't know anything much at this point. He still hadn't opened his eyes, hadn't responded to any stimuli at all since I'd battered him with my car.

Oh, God...

Nausea roiled through me, and I swallowed hard to keep from dry heaving.

"We're doing everything we can for him, ma'am," the paramedic said, seeing my distress.

He was good at his job, kind and soothing and calm. I focused on him to steady my crazy, tilting reality. He looked to be in his early thirties, African American, tall and muscular. His name patch, stitched into his lab coat in flowing cursive font, was *Johnson*.

"Is there someone I can call for you, ma'am? A friend or family member?" Johnson asked, shining a light into my eyes to test my pupils.

"M-my h-husband. G-george C-carson." The shaking was getting worse as the enormity of what had happened settled over me like a shroud. I'd hit a pedestrian with my car. If he died, I'd be a killer.

I closed my eyes and ran through the events in my head, like watching a video.

I hadn't been driving recklessly, had I? Surely not. I was a fast driver, aggressive, but competent. My mind had wandered. I didn't recall the moments before I saw him at the last second in the roadway.

Think about it, Willa.

I'd sped up. But Greta had been traveling well within the posted speed limit. Hadn't she?

The roads were wet but not overly slick.

Yet, I'd been unable to stop when that man...had what?

Fallen? No. Not fallen exactly.

I shook my head slowly. He'd stumbled. Off balance. Like he'd been drinking, maybe.

Bile rose again, burning my throat. I opened my eyes and glanced at the scene once more. Video. Were there traffic cameras close by? Would they find video of the incident?

Johnson said, "Stay with me, ma'am. We're almost done here, and then the police will want to talk with you."

Right. The police. I nodded, noticing more vehicles had arrived. Vans. White news vans with television logos on the sides.

"What day is it?" Johnson asked, jarring me back to the present.

I'd hit a man with my car, quite possibly killed him.

Even if he wasn't dead now, he might not survive much longer.

What were the chances that he'd survive after being hit with a car traveling forty miles an hour? Not good.

I shuddered. I'd experienced more than enough death, personally and professionally. My heart went out to his family. All too well, I knew the survivors' overwhelming sense of loss, the gnawing fear.

Even if I didn't end up in prison, things would never, ever be the same.

I shuddered again as the shock threatened to swamp me.

"Ma'am?" Johnson prodded. "Did you hear me? What day is it?"

I swallowed hard around the lump of dread in my throat. "Uh, Tuesday, November fifteenth."

"Good." Johnson shined a bright penlight in each of my eyes again, then stepped back. For a moment, I saw only glowing dots from the glare on my retinas.

My vision cleared, and another man moved into my line of sight—a uniformed police officer, his silver badge glittering in the flashing red and blue lights. *Here we go.* An overwhelming dread settled atop everything else.

He stepped forward and gave a slight nod. "Ma'am, I'm Officer Briggs, Tampa PD. I'll need your license and registration."

I told him where to find the documents and gave him permission to look. License in my wallet, registration in Greta's glove box. He dug them out and took them back to his squad car to run me through the system.

A few moments later, he came back and returned the documents to me. "Judge Carson, I need to ask you a few questions about what happened here."

I relayed the facts succinctly. The man darted out into traffic. He left me no time to stop. I administered CPR until help came.

When I'd finished, Johnson and his partner were loading the man into a second ambulance. His head was still uncovered, an oxygen mask now strapped to his face. His crisp, white shirt had been pulled open. The wet blue tie sat cockeyed around his neck.

The oxygen mask was a good sign, right? They wouldn't give oxygen to a corpse.

Briggs finished scribbling my words onto a small, square notepad, then gestured toward his squad car, which was parked diagonally beside Greta. "Ma'am, I'm going to need you to step over here with me so I can perform a field sobriety test and administer a breathalyzer and a couple of presumptive drug tests."

He didn't ask for my permission. He wasn't required to. I was well aware that I could refuse, and any half-witted lawyer would have. But I'd had nothing to drink, ingested no prescription meds, and I never took illegal drugs of any kind. Nor would they find anything of the sort in my car.

I had nothing to hide. A search and presumptive tests that returned negative results would exonerate me in several respects. I was confident the results would be negative, and the sooner that was settled, the better.

So I consented, nodding.

My legs quivered as I slid down off the back of the rig, and for a moment, I worried they wouldn't support me. A small knot of onlookers had gathered around the accident scene. The rain had suppressed the size of the crowd. Low murmurs filled the air. Gawkers took photos, and several others appeared to be videotaping using the scourge of modern America, the smartphone.

Had anyone called George?

"D-do you know who he is?" I asked, noticing the catch in my voice, probably caused by excess adrenaline. But it made me sound weak and vulnerable, and I didn't like it. I cleared my throat and tried again. "Why did he dart into the street? For that matter, why was he outside at all on a night like this?"

Briggs asked me to perform a few simple tasks, which I did. He pulled out his breathalyzer.

"Please breathe into this, ma'am," he replied, in lieu of answering my questions. He thrust a small, gray plastic box in front of my face.

I did as he asked, watching the second paramedic rig.

The fire-rescue team was now assisting the police with crowd control. A tow truck grumbled toward us on Bayshore Boulevard to haul my poor Greta away.

The odd numbness in my body lingered, which was probably good, given the amount of adrenaline in my system. I peered in the direction of my home, hoping to see George. He was my rock. We'd been through so much together in our seventeen years of marriage. This would be yet another chasm to cross.

Shouts echoed off the buildings surrounding the scene and drew my attention back to the crowd. Seemed odd so many people would flock to this area on a Tuesday night. Until I heard my name being whispered by the onlookers. Someone had recognized me.

In the technology age, my identity was always just a click or two away on those damn smartphones. Nothing drew rubberneckers like a potential scandal.

I turned back to Officer Briggs and asked again, "Have you discovered who the man is?"

"Not yet, Judge Carson." His attention was still focused on his notes and not me.

"Okay." I clutched the damp blanket tighter and stared through the darkness at the lights on Plant Key Bridge, hoping George would arrive soon. He'd be in the middle of dinner service now, his restaurant packed with diners. It might take him a bit to get away.

The doors to the ambulance slammed shut, and I jumped. Through the back windows of the rig, I spotted Johnson, the paramedic who'd helped me earlier. Our gazes met. In his dark eyes, I saw resignation and a flicker of judgment before the ambulance drove off toward the nearest hospital, Tampa Southern.

Officer Briggs had me repeat the breathalyzer again, pursuant to protocol. By then, the crime-scene techs had shown up to begin their work. They were still cordoning off the area when George arrived.

"Willa, are you okay?" George rushed over to me and pulled me into a tight hug. I was tall for a woman, almost six feet. But he towered over me.

People who knew my husband—and really, around Tampa anyway, who didn't?—described him as handsome in a Tom Selleck at fortyish-minus-the-mustache sort of way.

But there was more to George than good looks. He was also keenly intelligent, affable, fair-minded. And honorable to a fault. I'd never been happier to see anyone in my life.

"I'm o-kay," I said, my face muffled by the front of his yellow polo shirt. I held on to him like a lifeline. Involuntary tremors ran through me. I wanted to sit, and at the same time, I wanted to walk around to burn off the energy zinging through my system. I didn't know what was best at that point. The whole experience was horribly surreal.

George pulled back and frowned.

"Let's get you to the ER and have you checked out." He glanced toward Officer Briggs. "Is that all right? Do you need her for anything else here?"

"Not at the moment, sir." Briggs straightened. "I'll catch up with you two again at the hospital."

I didn't need medical attention—I wasn't the one who'd been slammed by a car—but I let George lead the way.

CHAPTER FOUR

Tuesday, November 8
11:15 p.m.

"I'M FINE. REALLY. JUST a bit shaken up," I told Dr. Parker, the young ER resident who was examining me at the hospital. Was it my imagination or did these doctors keep getting younger and younger?

He requested, and I supplied, consent to draw and test bodily fluids. He drew a couple of vials of blood. Swabbed my cheek for DNA. Requested and received a urine sample.

When I came back from the toilet, I glanced at George, who was leaning against the wall in my trauma bay while talking quietly on his cell phone. He'd picked up his calls and waited until after the doc began questioning me to return this one. From the sourness of his expression, it was probably our insurance agent.

I turned my attention back to Dr. Parker. "Any word on the victim?"

He gave a brief shake of his head. "I'm not allowed to discuss other patients, ma'am."

Once the initial shock had worn off, a needling unease had settled over me. I was not normally on the wrong side of the law. Quite the opposite. Not only did I administer the law daily in my courtroom, but I was also a lawyer, and a damn good one. My friends and many members of my family were lawyers. Even now, years after I'd stopped practicing, folks asked me for legal advice at parties and social gatherings all the time.

I usually demurred because judges aren't supposed to give legal advice. Or take cases.

But never had I been the one responsible for any injustice or harm to another person in my life. Certainly, I'd never battered anyone with a deadly vehicle, or anything else.

This was all a first for me, and I couldn't quite comprehend it. So far, no one had suggested arresting me, which was about the only good news.

George hung up and headed over to the exam table, taking my icy hand in his warm one and forcing a smile that didn't quite erase the anger in his eyes. "You okay?"

I nodded. "Who were you talking to?"

He looked away, and the lines between his brows deepened. "Oz."

He meant Chief Judge Ozgood Richardson. The man we usually called CJ if we were discussing his professional role. Oz was what we called him at dinner parties when we couldn't avoid being in the same room at a social event. Which was as rarely as I could manage without being downright rude.

My heart stumbled. I'd expected to have to deal with CJ at some point about all this, but not so soon.

Not that CJ was my primary concern at that moment. He wasn't my boss, and he had no control over me, even if he pretended he didn't know that.

Federal judges couldn't be fired. We were appointed for life, unless we were impeached for bad behavior. Problem was, according to CJ, the only kind of behavior I ever engaged in was bad. He'd been gathering black marks against me since my very first day. At least it felt that way to me, and he never bothered to deny it.

I shook my head. Tonight's events would be spread far and wide by social media vultures. Which would give CJ the ammunition he'd been hoping for, allowing him to bring formal charges against me. Which he would do in a hot New York minute. No doubt about it.

"How did he find out so soon?" I croaked.

"Willa, it's all over the news." George sighed. "Those crews at the scene were feeding live to the stations. They're legitimate news agencies, so they won't sensationalize this thing. But I'm guessing everyone in Tampa knows by this point."

"Swell," I said sourly.

Those needles I'd felt inside jabbed harder than the ones the young doc had used to draw blood. The legitimate news teams were okay. They'd report the facts and keep it fair and balanced. But the tabloids and amateurs looking to go viral online were bound to follow. Just a matter of time before they swarmed all over me like ravenous snakes on a dead rat. And not too much time, either.

I forced words past my constricted vocal cords. "What did CJ say?"

George exhaled slowly, a small muscle ticking near his tense jaw. "He's…not happy."

I expected that. Hell, I wasn't happy, either. Neither was the poor man I'd hit with my car. Nobody was happy tonight. How could we be?

I squeezed my eyes shut against the unexpected sting of tears. I wouldn't cry. I never cried in public, and I did not intend to start now. Besides, I had nothing to cry about. I was alive and well, unlike that poor man who had been lying under my car in the street...

Anxiety threatened to overwhelm me again. My heart raced, and my breath quickened. I deliberately took long, slow breaths. The last thing I needed was to give the hospital a reason to keep me here overnight. All I wanted was to go home.

"I need to check on some lab results, Mrs. Carson," Dr. Parker said, scribbling something on the clipboard he held in his hands. "I'll be back in a moment."

The industrial-gray curtains fluttered behind him as he passed through on his way out.

I turned to George. My tone was surprisingly flat despite the urgency raging through my system. "Have you heard anything about the man? Will he be all right?"

"I saw Chief Hathaway in the corridor. He'll be down to talk to us." George rubbed my chilled fingers, trying to warm them. It was no use. I might never be warm again. "He said the official word is that the man is in critical condition."

"Do they have an ID on him yet?" I'd been asking this question since the incident. If I focused on the practical, I could function. The man's identity seemed like a concrete step in the right direction.

"No." George inhaled sharply and rubbed his eyes with his free hand. "No wallet or anything in his suit. Officer Briggs said they put him at about thirty-five years old, give or take. That's the best they've been able to do so far."

I nodded miserably and said nothing more.

Dr. Parker returned. "Your breathalyzer tests, both at the scene and here in the ER, were negative. We won't have full toxicology results on your blood tests for a while, but preliminary results are negative for controlled or illegal substances."

Irritation bubbled inside me. They had rules. Protocols to follow. But I wished they'd quit concentrating on advising me and double down on the victim instead. Without a positive ID, his family couldn't be notified. The people who loved and missed him would have no idea where he was. And we wouldn't know why he'd walked in front of my car. Which was important, too. First things first.

Dr. Parker handed me final papers to sign, then discharged me. Cut and dried. Over and done. I slid off the table, my balance still a bit unsteady. It was past eleven o'clock, and I felt like the walking dead. Body achy and sore from the tension more than anything else, and spirit defeated.

George walked me out into the hall, his arm around my shoulders like a shield. I was more than grateful for his strength and quiet presence as we headed toward the mob of gawkers, legitimate media, and wannabes.

Thankfully, no cameras had been allowed inside, though I could see them through the floor-to-ceiling glass windows lining the front of the waiting area.

The waiting room was deserted except for a couple sitting in the corner. A woman with shoulder-length, medium-blond hair was crying softly on the shoulder of a large, attractive man sporting a dark buzz cut and a beard. Of course, I wasn't the only one involved in a crisis tonight. I hoped these two would weather whatever storm they were passing through.

Tampa Police Chief Ben Hathaway waited for us near the front doors. George headed straight for him.

Ben was a burly guy, not fat, but not exactly a bodybuilder type, either. He was dressed in his usual rumpled navy-blue suit.

He met my gaze directly, expression somber, and cleared his throat. "I thought you should know they called him."

I understood what he meant. The doctors had pronounced him dead and stated the time. The man I'd hit with my car was dead.

It felt like the earth had vanished from beneath my feet. Thank God for George's arm around me or I might've crumbled to the floor.

I'd killed a man.

Not intentionally. And not immediately. He'd been alive at the scene, right? I'd felt his pulse myself. Maybe.

But he was dead now. And I was at fault. One more thing I couldn't fathom. Not yet.

"He was alive when they brought him in, wasn't he?" My voice was barely more than a weak whisper.

"Don't know all the facts yet. I'm sorry." Ben shook his head, pulled out his buzzing cell phone, and frowned at the screen. "I need to get back. I'll come by your place as soon as I can. Could be tomorrow, though. We still have a lot to do here and at the scene. Please go directly home and stay home until I get there. Please. Save all of us from having to defend ourselves against the publicity. You know how out of control these things can get, very quickly."

I searched his face for hidden messages. "Are you saying I should call a good lawyer, Ben?"

"I'm not in a position to answer that question. But in your shoes, I'd certainly consider it." With that, he walked away, leaving us to stare after him, stunned.

CHAPTER FIVE

Wednesday, November 9
12:25 a.m.

I WAS ALL TOO familiar with the rules in a vehicular homicide case. I knew I could be arrested and charged.

Except I hadn't been drinking, hadn't been speeding, hadn't done anything reckless. Not in the least.

The man had leapt into the path of my vehicle with no warning.

And now he was dead. Dead.

The word kept ringing in my head like a gong.

I glanced toward the couple in the corner again. She wiped her eyes with a tissue while he rested his hands on her shoulders. She reminded me of someone, a singer.

Sheryl Crow—that was it. Pretty. Blonde. Willowy. She was obviously distraught, and I wondered why she was at the hospital tonight.

My trembling started anew as shock and exhaustion overtook me.

George must have sensed my growing dismay, or maybe I looked like I might pass out. He guided me to a row of plastic chairs and pulled me into one.

"Whatever happens, we'll deal with this together. Like we always have. This was an accident. You weren't at fault. Notice that Hathaway didn't call the man a 'victim.' That means something. At the very least, he hasn't made up his mind about who's at fault here."

I nodded. His voice held true conviction, for which I was grateful. I wasn't feeling all that strong myself and having him to lean on helped.

His voice was angry when he said, "I won't let CJ railroad you into anything. Don't worry even a moment about that."

I frowned as my mind snagged on his words. "Did CJ say something about that when you talked to him?"

"He's too clever to tip his hand. And he didn't have to say anything specifically. He's had it out for you for a long time. You've always been too independent, too stubborn. Which is one of the many reasons I love you, by the way." George smiled, nodded once, and then gave a derisive snort. "I'm sure he'd like nothing better than to end your career and replace you with someone more amenable."

"Oh, God." I squeezed my eyes shut, hoping that when I opened them again, I'd be awakening from nothing more than an exhaustion-induced nightmare.

No such luck.

I peered around the ER. Still the same old tile floors and antiseptic smell in the air. Guilt and sadness threatened to pull me under like a riptide.

I'd killed a man. Run him down with my car. Killed him. Dead.

I shook off the errant thoughts clogging my head and darting around the corners like cockroaches in the dark. *Focus, Willa. Focus.*

George squeezed my shoulder reassuringly then stepped toward the doors. They swished open, allowing a gust of humid, rain-scented air inside. "I'll pull my car around to the entrance. You can wait here."

"Why?" I squinted up at him, the beginnings of a monster headache coming on—whether from lack of food or overwhelming stress, I wasn't sure. Probably both at this point. "It's not that far to walk. Let me go with you."

"It's better if I drive around and pick you up." He pointed outside, and I turned to see the vehicles circling the hospital parking lot. If we didn't get out of here soon, we'd be stormed by gawkers, not all of them friendly.

My stomach lurched.

"Trust me, the last thing we need right now is a public flogging," he said.

Reluctantly, I watched him walk through the automatic doors alone, head down, as he barreled toward the outpatient parking area.

George had experience avoiding nosy reporters, but these gawkers were different. The legitimate press had better things to do than follow me around, but the tabloids and social media junkies could be relentless.

Several gawkers were setting up cameras on the sidewalk as George walked past. Amateur video was worth a thousand words online these days, even if the video was poor quality.

One of the men was holding a microphone attached to his cell phone by a cable. He looked somewhat familiar, but I couldn't see him well from this distance. He wasn't one of the local reporters I knew. But he was wearing a jacket and tie, which meant he was overdressed compared to his compatriots standing around out there.

The couple in the corner of the waiting room stared at the developing circus, too. He whispered something into her ear, then dropped a quick kiss on her cheek before leading her across the room and through the double doors into the ER.

Headlights gleamed past, and then George was there, his massive black Bentley idling just beyond the throng. A small smile glanced across my mouth of its own accord. He'd acted like a knight in shining armor tonight, riding to my rescue. The least I could do was deserve him.

But I seemed to have left my courage with Greta back at the accident scene. I felt frozen in place.

I'd watched many a guilty defendant duck and cover their faces to hide from the cameras. Never thought I would need those skills, but perhaps I'd picked up some pointers.

After a deep inhale for courage, I squared my shoulders, clutched my impossibly tiny purse tighter, and hurried toward the exit.

The cold, rain-soaked air slapped my cheeks, rousing me from my post-accident stupor. Shouts issued from the gathered chroniclers, demanding to know everything, asking how I felt, seeking my side of the story.

I'd talk to the right people at the right time. For now, I ignored them all, making a dignified beeline for George and the refuge of his sedan.

Grace under pressure, Willa, my mother used to say. I did the best I could.

As I passed in front of a bank of photographers, I kept my head up and my steps even. My heart pounded loudly in my ears, drowning out all ambient sound.

George was holding the passenger door open. He waved for me to hurry.

A microphone with no legitimate network flag on it was thrust in front of my face. It was the young man wearing a coat and tie. He held the microphone as close to me as he could get and yelled, "Judge Carson, Rinaldo Gaines. The People's Champion. Did you know that man? Did you deliberately hit him with your car?"

The question was so outrageous that it stopped me in my tracks. I looked straight at him, which meant directly into his camera lens, which he held in front of his face.

"Of course not. What an unbelievably tasteless thing to say, Mr. Gaines. Your mother must be ashamed of your behavior," I said before I reined myself in.

"Probably not as ashamed as your mother is of yours," he replied. Cheeky little bastard.

"You're about the rudest young man I've ever met." I gave him another full second of my patented Judge Willa Carson stare before I turned, hurried across the last few yards, and climbed inside the car, slamming the door behind me. George sped away before I'd even latched my seatbelt.

"Who was that reporter you were talking to?" he asked.

I was still shaking with anger at the man's impertinence and lack of basic human decency. "That was no reporter. No news agency in this town would employ a man like that. I don't know who he is, but I intend to find out."

The entire evening felt surreal and scary and sickening. A man was dead. Most likely, my career was over. I'd be lucky to stay out of jail.

In fact, given the number of powerful people around town who'd like to see me removed from the bench, CJ was probably cackling gleefully like a demented munchkin at that very moment.

I scowled as overwhelming doom swelled in my chest.

George reached over and took my hand as we headed across Plant Key Bridge at last. "Don't worry. We'll get through this. I promise."

I smiled weakly and nodded. But I knew he was wrong. I'd killed a man. There was no way to erase that reality.

And I probably hadn't seen the last of Rinaldo Gaines, either.

CHAPTER SIX

Wednesday, November 9
10:00 a.m.

THE NEXT MORNING, I rolled over slowly, wincing as my sore muscles protested, and peered at the clock beside the bed. Ten a.m. I couldn't remember the last time I'd slept so late. I sat up and rubbed my tired eyes. I'd collapsed as soon as my head hit the pillow last night, but I still felt exhausted. The emotional turmoil gurgled inside my veins like hot lava.

Half awake, my mind indulged magical thinking. Last night never happened. I'd turn on the news this morning, listen to the local weather report, take the dogs for a run around the island, have breakfast, drive Greta to work. The same as always.

But as I came awake, I knew nothing was the same. The yellow and purple bruises on my chest from the snap of Greta's seatbelt were a vivid, painful reminder.

I'd killed a man with my car. There was no way to undo that reality, and things were likely to get a lot worse. This might be the last morning I would awaken in my own bed for a good long time.

Suck it up, Willa.

Yeah, yeah.

I threw the covers aside and sat on the edge of the bed.

George had left a note on the nightstand. He'd called my office. Advised Augustus, my judicial assistant, that I wouldn't be at work because I'd been involved in a car crash. He'd offered no further details. He didn't need to, given that the story was all over the news.

Augustus had promised to clear my schedule for the day and postpone everything on my calendar until the end of the week.

After a hot shower to soothe my aches and pains, I tugged on a pair of comfy sweats and wandered into the kitchen. George was fielding calls while he made breakfast. Omelets with cheese, ham, and peppers, judging by the ingredients on the counter. My stomach growled. I hadn't eaten since yesterday morning, and twenty-four-hour fasting wasn't my preference.

George looked over at me as I poured coffee into a big mug. "Good, you're up. Ben's on his way over."

I stopped mid-sip and stared at him. We'd waited for Chief Hathaway until midnight before we gave up and went to bed. I nodded.

George looked as exhausted as I felt. Dark circles rimmed his kind hazel eyes, and the fine lines at the corners were more pronounced than usual. We'd been through a lot already. You'd figure by now the universe might give us a break.

No such luck.

His cell phone buzzed, and he shook his head. "Carson."

With the phone pressed to his ear, he shrugged and lowered the burners on the stove before he walked away.

I slipped my feet into a pair of flip-flops, gathered our Labrador retrievers, and hurried down to the beach to give Harry and Bess a quick romp in the waves.

There were advantages to owning your own island. Privacy was the best one. I hoped the fresh air and exercise would help clear my head. But as I watched the dogs frolic in the water, last night's events refused to be shoved aside, which only made me tenser.

The moment of impact replayed like a video loop in my head. The dull thud of his body hitting Greta. That one loafer sticking out at an odd angle in front of her tires.

I whistled for the dogs and walked farther down the beach. Maybe a bit more distance from the house would separate us from the ghastly memories, too.

Didn't happen.

Next, I tried to focus on work instead.

Given my packed docket, I shouldn't have time to dwell on anything else. Hard-hearted as that sounded, keeping busy was often the best distraction. My caseload of nearly a thousand active cases meant there was more than enough on my plate to keep me out of trouble.

Yet, I dwelled anyway.

Before I realized it, the dogs and I had walked too far. Ben would arrive any minute. I didn't want to greet him in my pajamas.

I whistled and turned to jog. Harry and Bess caught up easily and trotted alongside me as we headed home.

Now was the time to hear whatever Chief Hathaway had to say and answer his questions. The facts were firmly consigned to history and couldn't be changed. The consequences would fall as they may. Next week, I'd be all but chained to my bench every day as the *Stingy Dudes* trial droned on and on, marching way too slowly toward completion. Which didn't matter really, since the next trial would slip into place when that one finished. The line of cases never ended. I'd always viewed the workload as total job security for me, even as the weight threatened to crush me daily.

A helicopter flew overhead, penetrating my concentration. My heart skipped a beat. These days, privacy was a myth, even on a private island like Plant Key. Helicopters and drones invaded our solitude way too often. Now they had a reason to focus on us.

The tabloid headlines wrote themselves. *Flamboyant Federal Judge…Wife of Celebrity Restauranteur George Carson…Kills Pedestrian.*

Yep. Too juicy to ignore.

I cringed and squinted up as the helicopter flew closer.

Was that a person leaning out the door with a camera? Or was I imagining things? What were they looking at? I turned fast, but only lush tropical foliage and white sand stretched behind me, with the city in the background. Same as always.

So the only thing to see here and now was me. They were filming me. Running on the beach of our private island with my dogs the day after I'd killed a man. I cringed because I knew exactly how they'd make me seem. Cold, uncaring.

"Stop. Just stop," I ordered my spiraling thoughts under my breath.

The dogs ran ahead, and I slowed to a walk until we reached the house. I hosed the dogs down out back, put them in their kennels to dry off, and then climbed the stairs to the deck.

Peering around the side of the house, I spotted Ben's unmarked sedan parked out front. Good. If he was planning to arrest me, he might as well do it now and get it over with, since I already had the day off. I might make bond and get released today. Be back at work tomorrow. Maybe.

I opened the back door and inhaled the delicious aromas of fried peppers and onions, but food was now the last thing on my mind. Ben stood near the stainless-steel fridge talking with George in hushed tones. George's hands moved animatedly, as they typically did when he was speaking on a topic he was passionate about. Which, in this case, probably meant me.

Ben looked a bit haggard, as if he'd not made it home last night. His shirtsleeves were rolled up, and a shadow of stubble darkened his usually clean-shaven jowls. His expression shifted from harried to guarded when he noticed me standing by the sliding doors.

"Willa," he said, walking toward me.

We weren't exactly friends, Ben and me. More like wary associates. He did his best to play nice with the federal judge, and I did my best not to annoy him any more than was necessary. Which was often difficult to do. He was prickly and so was I, and neither one of us was getting any softer.

George reached me first and slid his arm around my waist. He meant well. But his display of solidarity only made the knots in my stomach clench.

Ben cleared his throat, uncharacteristically hesitant. "Uh, I've got word on the deceased. He wasn't alive when he reached the hospital. The doctors officially declared him DOA when they brought him in last night. I'm sorry."

My heart plunged into my gut. I'd never swooned in my life. Not once. But I slumped against George and groaned.

George asked, "Do you know anything about the cause of death yet?"

"Not much. But what we do know is helpful for Willa." Ben placed his hat on the table and rested his hands on his hips. "Early presumptive tests showed high levels of illegal substances in his system. They're still determining exactly which drugs he consumed. Sometimes the presumptive tests show false positives, as you know, and the confirming tests will take weeks. But it looks like he'd taken fatal doses of illegal drugs."

"Are you saying it was the drugs that killed him?" I frowned.

Ben replied, "I'm saying it's possible but too early to know."

"So, he was an addict, then?" I cocked my head. "That could explain why he lunged into traffic, couldn't it?"

"Hard to say at this point. All I'm saying right now is that whatever drugs were in his system, it's possible he'd overdosed and died before your car ever hit him. If that's the case, he might have just collapsed into the road as you were driving past." Ben shrugged and cleared his throat again, as if he didn't want to deliver the obvious alternative. "It's also possible he'd be alive now had you not run him over."

"Right." I squeezed my eyes shut. "So the medical examiner hasn't pinpointed time of death, either?"

"Not yet. The lab results are preliminary as well as inconclusive. But it's gonna be close to the moment of impact. Less than a minute one side or the other."

"I understand." I'd never wished anybody dead in my life, but I was silently hoping that the man had been dead before he fell into the roadway. Not that hitting a dead man was a lot better than hitting a live one. But at least it would mean I hadn't killed him, and I wanted desperately not to be a killer.

I also realized the medical examiner might never be able to pinpoint the time of death so precisely.

Ben stepped closer and placed a hand on my arm. "I wish I had better information, but it's still too early. You know these things take time. I'll keep you posted as we learn anything new."

"Thanks, Ben. I know you don't have to keep me in the loop. But I really appreciate it," I said.

He nodded. "George told me you're not going to work today.

That's good. The vultures are swarming out there. I swear, if I had my way, we'd do away with social media completely. Everybody with a cell phone wants to be famous, and they think posting the most outrageous things they can find is the way to do it."

I nodded quietly. Ben and Tampa PD had experienced plenty of nasty run-ins with so-called citizen journalists like that toady Rinaldo Gaines. Ben had good reason to distrust and dislike them. But most of his annoyance was due to his crusty personality.

Our police chief suffered an uneasy relationship even with the legitimate media. In his view, they highlighted the details of their stories as salaciously as possible to grab public attention, blame his people, and make his job harder. Sometimes, he was right. But more often, he was being too defensive.

Of course, he also held low opinions of lawyers. Truth was, even though the police and the judiciary were supposed to be on the same law-and-order team, he wasn't all that fond of judges.

To be fair, not many media, lawyers, and judges would feature Ben Hathaway on their top-ten most-favorite lists, either.

Still, he was here when he wasn't required to be, offering me information he wasn't required to share, mostly because he was a decent human being and he knew I'd be grateful. Which I was.

"What about the man's identity?" I moved away from George toward the coffee. I needed more caffeine, and lots of it. "Who was he?"

"Still don't know." Ben took the java refill I offered.

I waved him to a chair and sat across from him. The coffee was too hot to drink, so I waited.

"There weren't many people walking around on Bayshore last night because of the nasty weather. But by the time we arrived, you'd drawn a small crowd. None of them admitted to seeing him until after he was hit," Ben said.

I nodded and said nothing, although the man's story seemed stranger and stranger.

"We went through his pockets. No wallet, no phone, no credit cards, no cash. Not even a house key." Ben cringed and ran his hand across the back of his neck. "We're looking at missing-person reports, but its tedious work, and we've had no luck yet."

I carefully sipped the coffee. "What about the fingerprint match?"

"Well, that's the weird thing, Willa. The guy had no fingerprints."

"No fingerprints?" George scowled. "You mean they were removed? Like in the movies?"

"No." Ben exhaled slowly. Poor guy really must have been exhausted. He was no spring chicken. All-nighters were unusual for him. "From what the medical examiner told me, he could have been born that way. Seems it's a condition. Affects a certain percentage of the population for various reasons."

George cocked his head. "So, no witnesses, no fingerprints, no wallet, no way to ID the body."

"Yet. No way to identify him *yet*. But we're working on it. And before you ask, yes, we've got DNA pending, which also takes a while."

"You've got nothing but prison, military, adoption, and maybe organ-donor records on file, right?" I asked. "From that cohort, you think you might get a DNA match to a guy wearing thousand-dollar loafers?"

"It's a long shot, I agree. We do what we can. He's young enough; his parents might have preserved cord blood when he was born. And we've got some feelers out to those ancestry websites that collect DNA, too. We might get lucky. You come up with a better idea, let me know." He glanced at the clock, drained the last of his coffee, and stood to leave. "I can let myself out."

With that, he gave a curt nod and turned to leave. Then he turned back. "Willa, have you seen the video clips from last night from that Rinaldo Gaines? You should look. And then steer clear of that guy. Nothing good ever comes out of his mouth."

I nodded. "Okay. He didn't seem like the kind of man I'd be inviting to dinner anytime soon."

"He's camped out at the entrance to your bridge right now. Don't go outside. He'll probably have a drone and use it to his advantage, not yours." His words were gruff, but the warning was appreciated.

"Thanks," I said, and he left. Which probably meant I'd pissed him off again. But we both knew a DNA match on the dead man was less likely than me winning the Powerball lottery. He needed a much, much better plan.

George kissed the top of my head and moved to the stove to plate our breakfast before it became dog food. "Are you doing okay?"

"Not really, no," I mumbled. "I just keep replaying the drive home last night in my head. Maybe I could've reacted quicker. Maybe I could've stopped. But I didn't even see the guy. He just showed up in the road. How does that happen? Where did he even come from?"

George set the plates on the table and rested his hand on my shoulder for several long seconds, infusing me with his quiet strength until a bit of the tension drained from my muscles.

"Let's eat before the food gets any colder." He sat across from me and waited until I reached for my fork and took a bite of the omelet.

I was hungry, and the omelet was delicious. I chewed a few bites and swallowed. "He's dead because of me, George. This is not something we can simply wish away. I'll be surprised if Ben doesn't come back here with a warrant for my arrest."

He opened his mouth, and I could tell what he was going to say, so I headed him off. "And don't suggest I call a lawyer. If I need to, I will."

He snapped his mouth shut, and we both ate a couple of bites before he spoke again.

"Listen, last night you said it seemed like the guy stumbled into your car, giving you no time to avoid him or to stop. You didn't so much hit him as he hit you. You were just unlucky. If you'd passed that point in the road, he'd have been hit by the next car. This guy wasn't going to make it out of the situation alive, Willa. No matter what." George ate a few more bites and waited for me to comment. When I didn't, he said, "Don't get ahead of the evidence. Let's wait until all the facts are in."

"Yeah," I said, nodding. I'd given countless others the same advice. But my doubts lingered. Yes, that man may have stumbled into my path. But Florida law required every driver to have her vehicle under control at all times. I had failed to stop within a safe, assured, clear distance. Simple as that. I'd still done that deed, even if he was dead before I hit him. Which was really unlikely anyway.

But what if George was right? What if *he* hit *me*? Then he'd timed his own execution. Was this a suicide after all?

Even in my own heart, I knew I was grasping and selfish to hope so.

I'd never killed anyone in my life. I desperately didn't want this to be the first time.

But wishing didn't make it so.

Hell, wishing couldn't even get Rinaldo Gaines off my lawn.

CHAPTER SEVEN

Wednesday, November 9
11:30 p.m.

WE SPENT THE REST of the day and evening at home, doing our best to pass the time. We heard nothing more from Ben Hathaway, and the legitimate news accounts dwindled to almost nothing. The citizen reporters and gawkers trolling for clicks pumped up their online speculations, but they had nothing new to fuel the fire, either.

Finally, I gave up and went to bed around midnight.

George drove me to the Sam M. Gibbons Federal Courthouse the next day because Greta was still damaged and sitting in the police impound lot for further processing. The *Stingy Dudes* trial was set to resume at ten o'clock.

Hillsborough Bay glinted in the sunlight as we traveled Bayshore Boulevard. The familiar sights along the way seemed oddly out of place under the circumstances.

Downtown Tampa was both bustling with workday activity and annoying because of all the new construction going on. The ever-improving scene gave the city a youthful vibrancy that encouraged people to move here and kept the tourists happy. But it made traveling to work and back a bigger hassle every day.

Harbour Island and the Marriott Waterside, across from the hockey arena, stood proudly welcoming at the waterfront. Shops, theaters, galleries, and restaurants in the popular riverfront districts were teeming with people.

I loved the drive. But today I wasn't behind the wheel, and no matter how many times I tried to drag my thoughts into the long list of work I had to do, all I could think about was the accident.

We continued over Platt Street Bridge, under the convention center, and on toward downtown, where many of the beautiful historic buildings were disappearing to make way for newer projects. My building was one of the newer ones.

Chief Justice Ozgood Livingston Richardson—CJ—had finally found money in the budget to move me from my decrepit chambers in the old federal courthouse to shiny new offices in the Sam M. Gibbons Federal Courthouse on North Florida Avenue with the rest of my colleagues.

To say I'd been surprised by his call was an understatement. Later, I'd learned from a colleague that he'd been ordered to move me because the building had been sold. CJ wanted me under his thumb, and I was never going to be in that particular spot, regardless of the location of my office. Keeping the upper hand with CJ was one of the fun things about my job. I grinned.

My chance to get out of the crumbling 1920s building happened in mid-July, and we were finally settled into the new space. Now I had a lovely view of downtown Tampa and the Hillsborough River beyond instead of overlooking the HVAC units on the old parking garage.

George stopped at the private judge's entrance, gave me a

quick kiss and another reminder not to worry, and dropped me off. Then he hurried back home to get things ready for tonight's dinner crowd.

Regardless of why I was moved to the new building, I loved everything about it. The new life was always better than the old, as my mother used to say. I greeted the guards and stepped into the elevator. Even the elevators were better. I rode the clean, roomy, zippy cars up to the third floor. I hadn't become accustomed to the smooth and fast lift, so unlike the rickety death trap in the old building. Every time I exited the elevator, an involuntary smile crossed my lips and lifted my spirits. Today was no different.

The doors sucked open to a reception area decorated tastefully in shades of cream and taupe. My chambers were located on the right. There were several judges on this floor, each with our own individual chambers. Inside, separate assistant offices and offices for our clerks completed the spacious suites.

My judicial assistant, Augustus Ralph, was at his desk, impeccably dressed and ready for the day, as always. I gave him a weak smile as I passed. I wanted a few minutes of solitude before diving into my cluttered calendar.

"You'll want to check these." He followed me into my private office with a stack of pink phone messages and a cup of strong Jamaican coffee in his hand.

We had a computer system for messages now, but Augustus said he preferred the old-school pink slips we'd been stuck with in the old building. I suspected he was simply rebelling against CJ in his own way, but I didn't mind. Thwarting CJ was a game many could play simultaneously.

"Thank you." I flopped into my chair and set my briefcase down. He lingered at the door, looking a bit concerned.

"Is there something else?" I asked.

His brown gaze narrowed. "That's a terrible thing that happened Tuesday night. I'm sorry."

"Yes," was all I managed to say.

He watched me another couple of seconds before he nodded and left, closing the door behind him. I flipped through the stack of messages. Most were from local reporters and news outlets, and I put them aside.

Three were from Chief Hathaway, requesting that I call him right away to discuss developments.

I dialed the phone, and an officer answered, cool and efficient. She put me on hold. Ben picked up a few seconds later.

"Thanks for getting back to me." He sounded slightly out of breath.

"Thank you for calling," I said, and meant it. This kind of VIP treatment wasn't the norm between us, and certainly not how he treated suspects. Which gave me a bit of hope. "You want to question me further?"

"Your involvement in this thing seems straightforward. All your lab work was negative," Ben said. "We can't find anything wrong with your car, although we're not done with the black box. We don't have that expertise in-house, and Mercedes is being difficult about it."

I simply nodded. Not many traffic incidents were tried in my courtroom, but I'd handled more than one product-liability suit against car manufacturers over the black boxes installed in every car by law. The data recorders had become much more sophisticated. It would reveal, for example, how fast I'd been driving and whether I was wearing my seatbelt. It would also show when and how I deployed the brakes.

There were limitations, too. The black box only recorded twenty seconds around the impact. And it didn't record video or audio. Or at least, that's what the manufacturers claimed. My guess was the temptation to do so would prove too great at some point. Maybe that point had already passed.

Like the blood tests and the search I'd consented to at the scene Tuesday night, I felt confident that Greta's black box would back me up. I wasn't worried about it at all.

"We might have a line on a couple of video cameras operating in the area at the time of the incident. Until we get them, we have your official statement, and that'll be enough for now, unless something else comes up." He exhaled slowly. "We're just waiting for the autopsy results to confirm the cause, manner, and mechanism of death. All of which can take a while."

"The medical examiner doesn't think the manner of death was obvious?" The news about the video felt promising, but the lift was temporary and eclipsed by the autopsy news. I pinched the bridge of my nose between my thumb and forefinger, feeling the headache throb behind my temples.

"You know how this goes, Willa. There are five options." I visualized him holding up his five fingers as he ticked them off, one at a time, starting with his pinky finger and ending with his thumb. "Accident, homicide, suicide, natural causes, and unknown. At the moment, the ME is calling this one 'unknown.'"

The comment stung. If the medical examiner couldn't say for sure how the man died, then his death could still be ruled a homicide. Which was just another way of calling me a killer. Whether they charged me with a crime or not.

Somehow, I found the presence of mind to ask, "What about the man's identity? Any luck with that? If we know who he was, maybe we can find out how this happened."

"We've pulled all the missing-person reports for the last thirty days. We'll go back further if we need to. I called to tell you that we've set up a tip line for people to call in, and we'll follow any leads we get. This is one case where the legitimate media can help, and they're trying. Hang on a sec." Ben mumbled something she couldn't hear and then came back to say, "Sorry, Willa. I need to go."

"Okay, but—" I heard nothing but the dial tone. He'd already gone. I hung up in a daze. My hands trembled as I raised my coffee mug. So many lingering questions.

The mystery man had been well dressed, well groomed, obviously not a street person. So why didn't he have ID with him? Technically, it was the crime of vagrancy to walk around without identification. He wasn't dressed like a vagrant or a lawbreaker of any kind. Quite the opposite.

And why was he out there alone? Why hadn't someone come looking for him already? The story had been all over the news since Tuesday night. Surely, someone out there knew who he was.

Maybe video of the scene at the time, if it existed and if Ben could find it, would show us something useful. At the very least, we'd know how the man had lunged in front of my car. Which wasn't much. But it was more than we had now.

I slipped into my robe and made my way to the courtroom. The *Stingy Dudes* lawyers had taken advantage of my day off to file about a dozen motions each. Most were nothing more than clutter for the record, but both sides were trying desperately to create and preserve appealable issues. They wanted a do-over if they lost the jury trial. The mere suggestion that I might have to try this case twice practically gave me hives.

We spent the rest of the day hearing and disposing of the motions. By the time we finished, it was too late to bring the jury back in for testimony. I released everyone about four o'clock.

Back in my chambers, there were no new messages from Chief Hathaway. I flipped on the television to the local all-news station. After half an hour of nonstop local coverage with not a single mention of Tuesday night's fatal accident, I breathed a bit easier. The legitimate news outlets had moved on, just as I'd expected.

Unfortunately, the internet had not settled down at all. Judges had become something of a trophy kill for a certain segment of the online population. They looked for judges they didn't like, cases they didn't approve of, just about anything they could use to capture eyeballs on their video channels. It was a crazy development, and one I didn't approve of in the least.

Not a thing I could do about it, either. I packed up my briefcase with enough work to hold me through the night, said farewell to my staff, and headed out.

George planned to pick me up at the judges' private exit where he'd dropped me off this morning, but the citizen journalists were wise to that. They'd gathered around the exit like a human blockade. I hurried through a deafening blast of screeching questions, all of which I ignored, and made it to the Bentley with all my limbs intact. Barely.

"Those vultures are still hot after my carcass," I complained, looking through the side window at the noisy mob, holding up their cell phones and their microphones, filming every second. Rinaldo Gaines was out there, wearing the same coat and tie, even in the sweltering sunlight.

"Did you know that vultures are social creatures?" George said conversationally, after I'd struggled my way into the passenger seat and harrumphed behind the closed door.

I knew he was only trying to cheer me up, but I glared at him anyway and replied sarcastically, "Do tell."

"I looked it up," he said, a grin on his face. "Turns out vultures roost, feed, and fly in large flocks, which are called a committee, venue, or volt."

"You make a comparison to lawyers, and I'm going to smack you with my purse," I said snidely.

He laughed as he pulled into traffic, leaving this particular committee of vultures behind. "It gets better."

"I'll bet." I slumped back into the plush seat and fastened my seatbelt. I sighed. "Okay. Why the ornithology lesson?"

He wiggled his eyebrows and kept talking. "In flight, a group of vultures is called a kettle. And when they're feeding together at a carcass, the group is called a wake."

"Isn't that special," I said sourly, causing him to laugh again. "So when they're chowing down on my carcass, I'm supposed to do what?"

He reached over and patted my knee. "The smart thing to do is not to give them a carcass to feed on."

"Yeah, well, it's a little too late for that," I replied, deliberately twisting his meaning. I was in no mood to be Pollyanna about any of this situation. He frowned and said no more. I was instantly sorry for thwarting his good humor, but I was worried. Really worried.

By the time we made it to Plant Key, his mood had changed, too. Because a smaller flock of vultures was camped out at the entrance to our home. We slowed to pass them, which gave a couple of the dumber ones the chance to bang on George's car and shout more questions, all the while running their video cameras. He slowed down to a crawl to avoid running over one of them, which was the very last thing we needed.

What a mess.

CHAPTER EIGHT

Friday, November 11
6:50 a.m.

EARLY THE NEXT MORNING, I sat on our veranda and stared out into the pink and gold sunrise. I liked to go for my run and then have a mug of my favorite Cuban coffee on the veranda while I wrote in my journal. I'd taken up journaling several years ago during a crisis to make sense of all the details swirling around in my head. It was like having a long chat with my subconscious, where all the answers seemed to be stored.

Journaling had saved my butt more than once since that first time. Maybe it would do so again.

I reported that gruesome moment when the front of my car collided with a human body. The devastating silence after I skidded to a halt grew to monstrous proportions. Nothing but Greta's engine and the plink of raindrops against the windows interrupted.

I wrote down my efforts to administer CPR to the poor man and how I'd thought I felt his pulse. *But had I?*

My chest squeezed, and the ever-present knots in my stomach pulled tighter. My day at the office yesterday was productive but seemed unimportant. Managing my packed docket, ticking off the boxes for the *Stingy Dudes*, dodging the vultures, making no sense of the chaos that had invaded my heart with the dead man.

One good thing happened when the attorneys on the *Stingy Dudes* case had asked for additional time before they resumed presenting witnesses. They wanted to regroup in light of the rulings I'd made on their various motions. I was relieved to grant the request and give us all a break. The jury had seemed pleased to have Friday off, too. The case would resume on the following Monday.

When I finished writing everything down, I closed the journal and sat with my thoughts. Had I killed that man? Where had he come from? Who was he?

None of these questions were answered by my subconscious today, but writing everything down did reduce ruminating. The facts were right there, in blue and white, if I needed them. I didn't have to hold them all in my head anymore. Which was a relief.

I set the journal aside and looked at the clock. Yikes!

I was due in chambers in less than an hour. Good thing I was fast for a girl—or so George liked to tell me. I shook off my mood as best I could and headed for the shower.

It took me not more than ten minutes to scrub down, rinse off, and blast my pixie-short red hair with the dryer. A light coat of makeup before I donned black jeans and a crisp, white shirt, and then slid my sockless feet into a pair of supple leather Tods. A quick examination of the effect in the mirror was the last step.

Competent, efficient and steadfast. Not a killer. Not even close.

"Precisely," I said before I headed out.

George waited downstairs to drive me to work. Greta was still impounded, release to the local Mercedes repair shop pending. Mourning the loss of my car seemed silly and insensitive under the circumstances. So I didn't. But I wanted to.

I'm from Detroit, where cars are the essence of life itself. A car means independence. And I was feeling the loss of both my car and my freedom. Justifiably so on both counts.

We headed along Bayshore Boulevard again, both of us quiet and subdued. George wanted me to stay home again today, but I'd flatly refused. I wasn't sick. I wasn't injured. There was nothing remotely wrong with me to justify another day off. I knew George was worried, and I appreciated his concern, but action had always helped me cope more than hand-wringing ever did.

Being a federal judge was more than a job, it was a calling, and one I took very seriously. My colleagues and my staff depended on me to handle my docket well. Litigants, lawyers, and the public expected me to deliver justice effectively, fairly, and promptly. I needed to be there. For them and for me.

Besides, the *Stingy Dudes* case wouldn't last forever, and I still had pre-trial matters to wrap up for several upcoming trials. Waiting around twiddling my thumbs while Ben Hathaway and Tampa PD handled my accident case wouldn't make time elapse faster, anyway.

"Are you sure about this, Willa?" George asked one last time as he swerved up to the curb. The large, boxy building's windows sparkled in the sunlight. "No one would blame you if you took another day off right now."

"I'm fine. I've got a lot to do. I'm too busy to stay home." I gave him a quick kiss before sliding out of his Bentley. Before I closed the door, I leaned inside and said, "I'll call you later."

"Be careful, Mighty Mouse." His expression concerned. "I'm here if you need me."

I smiled to reassure us both, shut the door, and strode through the committee of vultures on my way inside. When would they give up? Not until something more salacious came along. Was it wrong to wish for a royal wedding or a popular celebrity's baby to capture their attention?

Augustus was seated at his tidy desk. He was dressed to the nines in a gray pinstripe suit with a burgundy-colored tie. He looked up as I entered, and his gaze narrowed.

"If you'll forgive me, you look like you haven't slept in days." His lilting Jamaican accent followed me into my chambers, where I deposited my briefcase on one of the tasteful cream-upholstered client chairs in front of my desk.

The last thing I needed was him fluttering around me all day like a mother hen. A handsome man by any standards, Augustus was clean shaven, his dark hair cropped short, his nails buffed to a high sheen and well cared for. "Are you all right, Judge?"

I waved him inside. "Close the door behind you, please."

He did as I asked, then took a seat in a client chair while I waited. Legs crossed, he clasped his hands in his lap, careful to keep the crease in his trousers sharp.

"Please don't worry about me, Augustus. I'm getting more than enough of that at home right now from George." I did my best to look as commanding as possible, but Augustus's raised brow conveyed skepticism. He didn't take my power trip seriously. He knew he was indispensable. "We've got several pre-trial motions and hearings and—"

Augustus cut me off. "Chief Judge Richardson called. Several times. He said it's urgent."

I groaned.

Something akin to sympathy flickered through his brown eyes, and he broke what must have been his self-imposed vow of silence. "How did this happen? How did you not see that man right in front of your car? Why didn't you stop?"

"The truth is that I'm not exactly sure." With a sigh, I sat back. "Everything happened way too fast. One minute I'm driving along, the next he was just there, very close. I had no time to react or stop or anything. It's almost like…"

"Like he wanted you to hit him?" Augustus finished helpfully. "Wouldn't be the first time someone committed suicide by walking into traffic."

I nodded. "True."

He handed over the pink slip with CJ's message on it.

I groaned and dropped my head into my hands. "I really don't want to talk to CJ this morning."

Augustus nodded sympathetically, but he didn't relent. "He's been calling for three days. The longer you put him off, the worse he'll be."

He spoke like a friend, not like a subordinate. I cocked my head. Not for the first time, I wondered about him. At the very least, Augustus's presence in my life was shrouded in mystery.

He had been thoroughly vetted for the job, of course. He was working his way through college, and he was the nephew of Tampa power broker, Prescott Roberts. Which would have been enough to disqualify him from working for me. The last thing I needed was Prescott Roberts on my butt every minute, privy to whatever happened in my life because he had a mole inside my chambers.

But on the plus side, Augustus had learned about the vacancy through my mother's best friend, Kate Austin, and her new husband, Leo Columbo. Kate had practically forced Augustus on me, but even if she'd merely asked, I could refuse her nothing.

Kate had been the only mother figure in my life for a long, long time. Simply put, she'd done so much for me that I could never repay. Giving a job to Augustus was no hardship at all. Just the opposite, as it turned out.

But how did Augustus know Kate? Or Leo, for that matter? These were questions without answers at the moment. I made a mental note to move Augustus and his secrets closer to the top of my to-do list when things calmed down.

Augustus stood and walked to the door. "I'll bring you a cup of coffee after you finish your call to Chief Judge Richardson."

He walked out, leaving me alone with my pink message slip held between my fingers.

"What the hell," I murmured. After a deep, calming breath, I dialed the number. CJ picked up on the second ring. Of course he did. Dammit.

"I need to see you. In my office," he said without preamble, as if he had a right to order me around. He didn't. He held no real power over me at all, and we both knew it. I almost refused, just for the principle of the thing.

Before I had mustered the right retort, he'd hung up. The little twerp.

I replaced the receiver and shrugged.

Maybe a good battle with the great and powerful Oz was the very thing I needed to get me back on track. Then again, most days he was hardly worth the energy it would cost to put him in his place.

Like a kid headed to the principal's office, I trudged to the elevators. I rode up one floor and walked out into a fancy wood-paneled room, where a snooty-looking woman of about thirty sat guard outside CJ's door. She was new on the job, and I didn't have a clue who she was.

"He's expecting you," she said, her tone clipped. As if CJ's wishes were the same as orders from God or something. She waved me through.

The tiny hairs on the back of my neck stood up.

When I entered his chambers, he was sitting behind his massive mahogany desk. His desk rested on an elevated platform to make him seem more imposing than he was, but it served to do the opposite. He looked like a good facsimile of a tiny Godfather from up there. Perspective was a funny thing. I stifled a grin.

He'd always had a rather inflated opinion of his own importance. He believed his title of Chief Justice meant "the boss" instead of "the bureaucrat who controls nothing important and possesses no real power."

"Willa." CJ gestured toward one of the wing chairs in front of his desk.

"Oz," I replied, towering over him for a moment, just to give him a clear picture of his relative importance from my point of view.

He frowned and gestured again. "Please take a seat."

I made my way over, warily. I shouldn't have been there. I should've been playing phone tag with the guy. My plan was to avoid him at least until the Devil Rays won the World Series in the same year that the Bucs won the Super Bowl and the Lightning won the Stanley Cup. In other words, until the end of time. That was the game. A game, until now, I'd been winning.

Yet here I was, sitting in front of a man ready to pounce on my misfortune like another vulture chomping my carcass. I wouldn't be surprised if he was feeding juicy details to the rest of his flock.

CHAPTER NINE

Friday, November 11
9:50 a.m.

FROM MY SEAT, OZ up there on his perch, we were eye level.
Oz looked the same as always, sixty-five going on ninety.
Everything about him screamed staid and old and boring, though it
would be stupid to consider him harmless. Prescott Roberts, that
Tampa power broker I mentioned, was his brother-in-law.

In short, CJ was well connected and fairly well preserved—
and a major pain in the ass. I was already regretting my temporary
lapse in judgment that put me right here, right now.

He came directly to the point, emphasizing my abject failure,
as he saw it. "Willa, not for the first time, your behavior has
caused a fair bit of trouble for the court and *everyone* who works
here."

"*Everyone,* Oz? My conduct is causing trouble for the
cleaning crew and the parking attendants?" I sneered. "Seriously?
Who knew I had such far-reaching influence? I've been
underestimating myself all this time."

He narrowed his eyes and glared as he admonished me, as if I were a recalcitrant child, which just pissed me off. "Vehicular manslaughter is no joke, Willa."

I narrowed my eyes and glared right back, saying nothing.

"A complaint has been filed alleging that your conduct is prejudicial to the effective administration of justice," Oz pronounced officially, then sighed and sat back, as if his was a grievous duty. But his eyes gave him away. His solemn tone was at direct odds with the flicker of glee I saw in those old, crinkled, rheumy browns.

"A complaint? Filed by whom?" I cocked my head and kept a steady gaze aimed right at him. But my heart was pounding hard in my chest, and I held my churning gut in check with sheer force of will alone. *Grace under pressure.* Good goal. Hard to master.

Oz wouldn't be attacking me unless he had support. What kind of complaint was it, and who had made it? Litigants assigned to my docket who thought they could get a better shot with a different judge? One of my colleagues? Someone higher up the food chain who didn't like me? Maybe some politician who wanted his son installed in my job?

Could have been any or none of those options.

Even federal judges were entitled to confront their accusers. Which meant Oz would have to give me a good reason for whatever it was he meant to do. Eventually. I could wait. No rush, as far as I was concerned.

He nodded, folding his hands pompously on the desk. "A special judicial review committee has been appointed to investigate the facts and allegations contained in the complaint. You'll be interviewed as a part of that process. And you'll receive a copy of the report when it's finalized."

I gritted my teeth and stared at him in disbelief. "You mean to say you've started *impeachment* proceedings against me?"

"Please don't make this more difficult, Willa. A man is dead. Your name is all over the internet. Courthouse personnel can't even get our cars into the parking garage without fear," he intoned.

"What are you talking about?" I said, dangerously calm.

"We can go through the entire process, but don't imagine that you'll come through this unscathed." He looked so smug that I gripped the chair arms to avoid slapping that smirk off his face.

I held my tongue while he said all he wanted to say.

He puffed up his chest with righteousness like a Saturday night preacher in a hot, dusty parking lot. "I suggest you resign. Immediately. Save us all the scandal. Neither we, nor you, nor *George* for that matter, can afford any more embarrassment than you've already caused."

"Resign?" I was flabbergasted. And angry. Angry, more than anything. How dare he even try to speak for George! My nostrils flared, and I struggled to control my breathing. I clenched my jaw. "No."

"No?" Oz's smirk surfaced again, a little longer and more gleeful this time.

"No. I'm not resigning. I'm not going anywhere." I crossed my arms, allowing my fury to overtake the growing dread creeping up from my toes. "They haven't even identified the man yet. Or established the manner, cause, and mechanism of his death. For all we know, he jumped out in front of my car on purpose."

A small muscle worked in CJ's jaw, a sign he was highly annoyed with my answer. Good. He'd be a lot more than simply annoyed by the time I finished with him.

He said, "If you can't be reasonable, then at least show some consideration for the court. Take a leave of absence until the impeachment investigation proceedings are concluded."

"Not only no, but hell no. Who do you think you are?" I pushed to my feet, indignation swelling in my chest, even as my tone remained level. *Grace under pressure*. The jerk.

Calmly, I said, "I've got work to do. My docket is crammed full. Like all the other judges here. Litigants are depending on me to do my job, and I won't simply quit because you think you've finally found a way to get rid of me."

"I had hoped you'd be reasonable. But since you've refused…" He puffed up his puny chest again and spoke in his most officious tone, "I'm sorry you're unable to continue with your work, Judge Carson. We're all very concerned about your predicament. Of course, I will reassign your cases during your absence."

I widened my eyes in flat astonishment. "What? You can't do that! You'll create enough reversible error to clog up our dockets for years."

Even as I said it, I realized I was wrong.

Our entire legal system assumes that people will follow the rules. When they don't, we can't force them. All we can do is punish them after the fact. And the truth was that we mostly failed on the punishment side, too.

The practical reality was that CJ could absolutely do precisely what he'd threatened, with nothing more than a few keystrokes on a computer.

There was no way to stop him. He was the court administrator. If I'd had to take a leave of absence due to illness or something, he'd have the power to reassign my cases. A few lawyers or litigants might object, but they'd have no real legal grounds to do so.

By reassigning my cases, CJ could effectively remove me from office.

Maybe I could get the situation turned around. Refuse to just lie down and take this. But really, what was I going to do? Sue CJ to make him stop? Beg the lawyers and litigants not to leave me? Throw a tantrum like a petulant child? Make a spectacle of myself with all the judges and lawyers in town by demanding to have my cases back? File a motion with the Court of Appeals to get rid of *him*? Call the president?

CJ watched as the truth made its way through my head, one crazy idea at a time, until I reached the last one and my shoulders slumped. He smirked and nodded. "It's already done."

I began to sputter, but he kept talking.

"We're not going to leave you on the bench, Willa. Get used to that reality. You'll be totally out of the way now. The last thing we need is to spend the next two years redoing everything on your docket after you're convicted. We'll handle your cases once and do them right the first time." Oz, in his role as chief judge and court administrator, nodded once as if the matter was totally settled. Because, in effect, it was. At least for now. "Augustus Ralph will be instructed to be sure all documents are smoothly transitioned."

He paused. I said nothing because I could think of nothing to say.

"Go home, Willa. I can't have you removed from the building. Yet." He smiled again. That smarmy smirk that made my palms itch to slap him. "But you'll be effectively invisible if you insist on hanging around."

What I really wanted to say was how dare he take it upon himself to hand off my docket and command my judicial assistant around like his own personal lapdog.

Instead, I gritted out the only words that came to mind. "There was no vehicular homicide, Oz. A man is dead. We don't know how or why he died. It's looking like a drug overdose. Regardless, his death was not my fault. I will not be charged with any crime. I certainly won't be convicted."

"Just bad luck, then? Do you think that excuse will help you? The victim's family will be calling for your head on a stake before this is all over." Oz quirked a sarcastic brow at me, and then his tone turned positively mean. "Social media is already sucking up every drop of oxygen out there, slamming you, all our judges, and our jurisdiction. The other judges can barely enter and leave the building or even go to their homes. One of those damn bloggers followed me into the club last night and interrupted my meal. I won't have it, Willa. No one is on your side in this. *No one.* We're done here. Go home. Don't come back."

I glared at him. I wasn't usually a violent person, but I had the sudden urge to beat him to a bloody pulp. I was pretty sure I could do it, too. The little twerp. Something close to rage filled my heart, even as I heard my mother's oft-repeated admonition in my head again: *Grace under pressure, Willa. Hold steady.*

He must have sensed my hostile intentions because he quickly lowered his brow and cleared his throat. When next he spoke, he backpedaled a little. His words were almost conciliatory, and I figured what he said next would become the public version of this meeting.

"Look, Willa. I realize this must be difficult for you, but I have to do what's best for our jurisdiction. You're not the only one under the microscope here. We're all being watched to see how we handle things." He paused and then spoke as if we were friends. "Take some time off. It's the smart thing to do. Until all of this sugars out."

What a liar. Without another word, with as much dignity as I could muster, I stalked out of his private office and past the gargoyle standing watch, hoping the angry tremble in my body wasn't as visible as it felt.

I jabbed the elevator button, and the doors slid open immediately. I stepped inside.

Until all of this sugars out...

CJ's words sounded like a death sentence to my career. Which was exactly what he intended, make no mistake.

I rested my head against the shiny, metal elevator wall on the way down to the third floor.

Before the elevator stopped, at least one thing became crystal clear.

The dead man could no longer be left to Ben Hathaway and his team.

Thanks to Chief Justice Ozgood Richardson and his anonymous complainant, my career was now hanging in the balance.

I might not survive his kangaroo court impeachment, anyway. I knew that. CJ was a buffoon, but he was a sly one. He was right when he said I had enemies. Powerful enemies.

And I certainly wouldn't get back to my regular courtroom duties unless Tuesday night's accident was brought quickly to a conclusion that exonerated me completely.

Bottom line? I was the only one who could save myself.

CHAPTER TEN

I SPENT THE NEXT hour or so hovering between abject depression and determined anger. Yes, I'd complained about my busy schedule and all the mundane details involved in the day-to-day running of the American judicial system. But with a blank docket for the first time since never, I didn't like it. Not at all.

Augustus bustled about, wrangling the men who'd arrived to remove the *Stingy Dudes* case along with all the others. Boxes and reams of paper, assorted binders, and other documents were stacked high on each load.

As the handcarts rolled through the door, my spirits sank lower.

There was nothing I could do about any of this. But I wouldn't sit there and feel sorry for myself, either.

I'd been knocked around by life before. The worst thing was when my mother had died. I was sixteen, and my stepfather bugged out because he couldn't cope with his grief. Through it all, I'd learned a lot about independence.

Mainly, not to go down without a fight.

"Has the coroner's office called yet?" I asked Augustus when he brought me a glass of iced tea. "I'm expecting the autopsy reports."

A hint of pity entered Augustus's dark eyes as he stared at me kindly. "Not yet, ma'am. Perhaps you should take an early lunch, go for a walk. The sunshine will do you good."

"Oh, should I?" I snipped, more harshly than I'd intended. The last thing I wanted was to hurt Augustus. None of this was his fault. I winced. "Sorry. Lots of stress right now."

"How about I schedule you a massage for later?" He took a step back, as if I might flip out and bite his head off or throw something heavy in his direction. Which I really wanted to do, surprisingly.

But I didn't. Like a lot of other things he's wrong about, CJ is wrong when he says I have no self-control.

Augustus kept talking. "A new spa just opened near Channelside. Very chic and expensive."

I sighed. A day of pampering sounded lovely, but I didn't want to waste the time. Plus, CJ would have a field day if the vultures caught me lounging around at some fancy spa while police investigated the death of a man I'd struck with my car.

Besides, I had more important things to do. Starting with identifying the dead man. As a private citizen, I could investigate in ways the police could not. Witnesses were more likely to chat casually with me. I could snoop without a warrant, too. Which was precisely what I planned to do.

George wouldn't like it, and Ben would squeal, but why not? No one had more at stake here than me. And no one could accuse me of shirking my judicial responsibilities, either. Thanks to CJ, I didn't have any.

"Another time, Augustus. I've got research to do." I squared my shoulders and nodded toward the door as a suggestion that he'd overstayed his welcome. "Please let me know as soon as the coroner's office calls."

He gave me a puzzled stare as he left my chambers, closing the door behind him.

Research. First, who exactly was this guy? No ID when they'd searched his body and the surrounding areas at the scene. Which was weird. Who wanders around alone in an expensive business suit without a wallet or a set of keys or anything personal in his pockets?

Chief Hathaway had also said the guy had no fingerprints. The DNA results were still pending. Ben said his officers were busy going over missing-person reports for the last month, but I knew they were short-handed due to budget concerns. Cops would be out on the streets, not stuck behind a desk scrolling through paperwork to identify an accident victim.

This was a situation where the media was our friend. The publicity alone should turn up someone who recognized the guy, at the very least. And it would. Probably. Eventually.

Being a federal judge allowed me access to lots of public and private databases, including those used by law enforcement—like CODIS, NCIC, even INTERPOL.

Alone in my chambers, I closed my eyes and forced myself to remember the accident in detail. I saw the man's body as he'd lain cold in the street. I had managed to get a glimpse of his face once they'd put him on the gurney.

Dark hair, dark brows. Maybe early thirties. His eyes had been closed, so I didn't know his eye color. I had no idea how tall he was. I typed in what I knew and hit the enter key.

Moments later, my computer beeped. No results found.

Well, damn.

"What did you expect? Ben told you there was nothing on the guy in any of the databases." I frowned as I chastised myself. "Get your head on straight if you're going to do this."

I moved on to the man's missing fingerprints. A few keystrokes later, I'd found info on a rare disease called adermatoglyphia, which caused a certain gene marker to be switched off somehow. Those individuals were born without fingerprints. A couple other diseases were known to affect fingerprints, too.

But there were also other causes of the condition. Damage to the skin was the most common. Trauma, burns, skin problems like eczema, psoriasis, or scleroderma could result in loss of fingerprints. Some nurses and doctors literally washed their fingerprints off, after so many handwashings. People who work with a lot of paper and woodworkers could wear off their fingerprints, too.

Good for cat burglars and mob bosses. Bad for me. I shrugged. Fingerprint identification was not an option.

Next, I did a search of the local newspapers for the last week or so, trying to find stories about dark-haired, thirty-something businessmen who might have had dealings in the area. There were quite a few. Tampa Bay is a bustling business and convention area. Well-dressed, brown-haired businessmen of a certain age were pretty common. I saw dozens in my courtroom every week, in fact.

This research was getting me nothing except a long list of where not to look further.

I glanced over at the contemporary-style glass clock on my wall and saw it was only a bit after noon.

A long, long day, followed by more long, empty days stretched ahead of me like an endless ocean. I didn't like it. Nor would I accept it. Not until I had exhausted every possible alternative.

CHAPTER ELEVEN

Friday, November 11
3:00 p.m.

BY THE TIME THE coroner finally called at three o'clock, I'd
reorganized all the file drawers in my office and dusted the
bookshelf that held assorted stuff—like photos of George and me
with the president and the chief judge of the US Supreme Court on
the day I'd been officially sworn into office.

I picked up the frame and studied my younger self, proud as
the president shook my hand. The confirmation hearings had been
tough. So many questions from politicians more interested in
being reelected than making sure I was qualified for the job. In
theory, it was a barrage of inquiry meant to weed out lesser
candidates for the federal courts. In practice, everyone had a
hidden agenda.

I'd withstood them all, kept my cool in the face of intrusive
and insulting questions, and emerged as a United States District
Court judge. One of the youngest in the country at the time. A job
I was well qualified for and very good at performing. Definitely

not something I would simply walk away from because that little dweeb Ozgood Richardson wanted me to. Not a chance.

If CJ wanted to get rid of me, he'd have to make it happen. I'd fight him all the way. And I intended to win. Only fifteen judges had ever been impeached in more than two hundred years. Of those fifteen, only eight had ever been convicted and removed from office. The last one was removed almost a decade ago, and he'd been convicted of fraud, lying under oath, and accepting bribes from litigants.

Not only was I not accused of anything even remotely close to an impeachable offense, but the entire process was also lengthy and complicated. Years could pass before the trial was completed.

All of which meant the odds were heavily in my favor.

I'd vowed many times over the years that CJ would be gone from the bench before I was. My plan was simple. I'd outlast the bastard. I was young. I could wait.

But I needed to get out from under this cloud of uncertainty and emerge unscathed first. Which shouldn't be too difficult. There had been federal judges who were convicted felons and didn't lose their jobs. But I didn't plan to take up my place in history as one of them.

So who was this guy? I refused to believe I'd killed him. There had to be a better answer. Which would be hard to find as long as he still had no name.

His clothing suggested prosperity. Wealthy people either flaunted what they had or lived like social hermits. Hermits didn't need pricey suits and handmade loafers.

Still, the thought that no one cared if the man lived or died tugged at my heart, and I lost focus for a moment. I'd been lucky after mom died. Kate had treated me like her own. Her family had become my family. Even her new boy-toy husband, Leo, was starting to grow on me. I adored Augustus, and he liked Leo. Which had to count for something.

As if I'd conjured him, Augustus knocked on my office door before peeking his head in. "Coroner's on line one, Judge."

My heart stuck in my throat, I forced a smile. "Thank you."

Slowly, I walked back to my desk and slumped down in my seat, staring at that red flashing light on my phone like it was a nuclear warhead about to explode.

If I had killed that man, I wasn't sure *how* I'd live with the knowledge.

I might very well be living with it behind bars, though.

Only a remote chance of imprisonment, really.

But not an impossible ending.

Finally, I shut off the back and forth in my head, summoned my courage, and picked up the receiver. "Good afternoon, Martin. What do you have for me?"

Martin Eberhard had become coroner a year ago, and he'd gone a long way in updating the office's policies and procedures. He was efficient, no-nonsense, and detail-oriented—all excellent qualities in a medical examiner.

"Afternoon, Willa." He cleared his throat and then spoke in his familiar brisk tone. "I don't usually inform judges of my findings, but Chief Hathaway asked me to call because you have personal involvement with the case."

I pictured him as he talked on the phone. Eberhard was in his late sixties, gray-haired and paunchy, sporting those black-rimmed glasses popular with geeks the world over.

"Thank you, Martin. I appreciate your consideration."

"I'll cut right to it, then," he said briskly. "We won't know for sure until the full confirmatory toxicology comes back in about six to eight weeks. But you'll be pleased to hear that the man would have died due to a lethal dose of heroin laced with fentanyl in his system."

"So, hitting him with my car didn't kill him? Officially?" I blinked at the desktop, my mind racing to process the information.

"I can't say that," Eberhard replied. "What I can say is that he overdosed on toxic heroin. He would not have survived, whether you hit him or not."

I'd heard about toxic heroin. I'd also read articles in the local papers about a recent spike in death rates among area drug users, some of them homeless, because of it.

"Willa, are you still there?" Eberhard prompted.

"Yes," I said and straightened in my seat. "Yes, I'm here. Sorry."

Then again, addictions were so easily hidden these days, everyone was susceptible. It had taken the opioid crisis reaching epic proportions and landing squarely on the doorstep of small towns and suburbia for lawmakers to finally notice the problem and start doing something about it. But it was a tough situation, and it was far from controlled.

Eberhard said, "We simply can't pinpoint the exact time of death. I doubt we ever will. At the moment, I'd say it's more likely than not that he was dead before you hit him. Which means you're not likely to be charged with homicide."

I remembered the flutter of a pulse I'd felt in his neck when I was administering CPR. Had he been alive? I'd wanted him to be alive. It was possible I'd imagined the flutter. I simply couldn't say.

I coughed to get his attention. "Martin, you know I administered CPR at the scene. I thought I felt a pulse in his neck. Are you saying you're sure I was wrong?"

He paused for what seemed like an eternity. "I'm prepared to testify that he would not have survived whether or not you struck him with your car. Let's leave it at that."

I sighed and swiped my fingers through my short hair. Softly, I said, "As much as I want that to be true, I absolutely need to know for sure."

"I've given you my medical opinion. I can't do any more than that. I wasn't at the scene. I didn't examine the man until he reached my morgue." Eberhard's tone was brusque.

"How did he end up in the street if he was already dead?"

"Several scenarios are possible. He might have self-administered the toxic heroin, seeking his next high, and then inadvertently wandered into the street in front of your car."

"Wouldn't he have collapsed on the sidewalk? Or at least closer to the curb? He was in the middle of the travel lane when I hit him." I was asking questions no medical examiner could possibly answer with certainty. But I needed to know.

Eberhard did not reply. I had the sense that he'd turned his attention to something else.

His explanation seemed odd to me, but then the whole incident was completely beyond the realm of normal. I returned to the conversation at hand before I lost his attention altogether.

"Tell me more about this toxic heroin."

"Nasty stuff, I'm afraid." He sounded distracted.

"Yes, but how so?"

"Toxic heroin combines heroin and fentanyl. Both have depressant effects on the body. Users feel exaggerated drowsiness, nausea, confusion, sedation, and—in extreme instances—suffer unconsciousness, respiratory distress, and death." The sound of pages rustling echoed through the phone line as Eberhard flipped through them.

"Sounds like toxic heroin should be deadly every time, then, shouldn't it?"

"It often is deadly," Martin replied. "A few lucky users make it to the ER for an antidote. Naloxone. It can be effective if administered soon enough."

"Does the dosage of toxic heroin he took make any difference?"

"Yes. And the elapsed time, too." He cleared his throat. "Obviously your victim wasn't one of the lucky ones."

"Right." I tapped my fingers on the desk, trying to fit the details into the story in my head and coming up empty. In all the scenarios for why the man had stumbled out in front of me, drug addiction wasn't one I'd considered. "Sounds like an awful way to die."

"It is. Unfortunately, the local drug dealers have found a way to turn that gruesome death to their advantage."

"What do you mean?"

Eberhard said, "They use the potential for death to entice thrill-seekers. Toxic heroin's bad reputation has become their best form of advertising. The dealers get a boost in sales after a string of fatal overdoses. I see the evidence here in my morgue."

I stared into the phone. "But that's crazy."

"It is," Eberhard agreed. "The lethalness attracts a certain kind of addict. They demand to try it for the thrills. Some don't live to regret it."

"And you think this guy was one of those thrill-seekers? That he simply overdosed?" I still couldn't believe it. He'd been bruised and battered from the accident, yes, but wearing clothes that would've paid rent on a tony Tampa apartment for months. Which meant he'd achieved some level of success in life. Why wouldn't he have been smarter about the drugs he ingested?

"I have no way of knowing, Willa." Eberhard's words were clipped now, perhaps annoyed because the answer was out of his realm of expertise. "What I can tell you, based on the amount of toxic heroin in his system, is that it's highly unlikely he simply walked into the path of your vehicle."

"Why?"

Eberhard explained as if talking to a very dense seven-year-old. "Because he wouldn't have had the ability to do so. According to my timeline, he would have already been dead or very near death before you struck him. Which means he wouldn't have been capable of walking at all."

"But if he didn't walk into traffic, then..." My voice trailed off as realization struck. "You're saying someone pushed him?"

"Not necessarily. He might have simply fallen."

"But a push seems more likely, given the distance he traveled to end up in front of my car, doesn't it?"

"Yes. Although accident reconstruction isn't my bailiwick. Or yours. That's a question for Chief Hathaway."

"But why? And who would do such a thing?" I'd heard testimony about all sorts of murders over the years. This was a first for me.

"I'm a medical examiner. Not a clairvoyant. I've said all I can about this until we get further lab reports, which aren't likely to change things much. The headline, for your purposes, is that in my very well-qualified medical opinion, you didn't kill the guy. If I was filling out the death certificate right now, which I'm not, I'd say the cause of death was a toxic heroin overdose. The manner of death remains undetermined but is most likely either accidental overdose or intentional suicide. The mechanism of death is related to the overdose, although I haven't pinpointed the exact biological reason yet." He paused, and when I asked no further questions, he added, "And if there's nothing else, I've got to go."

"Of course. Thank you, Martin. It was very kind of you to call and let me know," I said, but he'd already hung up.

I sank back in my chair again, a bit of the tension between my shoulder blades easing. The case of the mysterious well-groomed man kept getting more and more complicated. But maybe I hadn't killed him, and that was a thin reed I wanted to hang on to. The coroner had said I'd be pleased to hear the results. I wouldn't say that "pleased" described my current mood. More like relieved.

Whoever had given the dead man those drugs was his killer, even if he'd taken the drugs voluntarily.

The drugs were administered well before I'd arrived on the scene.

He'd have died alone in the cold rain if he hadn't somehow landed in the street half a moment before I arrived.

Which also meant that CJ would be sorely disappointed. Ben Hathaway wouldn't charge me with vehicular homicide for the death.

Which didn't mean, of course, that CJ would stop the impeachment investigation. He'd chosen his path, and he would stick with it. He might still prevail.

Florida law required a driver to have control of the vehicle at all times. I hadn't. I'd been distracted. I was driving faster than I should have been for the weather conditions that night. I was unable to stop before I hit that man.

None of my conduct was above reproach.

Neither was it criminal.

But the coroner's opinion meant CJ would be stuck with complaining about disruption to the court caused by my unjudicial conduct. Which he'd been complaining about ever since I took the job. Same old, same old.

My worst sin in CJ's eyes was that I'd caused a spectacle and brought unwanted public criticism to the court. If there was one thing CJ hated, it was public criticism. He took it as a personal affront. He simply wanted me gone, had from the start. Now, I'd all but handed him a means to do it, albeit unintentionally.

I shrugged. Nothing I could do about that. CJ was as uncontrollable as I was.

For the moment, though, I still had a lot of empty time on my hands. The best way to use it was to focus on my own investigation into what had happened the night of the accident.

Someone killed that man.

An unsolved murder or unexplained death involving a high-ranking federal judge would feed the conspiracy mongers for years. Decades, even.

My ability to do my job and even George's business would be impacted.

Speculation about me and my involvement in the poor man's death would never end.

Unless I ended the speculation myself by finding out who killed the man and why.

Which was exactly what I planned to do.

CHAPTER TWELVE

Friday, November 11
6:00 p.m.

WHEN I WALKED DOWNSTAIRS to meet George at the end of the day, I was feeling more optimistic. Until I stepped outside the courthouse and into the sunlit plaza in front. The vultures, protesters, and cameras swarmed like hungry mosquitos, forming a sea of humanity, all jostling and barking for attention.

"Judge Carson, is it true that you've been suspended from your position on the bench?"

"Judge Carson, do you have any comment about the impeachment proceedings filed against you today by Chief Judge Richardson?"

"Judge Carson, how do you and your husband plan to handle all this negative publicity?"

"Judge Carson, have you been in touch with the dead man's family?"

"Judge Carson, is this the first time you've ever killed a man?"

I kept my head high and forward, sunglasses firmly in place, expression deliberately unreadable. The questions pelted me from all sides, but I pressed on. By the time I'd waded through the firestorm to reach George's Bentley, I felt like I'd survived an epic battle.

The questions about the deceased were especially unfair and harsh, but these vultures weren't legitimate journalists, and they weren't our friends. They didn't care how we felt.

Some were only interested in salacious headlines and getting the highest ratings on cable networks. The so-called citizen journalists were looking to sell advertising on blogs and websites by creating viral videos, using any means possible.

Welcome to the twenty-first century. I scowled behind my oversized sunglasses and ducked into the sedan.

George looked as grim as I felt when I finally slid into the passenger seat and slammed the door behind me.

We were used to the occasional appearance on TV and even in local tabloids. The stories were usually positive, puff pieces that made everybody feel good.

Around Tampa, we were considered a high-profile couple because of George's five-star restaurant and his amazing chefs, not because of my job. Being a federal judge made me kind of a big deal among lawyers and other judges, and even in certain political circles. Outside of that, though, most people only knew me as George Carson's wife.

The dead man had changed all that, and not in a good way.

"Bastards," George said under his breath as he eased the Bentley out of the path of the crowd ahead and into traffic. "They're like hyenas at a kill. Picking and tearing and scavenging for any crumb they can find. I'll bet you anything those protesters out there are being paid to show up and make this scene."

I slumped in my seat. "Last week you were excited about your upcoming interview on *Good Morning Tampa*."

"Yeah? Well, this is not that." He stared straight ahead, a small muscle ticcing near his tight jaw. "These idiots have completely shut down George's Place. Guests couldn't get past them today for lunch. I don't even have a restaurant if diners can't get to my food."

I crossed my arms and stared out the window. He wasn't really ranting at me. George and I had a strong marriage, a good partnership. He was under as much stress as I was. His restaurant was essential to him and our livelihood. But none of that made his words hurt any less.

Guilt—my new constant companion—swelled inside me again. Wonderful. Not only had this thing screwed up my career, now it was apparently ruining my husband's life, too.

We stopped at the light, and George clicked on his left turn signal. The route was the same one I'd taken Tuesday night. There was only one way on and off our island. We had to travel on Bayshore Boulevard to get there.

He made the turn, and the big sedan growled easily along the roadway until we veered to the right and the Plant Key Bridge shimmered in the distance, illuminated by the setting sun.

The island itself had been built back in the 1890s by the Army Corp of Engineers at the insistence of one Henry Plant, a local Tampa resident and real-estate mogul.

Back then, Hillsborough Bay had been too shallow for navigation and devoid of any landmasses. Using his money and influence, Plant had persuaded the engineers to dredge up enough solid land for what would eventually become Plant Key, at the same time they were dredging the bay to allow more commercial freighters to pass through to the Port of Tampa.

The result was our egg-shaped island. It was about a mile wide and two miles long and sat between the Davis Islands and Ballast Point in Hillsborough Bay. The narrow end faced Bayshore Boulevard on the north while the wider southern end faced the Gulf of Mexico.

Plant Key Bridge was added near the end of construction and connected the island to Bayshore Boulevard just east of Gandy Boulevard.

If good ol' Henry Plant had tried to have his project built today, there would've been serious objections from several different marine-wildlife conservation groups. Both the island and the bridge carved out space smack in the middle of everybody's favorite view as well. But such things weren't a priority back then. And in Plant's opinion, if he owned an island, then he needed a way to get over there, didn't he?

George sighed and reached across the console to lay a hand on my thigh. "I'm sorry. This isn't your fault. It's just frustrating."

I nodded miserably.

He made a smooth turn onto the ramp leading up to the bridge. "How did your day go? Any word on the autopsy results?"

I laced my fingers with his as I relayed the information the coroner had told me.

"Well, that's good news, isn't it?" he asked.

"Yeah, but it's not good enough. I need to know what happened. I spent the rest of the afternoon researching toxic heroin and searching through missing-person records in the law-enforcement databases. Nothing."

"I'm sorry." George slowed as we crested the top of the ramp, and I spotted what looked like a roadblock ahead, lights and sirens flashing off the squad cars parked across the lane to block vehicles from crossing the bridge. George gave a disgruntled snort. "See what I mean? At this rate, dinner service will be empty, too. And we were fully booked for tonight."

These citizen journalists and protesters were turning out to be a bigger nightmare than the accident itself, which was saying something. We didn't want or need all these negative stories floating out there online. Unlike yesterday's newspaper that was used to wrap today's fish, anything posted online would last forever. These vultures were doing permanent damage to George's Place. Damage that might never be undone.

Minaret was the name of the nineteenth-century home George had inherited from his great-aunt Minnie. He was her only nephew and her favorite person, so when she died, Minnie passed the place on to him. The name reflected the polished-steel onion dome on top of the mansion.

The first floor housed the restaurant, called simply "George's Place." The second floor was our flat.

At first, back when we'd been living in Detroit, getting the call from Minnie's estate attorney had felt a little like winning the grand prize on some game show. But what they don't tell you is that those prizes come with hefty costs attached to them. Costs like taxes and upkeep. Hell, the air-conditioning bills alone were enough to fund a third-world country for a couple of years.

Not that George and I were about to hit the welfare line or anything, but all his long hours working at the restaurant, and mine sitting on the bench, weren't spent just because we loved our jobs.

I groaned and squeezed my eyes shut as George traveled closer to where the police vehicles were controlling access to our home. My head pounded, and my body ached, and all I wanted was a long, hot bath and a nice glass of gin on the veranda. I'd given up smoking again, but tonight called for a cigar to ease away the tensions of the day.

I straightened in my seat and faced forward like an adult, still wearing my sunglasses. George gave my hand a reassuring press as we pulled up to the uniformed officers. Chief Hathaway strolled over from his unmarked sedan.

George lowered his window, and hot air blasted in as Ben tipped his head to us while keeping an eye on the mob. "George. Willa. Glad you're here. I'll accompany you home, if you don't mind. We've finally got an ID on the deceased."

CHAPTER THIRTEEN

Friday, November 11
6:20 p.m.

"SO, WHO IS HE?" I asked as soon as we got inside.

Instead of heading upstairs to our living quarters as we usually would have, George led the way into the Sunset Bar. The place was deserted, which was strange given we were getting into tourist season. November always began the snowbird migration of part-time residents returning south for the winter and the first batch of vacationers fleeing the cold.

George waved to the bartender as we passed and then led us to an isolated booth in the corner. I slid into the seat. George sat beside me, and Ben took the bench across.

"Who is he?" I asked again.

Ben took off his hat and ran a hand through his flattened hair. "Charles Evan Hayden. Went by Evan. Worked for Foster & Barnes, a local financial services firm catering to sports celebrities, mainly. Small but successful, I guess."

"How did you ID him?" I straightened as the bartender

brought us glasses of water. I'd have much preferred a Bombay Sapphire martini with a twist, but that would have to wait.

Ben drained half his water and nodded. "Three of his coworkers contacted us after we ran his picture on the local news."

"Good. What'd they say?" I asked.

Ben cringed slightly. "Seems Hayden wasn't exactly Mr. Popular with his colleagues."

"Why not?" George asked, a troubled frown on his face.

"He was a financial planner for star athletes. Mostly local, but he had clients throughout Florida. His specialty, according to his coworkers anyway, was tax avoidance." Ben raised his eyebrows. "Which in his case was a euphemism for tax fraud, I gathered."

"Oh," George said.

Tax avoidance isn't illegal. Tax fraud is. I'd seen my share of fraudsters as a lawyer, a judge, and sometimes in our social circles. Motivations for tax fraud varied. Usually, they simply didn't want to pay taxes. Everybody understood the desire to avoid paying, but most people were law-abiding taxpayers anyway.

And some weren't.

I said, "Sounds like his colleagues weren't very fond of him."

"That's putting it mildly." Ben shook his head and snorted. "No one we talked to could stand the guy. By all accounts, he was arrogant and rude and a general son of a bitch. His nickname around the office was Chuckles."

George frowned. "Chuckles?"

Ben nodded. "Because he was so obnoxious, and he hated using his first name. Avoided it at all times, they said. Calling him Chuckles to his face was a sure way to get punched if you didn't duck out of the way fast enough."

"Well, that's just great. We're being flayed alive over a guy who was about as worthy as Bernie Madoff," George said snidely. I flashed him a glare, and he shrugged.

I looked at Ben. "The coroner told me Hayden was so doped up on toxic heroin there was no way he could have walked out in front of my car, Ben. That means either he fell or someone pushed him into my path."

Ben nodded. "Seems that way."

The cold water glass between my fingers was slippery with condensation. After a couple of sips and a minute of contemplation, I asked, "Do you think his coworkers might have despised Hayden enough to kill him?"

"Not sure," Ben replied. "I'm going over to the offices to interview them again myself tomorrow. It's Saturday, but I guess financial planners are like cops. They never take a day off."

"I'd like to come along."

He frowned, and George scowled.

"I know it's not normal procedure. But I've got the time," I said. "And I'm good at it. We've worked together before. You know I won't get in your way."

Ben narrowed his gaze. "When we asked his colleagues about drug use, they all gave a firm 'no way.' They say Hayden was a horse's ass, but he was also squeaky clean about his body. A real health nut. The coworkers all said Hayden would never have used drugs. Called him a straight arrow in that department, at least."

"If Hayden didn't take the drugs himself, how'd they get in his system?" George's scowl deepened. "You think someone else shot him up? Is that what you're saying?"

"Dunno." Ben shrugged. "A couple of his colleagues are claiming foul play."

"Murder?" I said.

"They didn't go that far. They just said if Hayden had drugs in his system, he didn't take them willingly," he said. "And if someone else gave him the drugs, maybe they unintentionally overdosed him."

Perversely, the word "murder" made me feel slightly better. Not that murder was some kind of stimulant for me. But if someone had deliberately killed Hayden, the investigation would pivot in a whole new direction. Meaning, away from me and my car and my driving.

"Is that what you think, Ben? This was an accidental overdose?" I asked.

"It's too early to rule anything out." Ben finished the rest of his water, then stood, collecting his hat. "I need to get back out there. Be careful tossing that information around. If speculation gets out that Hayden was murdered, you'll have even more people camped out at the entrance to your bridge. Looks like you might need to shut down your restaurant for a while, George. At least until all this blows over."

"What?" George sputtered. "I can't do that. Crowd control is your job. Put some more officers out there and keep those vultures off my property."

"We're doing what we can. We can stop them at the bridge, but we're likely to snag some of your paying customers that way. Besides, the airspace is open, and there's nothing we can do about drones flying overhead. Helicopters, either." Ben gave a curt nod and prepared to leave.

"What's next?" I asked.

Ben replied, "We've notified Hayden's parents. They live in Pittsburgh. They're flying in tomorrow."

"You told them about the toxic heroin?" George asked.

Ben shook his head. "Not yet. Figured that's the kind of news

I should deliver in person. No parent wants to hear that their son died of any kind of drug overdose."

We sat in silence for a few moments before I asked, "What about my request to go with you to Foster & Barnes?"

He looked at me a couple of long moments before he replied, "I'll call you in the morning, and let you know what time I'm heading over there. You've got good instincts and firsthand knowledge of the accident, which could be useful. That'll free up another man to secure your bridge, too."

George harrumphed.

Ben grinned and plopped his hat back into place. "Have a good evening."

I watched Ben's back until he left the Sunset Bar. The brief flare of adrenaline-spiked euphoria I'd felt over the possibility of Hayden's murder moving me out of the spotlight vanished. In its place came a heavy finality. I loved George, our marriage was good and strong and true, but we couldn't afford to shut down his restaurant. Simple as that.

"So," I said as George slipped off the bench and moved across to where Ben had been sitting. "Things are really slow?"

"Not just slow. Things are dead in here." I winced, and George reached across the table to take my hand. "Sorry. Bad pun."

"No. You're right. And Ben was right, too." I gestured around the empty bar. "Until something way more scandalous than me comes along to distract them, the tabloids, the curiosity seekers, and any paid protesters in the crowd will continue to block the bridge and keep diners away. Add to that group the citizen journalists. And then there's the legitimate press who are bound to do follow-ups as the case develops. Starving diners won't want to run that gauntlet, even for your menu. No matter how sublime it is. There are other restaurants in Tampa."

George looked miserable, but he didn't argue. There was no reasonable argument to be made.

I took a deep breath before I said, "So, until Hayden's death is explained, and the case resolved, and these people find other poop to scoop, I should move to a hotel."

"What?" George winced and squeezed my hand. "No way. I won't let these bastards split us up. That's crazy. This thing can't last forever. We'll just make do the best we can."

"No. That's not fair. And making do will not solve the problem." I shook my head, pulled free from him, and missed his warmth immediately. "This is our home, and we can't live like this. I'll keep getting paid, even if I'm not working, until CJ manages to get me impeached, tried, and convicted. Which will take a while. You know we can't give up the income from the restaurant for who knows how long. If you lose too much momentum, it'll be hard and expensive to get everything back on track. That's money we both know we don't have."

He lowered his eyes and didn't reply because there was nothing he could say. I was right, and we both knew it. Property taxes were coming due. He had staff to pay. The busy holiday season had already started. He needed to keep the restaurant open, and to do that, he needed paying customers.

I said, "If I leave, they'll stop hounding you, at least. Once they stop hanging around the bridge, your clientele will return."

His heart wasn't in the protest, but he mumbled, "Maybe. Maybe not."

"It's worth a shot. And it's only for a short while. Just long enough for me to figure out who killed Hayden."

"You?" Alarmed, his eyes opened wide. "I don't like that idea at all, Willa. Leave it to Ben. It's his job."

"Can't do that." I shook my head. "Ben's got too much on his plate. He'll get the job done, but how long will it take? Months will pass before he gets this thing figured out. I don't want to be separated from you for that long."

"If someone murdered Hayden, what's to stop them from trying to kill you, too?" George objected, shaking his head vigorously. "I don't like it."

"I don't like it, either. None of this has actually been a trip to the beach for me, you know," I snapped. Then I took a deep breath and blew out a long stream of frustration. "Look, CJ has made it clear that I can't work until all this is resolved. What would you have me do? Take up knitting? Or maybe I could invite some of those vultures out there to play poker?"

George looked away, his hazel eyes stormy. In all the years we'd been married, we'd never chosen to spend much time apart. He was my sounding board, my rock, my regular dinner companion. I served the same roles for him.

But I'd run smack into this mess, and it was only fair that I be the one to get us out. At least, I had to try. I couldn't simply twiddle my thumbs and wait for Ben Hathaway.

"I hate this," George said at last, still not looking at me. "I hate that you're being blamed for something that wasn't your fault. I hate that you're being dragged through the mud before all the facts are even in. On top of everything else, that jackass of a chief justice is using this situation to have you removed from the bench. It's horseshit, Willa. All of it. And it kills me inside to see you hurt by this load of crap."

"I know. I feel the same." I took his hand again, holding it tight. "But we'll make it through this. Just like we've made it through everything else. Besides, I have better access to information from my chambers than I do here. I'm sure Augustus can act as a go-between for us if we need it."

"Seriously?" George gave a mirthless laugh. "I can't even talk to you?"

"We can talk on the phone, but it's risky. Electronic eavesdropping is pretty simple to do these days. Those vultures will be watching my every move. The more time you spend with me, the more you'll stay in their crosshairs. We want you off their radar, at the very least. We want them to come after me and leave you alone." I forced a smile I didn't quite feel and gave his hand another squeeze. "Come on. It could be fun. Like our own spy movie."

"Carson. George Carson," he mimicked countless actors playing the role of James Bond, trying to be funny. Neither of us laughed. "Are you sure you can't stay at Kate's? She's got the room, even with Leo's daughters there."

I took a deep breath and shook my head. I could offer a few good reasons, but I didn't want to explain. Bringing my circus down on Kate wasn't going to happen. She had enough to deal with as it was.

He was quiet for a while, but George finally accepted that he couldn't change my mind. "When are you leaving?"

"Tomorrow morning will be soon enough. I'm already here now. Might as well enjoy our evening, since you won't be busy." I smiled at my weak joke, but he winced, which was when I knew for sure I was doing the right thing.

We'd have one last night together. It would have to be enough.

I pushed back into the bench seat. All business now. "I'll call Augustus tonight and let him know what's going on. Have him leak some story about me needing space or some nonsense. I'll let him make that part up. He's good at protecting me and keeping secrets."

George didn't reply. Nor did his frown ease at all.

I laced my fingers with his, and we sat silently across the table that might as well have been as wide as the Gulf of Mexico. "It will all work out in the end, you'll see."

"I hope you're right, Mighty Mouse." George exhaled forcefully. "I really hope you are."

I smiled and put as much bravado in my tone as I could muster, despite my misgivings. "Of course I'm right. I'm the judge. Haven't you heard? Judges are always right."

George nodded and sarcastically replied, "Uh-huh."

CHAPTER FOURTEEN

Saturday, November 12
9:00 a.m.

I HAD A RENTAL SUV delivered to Minaret, stowed a suitcase in the back, and made a show of leaving Plant Key the next morning. I slowed down and waved as I left because I wanted everyone camped out at the entrance to our bridge to see me go.

No doubt about my departure. Absolutely none.

If I could have figured out a logistical way to do it, I'd have announced that I wasn't coming back anytime soon, either.

Most of these people were paid protesters and the citizen journalists who paid them. The perpetrators were thinly staffed and thinly funded. I was betting that a company of one using credit cards and operating from his parents' basement hoping to strike it big in the world of internet gossipmongering wouldn't hang out here in the hot sun all day for too many days.

In short, I wanted them to give up and bug out. I hoped they wouldn't wait too long to do so. Saturday lunch was usually a busy crowd at George's Place. With luck, these vultures would be gone before noon.

I arrived at Ben's office right on time. Being Ben, he wanted to drive. I left the rental in his parking lot and let him win this small victory.

Foster & Barnes was located in Tampa's Rocky Point business district. Because of the Saturday traffic and the roadwork and his cautious driving, we reached the firm's offices twenty-five minutes late. I wasn't worried. These guys would be here a while, setting up to make more money. It was a game with them. And a dangerously cutthroat, addictive one.

The building was very posh and English-upper-crust-feeling. Pretentious stone pillars and fierce yew topiary were out of place amid the tropical stucco of its neighbors.

Exactly the kind of place I'd expect an arrogant jackass—as Charles Evan Hayden had been described by his coworkers—to work. I figured Hayden's colleagues were the same. Takes one to know one, after all.

We got out of the unmarked sedan, and Ben slammed his door. He didn't lock the car, but then, given the neighborhood we were in, no one was likely to bother it. There was a security keypad at the door, and Ben pressed the button on the intercom.

"Police Chief Ben Hathaway here to interview Kelly Webb and Tom Bradford," he said, giving me a flat look as he did so.

A woman answered, her voice clipped. "One moment please."

Seconds later, the door buzzed open, and she held it for us as we walked inside. Her face had that permanent wind-tunnel look, like she'd had too much plastic surgery. She didn't seem pleased that Ben was plus one. Good.

"This way, Chief Hathaway." She watched me warily from unnaturally widened eyes as she gestured toward a hallway across the airy, beige-and-white lobby from where we were standing. "We were expecting you earlier."

Ben removed his hat, grumbling, "Sorry. Traffic."

"May I have the name of your guest?" the woman asked.

"Wilhelmina Carson." I left the judge part off. People were usually reticent to confess to murder in front of a judge. "Everyone calls me Willa."

"Right this way, Ms. Carson," she said, ignoring my preferences and failing to offer her name in return. Her heels clicked on the granite tiles as she guided us into the back.

I'm a judge. I make judgments. This woman was both haughty and rude.

So I couldn't resist asking, "I'm sorry. I didn't get your name."

"Madeline Bishop," she replied without a pause in her rapid steps, as if I was rude to ask and she was annoyed with my behavior. There was a lot of that going around lately.

Ms. Bishop didn't see me smile unless she had eyes in the back of her head. But she'd confirmed my guess. Charles Evan Hayden wasn't the only socially inept jackass who worked here.

The offices were clean and tidy, if a bit stark. We walked past at least eight generously sized individual offices, plus two suites for the top executives. All the offices were occupied, mostly by youngish men with fashionably unshaven faces dressed in expensively casual weekend-in-Palm Beach clothes talking on speakerphones. It was Saturday in Florida, after all.

Through the windows, I spotted a lovely walled courtyard behind the building. Immaculate grounds. A marble fountain featuring two leaping dolphins. In the distance were spectacular views of Old Tampa Bay.

From here, with the sparkling turquoise waters and the

tranquil new-age jazz playing quietly in the background, we seemed a million miles away from the mundane world.

The celebrity clientele that Foster & Barnes catered to must have enjoyed the expensive, exclusive tranquility. All that money they were making had to be displayed somewhere, right?

Ms. Bishop led us into a brightly lit conference room with a long, glass-topped table and contemporary-style metal chairs. The same kind of black-and-silver slings found in airport waiting areas, but about a thousand times more expensive and two thousand times less comfortable.

Yep, Foster & Barnes was pretty much as I'd expected. The effort to be both expensive and appealing to all tastes meant the interior design was so sterile that any trace of human personality had long ago vanished. I much preferred Aunt Minnie's antiques and knickknacks.

A vase of calla lilies rested on a shelf along the wall sporting black-and-white photos of smiling business people glad-handing clients—some I recognized, some I didn't. I don't read the gossip rags much, but a lot of these folks dined regularly at George's Place or showed up at the charity functions we attended.

"Ms. Webb and Mr. Bradford should be right with you," Ms. Bishop said with a touch of disdain. She really didn't like dealing with public servants, or servants of any kind, I guessed. "May we offer either of you something to drink?"

"No thank you," Ben and I replied in unison. If we'd said yes, her gaze made it clear she'd have poisoned the water or something.

She nodded then clicked back out into the hallway, her footsteps echoing off into the distance. He chose one of the torture chairs, and I remained standing. We waited in silence. Which was fine by me. For the moment, I was content to soak in the sunshine from the plate-glass window that overlooked the pretty garden. It was a nice change after days of gloom.

Ben pulled out his phone and began scrolling through his emails while I enjoyed a rare spate of silence. A clock ticked rhythmically from its perch in the corner. Air conditioning blew down from the ceiling. Dappled sunlight played across the sparkling tabletop, and the rays danced along the imported rug beneath.

I wondered if this long wait in pleasant surroundings was the trick Hayden and his coworkers employed to relax their clients into releasing control of their assets. If so, it was highly effective.

Maybe I should rethink having Augustus book that massage at the spa. I might be relaxed into all sorts of things. I smiled.

A few lovely, empty minutes passed before a man and a woman entered the room.

The woman was attractive enough. Late twenties, shoulder-length blond hair, nice skin, not much makeup. She wore a pale-gray dress and pumps. She was petite, maybe five-four, with an additional inch or so of lift from her heels.

And she looked vaguely familiar. Maybe just because she was the type of young, successful millennial that roamed the best places in Tampa these days.

"Kelly Webb," she said with a friendly smile, extending her hand to me, then Ben. "Call me Kelly. Everyone does."

Kelly was pretty, but it wasn't her beauty that struck me. She had an ethereal quality about her, as if she inhabited the ruthless, cutthroat world of financial wheelers and dealers, but wasn't tainted by it. Whether she was truly ethereal or donned the façade to impress wealthy clients, I couldn't say. Perhaps she'd used it to woo Charles Evan Hayden, though. I wondered if the two had been lovers.

The man who followed her was Tom Bradford. He resembled Hayden in many ways. He looked about thirty, dark hair, pricey clothes. The cynical smirk on his boyish face might have been Hayden's go-to expression, too, if the intel Hathaway already shared could be trusted.

"Time is money, Chief," Bradford said, sprawling into a chair at the other end of the table away from the rest of us. "And your visits here are costing me big time. Do you know who I've got waiting in my office?"

"Nope." Ben yawned, completely unimpressed by Bradford's brash demeanor.

Bradford snorted. "A guy who could buy and sell your department a dozen times over. So I need to get back. I can't imagine what else we can possibly say that we haven't already. Hayden was an asshole. Nobody liked him. He's dead. End of story."

"Tom!" Kelly exclaimed, admonishing him like a younger sister would. "Be nice."

"You be nice. That's what you do, isn't it?" He leaned back in his chair, sneering. "I hear you've been real nice to Hayden's clients. Trying to steal them all for yourself."

Ben interrupted, slapping a lid on Bradford's adolescent antagonism. "Do either of you know of anyone in these offices who uses heroin?"

"Heroin…?" Kelly said, eyes widening like shocked camera shutters.

Bradford rolled his eyes.

"Is that a no?" Ben wagged his head to look at the two.

"How would I know?" Bradford shrugged. "We're not exactly best pals with each other around here. This is a competitive business, if you haven't already figured that out. We're best pals with our clients. With coworkers, not so much."

"So, one or more of Hayden's clients are heroin users," I said.

"They're sports stars and celebrities with too much money. All of them have dozens of hangers-on. What do you think?" Bradford narrowed his gaze toward me. He hadn't bothered to look at me before. "You're that judge. The one who mowed Hayden down with your car."

An involuntary gasp escaped my lips. "I didn't mow Mr. Hayden down with my car. Don't be ridiculous."

"Hell, I'm not complaining. Just the opposite. You got the guy out of my way quite handily." Bradford grinned at me and applauded. "Well done, Judge Carson."

"Please excuse my colleague. He isn't trying to be such a jerk. It comes naturally." Kelly shot him a withering stare before turning back to Chief Hathaway. "We're licensed here. Our activities are restricted and monitored. We have rules. Drug use is not one of the perks of the job. We can get fired for it."

She batted her eyelashes and damn if the stoic Chief didn't crack a smile. Yep. This girl definitely used her assets to distract and coerce. I made a mental note that she hadn't really answered Hathaway's question, either. Which meant drug use existed here, as it did in many offices. And she absolutely knew about it.

These two were far from model citizens. For sure. And probably no better or worse than Hayden. Yet, neither seemed to realize that they could have been in his place already. Or that they might soon be as dead as he was if they were among the drug users.

Which made me wonder just how far they'd go to keep their habits a secret. No time like the present to find out.

CHAPTER FIFTEEN

Saturday, November 12
11:00 a.m.

BEN CLEARED HIS THROAT and frowned down at the notes he'd written on his phone prior to us coming here. He'd shown them to me in the car to give me a heads-up about his interview plans.

"What about new people in Mr. Hayden's life? Girlfriends? Buddies? Did you see anyone new or strange lurking around in the last few weeks?"

"No. Sorry," Kelly answered, staring at her hands on the table.

Bradford shook his head, looking about as bored as a person could be and still remain conscious. In my courtroom, the ones that had the most to hide or to lose used the technique to mask themselves. Sometimes, it was effective to fool the jury.

Quantum physics claims that the very act of observation alters reality. I'd come to believe the same was true of interview subjects. These two knew things they weren't telling us. Lies of omission. Their answers teased the back of my brain.

Or maybe my judgment was clouded because I wanted this situation settled. I wanted my life back. Settling the Hayden matter was the first step.

Kelly looked up at me and blinked her pretty eyes, which didn't faze me in the least. "Judge Carson, I think you know my parents. They own Humidora. It's a cigar bar at Channelside."

Which was when the niggling sense that she was familiar clicked in my head. Of course.

George and I had frequented the Humidora smoke shop quite often last year. Then our free time had dwindled, and we hadn't been back lately. The owners, a lovely couple, were always friendly and helpful.

"Yes, I do remember your parents." I smiled and looked closer at Kelly Webb. Light-hazel eyes. Blond eyebrows. The resemblance to her parents was there. "You look very much like your mother."

She actually blushed and lowered her eyes. "Thank you."

I sat back and took in the room again. The office décor suited Kelly perfectly, too—pale linen, light hazel, and pastel peach. Maybe she'd been the decorator.

"Are you a heroin user, Mr. Bradford?" Ben redirected the conversation. "Just to be social with your clients, perhaps?"

The question jolted Bradford from his blasé attitude. Or maybe Ben's boldness had finally punctured Bradford's hard shell. He gave another shake of his head, not deigning to answer with words.

"What about pot? Cocaine? A few lines with clients to loosen them up?" Ben asked, and Bradford shook his head after each question.

"What exactly are you trying to get at?" Bradford glared. "I'm clean. We're all clean here, okay? We get random drug tests every month. Come back with a warrant, and you can search our offices."

He left off the foul epithet I expected to hear at the end of that speech, but it hung in the air anyway.

"Where were you Tuesday night between nine p.m. and eleven p.m., the night Evan Hayden died, Mr. Bradford?" Ben asked. If Bradford had an alibi, that would let him off the hook.

"Here. Working late. Kelly can vouch for me." Bradford glanced toward Webb.

She looked at him, then Ben, then me with another round of doe-eyed surprise. "Financial planning isn't all glitz and glamour. Usually it's long hours and lots of stress managing our clients' accounts."

She paused, and then, as if she'd just remembered something, she smiled. "There are security cameras in all the offices. You can check the videos if you like."

"With a warrant," Bradford repeated belligerently.

"I'll be sure to get one." Ben clicked off his phone and shoved it into his pocket, then pushed to his feet. "Luckily, I know a judge."

Webb frowned but didn't say anything else.

"Are we done here?" Bradford said, standing as well. "I need to get back to my work. And I've got lunch plans."

Ben gave a curt nod. "If I think of anything else I need, I'll call you. Or come back."

"You do that." Bradford jutted his chin forward and followed it out the door.

After he left, Kelly Webb led us out of the conference room toward the lobby, chatting amiably all the way.

"Before we leave, I'd like to see Hayden's office," I said.

Webb's eyes clouded. "I don't think we can let you rummage through his things."

"I just want to look at the place where he worked. Nothing more," I replied. This was private property. I had no right to be here at all. But if she didn't consent, that would tell me something, too.

Pleasantly, Hathaway said, "I can get a warrant for that, too. While I'm asking the judge."

Webb shrugged. "I guess a look around won't hurt. Evan's office was upstairs. Better views from the second floor. Follow me."

She led us to the elevator and down a corridor on the second floor that resembled the first-floor offices. These were also occupied, mostly by Young Turks dressed as casually as a *GQ* magazine fashion shoot.

At the end of the corridor, Kelly led us through an open doorway into an office much more spacious than any of the others we'd seen. The view of the garden and Tampa Bay beyond was spectacular. The same cold, unwelcoming modern furniture we'd seen everywhere else was artfully arranged to take full advantage of the view.

"This was Evan's office," she said.

"Who'll be moving in here now?" I asked. In law firms and courthouses, the moment an office as great as this one became vacant for any reason, eligible tenants practically leapt over one another to take up residence. I imagined the high rollers at Foster & Barnes would be the same.

Webb had the grace to blush again, at least. "I'm not sure. It hasn't been officially announced. But it won't be me or Tom, if that's what you're suggesting."

"Why not?" Hathaway asked.

"Because we don't qualify. Evan was one of the firm's top performers. He had a long list of star clients. Put simply, we don't." She didn't add a "yet" to that statement, but it hung in the air anyway.

"Aren't you wooing Hayden's clients?" I asked. "Or was Tom wrong about that?"

"Of course, I'm wooing Evan's clients. Tom is, too. We all are. They've all been reassigned to some of us already, but we have to make them want to stay," Webb replied matter-of-factly. "Like Tom said, this is a very competitive business. Not only within Foster & Barnes, but also from all the other firms out there who would like nothing better than to replace us."

"Right." I understood her point. Law firms were the same. Accounting firms and medical practices, too. Clients weren't chained to the firm. Personal relationships kept them in the fold, or out the door. It worked both ways.

Hathaway said, "Where are the files? I don't see anything at all in this office."

She nodded. "Computer servers. We work off laptops connected to secure servers. We keep them with us at all times."

"Where is Hayden's laptop?" I asked.

She shook her head. "I imagine you'd find it in his car or his apartment. He wouldn't have left it here on Tuesday, for sure."

"What about Hayden's assistant?" I couldn't run my office without Augustus. These high rollers had to have some kind of office spouse, too.

Webb frowned and cocked her head, as if she found the question puzzling. "You met her already. Madeline Bishop."

"Sorry," Ben said to me. "We interviewed Ms. Bishop. I'll fill you in later."

I nodded. Not because the offer was acceptable. I figured I'd get nothing out of Madeline Bishop if I tried to press her for answers here. An interview in her home was more likely to yield results.

We spent a few more minutes in the sterile room. There were no photos on the walls. No computer on the desk. No phone, even. The office was simply the most minimalist room I'd ever seen. Absolutely nothing was out of place. A wall of cabinetry lined one wall, and I suspected that was where Charles Evan Hayden's office paraphernalia had been stuffed.

If we opened the door, would everything come tumbling out onto our heads?

Kelly Webb glanced at her high-tech watch. "I'm sorry, but I've got a luncheon appointment, too."

"Okay," Hathaway said, following her back the way we'd come in.

We'd learned nothing. Something was definitely off about Madeline Bishop. Kelly Webb and Tom Bradford, too, for that matter. Given the way their client-assignment system worked, every analyst at Foster & Barnes probably had a motive for murdering Hayden. Every single one of them would have wanted his client portfolio.

But did they want it badly enough to kill him for it?

I glanced at Ben to see if he felt the same. His expression was unreadable.

At the front door, Webb stopped and smiled at me again. "Please visit Humidora again soon, Judge Carson. I'm sure my parents would love to see you."

"Give them my best," I said before I followed Ben back out into the afternoon sunshine, feeling a little less confused about Hayden's death. Not only was he a jerk with a lot of enemies, but he was also a wealthy jerk with a lot of clients just about any financial planner in the country would want to poach.

People had been killed for a lot less.

CHAPTER SIXTEEN

Saturday, November 12
1:00 p.m.

WE WALKED ACROSS THE hot parking lot and climbed into Chief Hathaway's even hotter sedan. He started the ignition and cranked up the air conditioning. Within minutes, we were headed back to the cop shop.

"Did you have any luck finding video of the accident Tuesday night?" I asked, snugging my seatbelt a little tighter as he accelerated around a tight curve. I loved to drive, but I was a nervous passenger.

"You know that stretch of Bayshore Boulevard as well as we do. If you'd been a block or two on either side of where it happened, we'd have video. But there's no traffic cams at that site. No commercial buildings with cameras, either. And it's dark there, between streetlight poles. We even checked with MacDill, but they said they don't regularly monitor the roads that far from the base." He glanced over with sympathy in his eyes. "It's almost as if Hayden chose that spot because he knew he wouldn't be seen on camera."

Which could have been precisely what he'd done if he'd committed suicide. Or what someone else had done, if they'd shoved him into traffic. At this point, either option was possible. But it wasn't likely that he'd simply been lucky enough to get hit by my car at the exact location where no one would witness his death.

Bayshore Boulevard is a picturesque linear park that runs the five-mile length of the shoreline between Gandy Boulevard and the Platt Street Bridge. The wide swath of traveled roadway and attractive buildings with spectacular views of Hillsborough Bay were bounded by green space and sidewalks. The area was heavily traveled by vehicles of all kinds at all hours. It was well lit and safe for pedestrians, bikers, rollerbladers, parents with strollers, joggers, and tourists simply enjoying the views, who were always present.

The wonder was that anyone could ever be on Bayshore without being seen, regardless of the time of day or the weather. There were always a few hardy (or foolish) souls out there even during hurricanes.

Sure, the incident happened late on a Tuesday night when most people were home preparing for bed, and the weather was lousy. Still, how was it possible that Hayden and I had simply been so unlucky?

It wasn't possible. Was it?

I closed my eyes and visualized the drive. I'd rounded the curve after the Platt Street Bridge, passed the hospital, and continued beyond the Davis Islands Bridge. Up until that point, there were commercial buildings and high-rise condos, all of which would have been equipped with video cameras, as well as traffic cams. Not an inch of Bayshore would have gone unwatched.

After the Davis Island Bridge, large, old homes replaced the high-rises for a long stretch of roadway. After that, more high-rises mixed with individual homes and shorter condos. A traffic light at Howard and another at Bay-to-Bay, which was about the halfway point.

I recalled the precise point of impact. Between South Boulevard and Howard Avenue. Bushy crepe myrtles blocked the headlights from oncoming cars to avoid night blindness. Stately homes were set back from the roadway on the right. Between them were a couple of empty lots where old homes had been demolished and new ones were not yet constructed. At that point, the streetlights were not illuminated for some reason. Greta's headlights were the only beacon in the darkness for about a hundred feet or so.

Right there. Startled by the memory, I jumped when I simply visualized the event again.

Hayden lunged into my travel lane. Back first, which was why I didn't see him as a person. In the darkness, his dark hair and dark suit, wet from the rain, looked like a shiny trash bag in Greta's headlights.

Until I slammed on the brakes. Hit him. Greta stopped. I got out of the car and went to help him.

The whole thing took a lot longer to describe than when it had actually happened.

"What about those construction zones? Neither one is directly adjacent to that dark stretch where…Hayden fell into my lane. But they might have video cams with wide-angle lenses to safeguard tenants at night."

"We've been making calls. So far, no luck." He paused and cleared his throat. "I'm sorry, Willa. We'll keep trying. But unless someone comes forward with it, looks like a no-go for video coverage."

I nodded. I understood. We rarely had all the evidence we needed in situations like this. All we could do was work with what we had.

After a while, I asked casually, "Where did Hayden live?"

Ben grinned. "Don't even think about going over there and hassling his neighbors."

"Oh, come on. Why would you even say that?" I pretended to be wounded by the accusation, and he fell into a belly laugh that threatened never to stop. Which got me laughing, too. Tension, of course. Neither one of us was truly amused. But the laughter felt good anyway.

By the time the hilarity died down and I wiped the tears from my eyes, we'd returned to the parking lot where I'd left my rental. Ben dropped me off next to it.

Before I climbed out of his sedan, I asked, "What time are Hayden's parents arriving?"

"Not until late tonight. Maybe let them alone until tomorrow. This won't be easy," Ben said.

"You'll call me?" When he nodded, I left the sedan, and he pulled away.

It was past lunchtime, and I was hungry. I couldn't go home, and I didn't want to go to the office. So I called Kate and invited her to join me at Bella's.

CHAPTER SEVENTEEN

Saturday, November 12
2:30 p.m.

I ARRIVED AT BELLA'S before Kate and found an empty booth in the back. She joined me a few minutes later. After we ordered, I said, "I'm checking into a suite at the Le Méridien this afternoon."

A bit of poetic justice, really. Le Méridien was the luxury boutique hotel that now occupied what was once the decrepit old courthouse where I'd been imprisoned by CJ for way too long after everyone else had moved to the new building.

Kate frowned and her tone was laced with concern. "What are you doing, Willa? Why in the world would you leave George at a time like this? You need his support now. You two should be presenting a united front."

"Even if that means George's business will suffer?" I shook my head. "We can't afford that, even if I was willing to punish him that way."

"George agreed to this?" Kate cocked her head and narrowed her eyes.

"You worry too much," I replied to avoid the question. I smiled. "Le Méridien is one of the nicest places in town. A little expensive, but if I can't live at home, I'll pamper myself in luxury and make sure CJ finds out about it."

"You're not usually so petulant," Kate replied, frowning.

"Not so much petulant as practical," I assured her. "Look, it's a short walk to work from Le Méridien, which is easier than getting a parking pass for my rental in the secured private garage at the new courthouse. For that, I'd probably need CJ's approval. Never gonna happen—because I wouldn't ask, and he wouldn't consent even if I asked."

The waiter delivered our food and I deftly turned the conversation to her children while we ate. Kate could always be distracted by family matters.

"You know you're just hurt and angry, don't you?" Kate asked me over cappuccino after we'd finished our pasta. There were many restaurants in Tampa, but Bella's was an old favorite of Kate's. It was intimate and comfortable. Not to mention that the food was excellent.

"Of course I'm hurt and angry," I replied in an angry tone. Kate smiled. Which annoyed me to no end. I took a deep breath. "Why does Oz hate me? Do you know?"

"Don't be so dramatic. Oz doesn't hate you. He just doesn't want you on the bench in his court. He made that plain from the moment your name was floated for the job," she replied as calmly as always.

My greatest sin in CJ's eyes was that I'd been nominated to fill a seat too many other people wanted. People who were much older and much more qualified, at least in their opinion. People who had paid their dues and waited in line.

None of them had been satisfied with the president's choice of a young woman new to Tampa and with no prior judicial experience. They'd used every opportunity since I'd been sworn in to try to oust me. Which CJ had helped them with whenever he could without showing his hand to the entire world.

I should have been used to it by now, but I had to admit, it still bothered me. No one liked having to constantly look over their shoulder to see what dangers might be looming.

"Well, he lost that fight a long time ago," I said.

"He's never going to give up. He's never going to give in, either." She smiled again and shook her head.

"It ain't over 'til it's over. Which will be when one of us is gone." I smiled back at her because, really, the whole situation would have been humorous if it hadn't felt so tragic at the moment.

"We both know Oz won't win this impeachment fight. The odds are against him. They always have been." Kate patted my arm. "Just take a little break and let things sugar out."

I wrinkled my nose. "That's exactly how Oz put it. When he asked me to resign or face the consequences."

"Come on. You told me yourself that fewer than twenty federal judges in the entire history of the United States judicial system have ever been removed from the job. You can do just about anything and not get fired. It's called an independent judiciary," Kate said.

"That's true. But Oz isn't completely wrong, either." I nodded. "I'm not worried about being arrested anymore. But public trust and confidence in the judicial system is as important as the rule of law. I can't be effective on the bench if I'm not trusted to deliver justice appropriately."

Kate had ordered a cannoli, and she took another bite of the crispy crust before she answered. "I know you're worried. What does Ben Hathaway say about all of this?"

"He's only just now identified the man. The parents are arriving tonight. I'll meet them tomorrow."

Kate's perfectly arched eyebrows dipped into a frown above the bridge of her nose. "Do you think that's wise? They're not likely to be kind to the woman who caused their son's death."

I widened my eyes. "But I didn't—"

"I know this wasn't your fault, Willa. Doesn't matter in this instance. The mother won't want to blame her son. I've got two sons and two daughters. Trust me on this. I know what I'm talking about." She patted my arm again when she said she had two daughters. One of the two was me. And I wasn't technically her daughter at all. But her words made me feel warm and fuzzy anyway. Even if she was essentially saying Mrs. Hayden would think me a killer.

This accident was a whole lot more complicated than a simple walking-drunk death by motor vehicle. I'd taken an oath to uphold the law, and I intended to do just that—and hopefully save my professional skin in the process.

But if Kate didn't support me, no one would.

Except George.

Which was a completely different thing.

I took another sip of my coffee then cleared my throat. Before I had a chance to reply, Kate abruptly changed the subject. "How is Augustus handling all this?"

The question startled me. "Augustus? He's fine. Why do you ask?"

Given his ties to other power-brokers in Tampa, people who were also friends of Kate's, I didn't want to say too much. Not that I didn't trust Augustus. It was his uncle, Prescott Roberts, and his crew of cronies, who were another thorn in my side.

But I still didn't know the full extent of my assistant's

connection to Kate's husband Leo Columbo, either. And I sensed this was a good opportunity to ask. On top of everything else, I didn't want to lose Augustus right now.

Kate finished her cannoli and pushed the plate aside. She didn't answer my question. Instead, she called for the check. When she did, another mutual friend noticed us and came over to chat. Just like that, I lost the chance to find out what I needed to know about Augustus.

Kate had to run out to another event. Something involving Leo's daughters, she said.

So I made my way to Le Méridien, my new home away from home. After I'd checked in, I unpacked and familiarized myself with the luxurious suite. I wasn't hungry enough for dinner, since I'd had a late lunch with Kate. A long, empty Saturday night stretched before me.

I ran through the channels on the television. Finding nothing of interest, I turned it off and plopped onto the bed. I opened my tablet and located a good book I'd wanted to read for a while. Shortly afterward, I fell asleep.

CHAPTER EIGHTEEN

Sunday, November 13
6:30 a.m.

AFTER SOME OF THE best sleep I'd had in days, I dressed for a leisurely run at Hixon Park and along the Riverwalk to Bayshore all the way to Gandy and back. The weather was beautiful, as usual for November in Tampa, and the exercise did me good. I craved the clarity that came with physical exertion. Running eight miles a day around the perimeter of Plant Key had long been one of my daily pleasures.

Today's run gave me the chance to check out the entrance to Plant Key. At six o'clock in the morning, there were no vultures staked out there. Which meant none of them had actually camped overnight. I took that as a good sign.

On the way back to my hotel, I jogged to the accident site. I stood in the median where Hayden must have waited for the next approaching car. The ground had been trampled by responders that night and dozens of vultures since, but the basic landscaping remained intact.

Half a dozen crepe myrtle bushes were clumped in a pedestrian refuge near the point of impact. It would have been a simple matter to use them for cover until Hayden's lunge or shove into the roadway, whichever one had happened.

Looking eastward, toward downtown, any observer would have had an unobstructed view of my approaching car, even in the gloomy nighttime. With Greta's headlights on and relative darkness surrounding the entire area. It would have been a matter of timing to wait until the very last minute.

This morning, there were a few lone runners on the sidewalk along the balustrade. On the opposite side, residents were indoors. It was too early for much activity. The forty-mile-an-hour speed limit paced traffic steadily during the work week, but I counted only five vehicles traveling past the impact point in ten minutes this morning.

After I'd seen all there was to see, I picked up my step and ran the rest of my route back to the hotel.

I showered, dressed, and ordered three Sunday newspapers, two large pots of coffee, an egg-white omelet, and toast. While I waited for room service, I dug out my laptop and the encrypted hotspot device I traveled with and found the articles Augustus sent me about toxic heroin.

Nasty stuff. As if regular heroin wasn't awful and addictive enough, now we had this new strain taking lives across the streets of America. As Dr. Eberhard had said, the "toxic heroin" was laced with fentanyl to create a powerful, often deadly, combo.

Fentanyl had been discovered in 1959 and was used as a morphine alternative to treat severe pain. It was also incredibly addictive. When fentanyl and heroin were mixed together, the potency of both drugs was increased. Once injected, smoked, or snorted, the new "toxic" heroin created a frighteningly powerful high.

Shortly thereafter, the depressant effects of both drugs kicked in and caused exaggerated drowsiness, nausea, confusion, sedation and, in extreme instances, unconsciousness, respiratory depression, and death.

According to what I read, most victims didn't know their heroin was laced with fentanyl at the time they ingested it. When they figured out what had happened, as Eberhard had said, they rushed to an emergency room. If they arrived fast enough, naloxone, an antidote, was immediately administered. Sometimes, it saved lives. Other times, it didn't.

In addition to the general information on toxic heroin, Augustus had included local news reports. At an electronic dance music festival this summer, hundreds of drug overdoses had occurred. Four deaths were attributed to toxic heroin. Other deaths were caused by Ecstasy.

One of the deaths was a young woman who left the venue alone. The news report said she was "drugged walking," which is really walking while high on drugs. She crossed in the middle of a busy street outside the concert venue and was hit by a car traveling fifty-five miles an hour.

"Pedestrian deaths have increased 27% while other traffic deaths have dropped. Drunken and drugged pedestrians are a significant number of these fatalities," Dr. Martin Eberhard was quoted in an interview in the *Tampa Times*. "Pedestrians hit by a vehicle traveling forty miles per hour are 90% likely to be killed. Impaired pedestrians are at least 50% more likely to wander into traffic and die."

By the time I finished reading the story, my entire body was vibrating. So was my phone.

I glanced at the screen and picked up the call. "Good morning, Chief Hathaway. What do you have for me?"

"Evan Hayden's parents arrived last night," he said, his tone quiet. "We had them in the lab this morning to give samples. But they've identified Hayden's body in the morgue. We're waiting for a quick DNA match, which might be conclusive. Then they'll take his body home. Maybe as soon as tomorrow afternoon. There's some red tape about transporting bodies on planes, but we're helping them expedite the paperwork."

"Surely the DNA match isn't necessary, is it? No one really doubts his identity anymore," I said.

Ben cleared his throat. "Because he died the way he did, no ID, no fingerprints, we need to be certain. None of us wants egg on our faces over this. They're being very understanding about it."

"Did they explain the no fingerprints thing?" I nodded, although he couldn't see me.

"Said he was born that way. Like we thought."

"How did they come across to you otherwise?"

"About what you'd expect." Ben sighed into the phone. "She's emotional. He's stoic. They're both devastated. He was their only child."

"Where are they staying?"

Ben didn't respond.

"You know I could make a few phone calls and find out where they are. I don't intend to harass them." I paused to let him reply, but when he didn't, I added, "I'd like to offer my condolences and learn more about their son. I'm good with people, Ben, and let's face it: you're not. They might tell me things they wouldn't tell you."

Still nothing from Ben on the other end of the line.

"I don't need your permission to approach them," I reminded

him. "You can save me some time, is all. We both know that I've got nothing but time these days. So it's fine if you want me to do this without you."

An aggrieved sigh echoed across the miles, followed by Ben's resigned voice. I could all but feel his scowl. "Fine. I'll call them and ask if they'll talk to you. I'll let you know. That's all I'm promising. But don't lead that crazy pack of attention-seekers toward them, Willa. That's the last thing these grieving parents need. And don't tell them that their son was shoved into your car. We don't know that. It's a theory at this point. Nothing more."

"Thanks, Ben." I paused a second. "When you call me back with a time, I'll fill you in on what I've learned since we left Foster & Barnes."

"Such as?" he said.

"Make the call. Then call me back with a time. I'll keep working here until I hear from you." I disconnected and returned to the recent official Bayshore Boulevard Pedestrian Crossing Study that Augustus had also included in his email. Among other things, it recommended reducing the speed limit on Bayshore Boulevard to thirty-five miles per hour to reduce crashes.

The reduced speed limits were scheduled to be implemented before the Thanksgiving holiday weekend. Meaning next week.

Because when a vehicle traveling at thirty-five miles per hour struck a pedestrian, fifty percent of pedestrians survived.

"Too little, too late," I murmured to the empty room.

CHAPTER NINETEEN

Sunday, November 13
4:30 p.m.

I LEFT LE MÉRIDIEN and headed toward the Sheraton Riverwalk Hotel located a few blocks from where I was staying. The weather was still nice, and I enjoyed the prickle of sunshine on my skin as I walked.

Ben had called just after lunch with the details, and I had to admit I was a bit surprised Mr. and Mrs. Hayden were willing to talk to me. After my mother's death, I'd wanted nothing more to do with anyone connected to her medical care during her last days. I was only sixteen. Coping with the overwhelming loss was a full-time project, and I could barely put one foot in front of the other.

Then, when my stepdad left a few months later, I felt totally bereft. Perhaps I reminded him too much of her and everything he'd lost. Mom's hair was golden blond, and mine was dark, but people always said we looked alike.

I don't know what I'd have done without Kate and her family. Sometimes I thought about that and tried to imagine how I would have survived. I'd have been sent to foster care, for sure. The rest of those scenarios simply didn't bear thinking about. Kate had been my guardian angel ever since.

While I waited at the corner for the light to change, I inhaled deeply and caught a hint of my mother's favorite lilac scent. Of course, the lilacs weren't really there. Whenever I thought of Mom, the fragrance was part of the sense memory, too.

The light turned green, and I crossed North Florida Avenue at East Kennedy Boulevard, then headed west toward the Hillsborough River. The Sheraton sat like a sentinel on its banks, nestled amongst the offices, parks, and hotels that had cropped up along the area.

Inside, the lobby was decorated in the usual tasteful shades of gray and taupe, with a distinct Florida vibe of potted palms and rattan furniture. I'd suggested we speak in the hotel's restaurant, which offered spectacular views of the Riverwalk.

Ben had explained their son's death to them. He'd assured them that I wasn't responsible. Toxic heroin had killed Charles Evan Hayden. It wasn't my fault. But I didn't know whether they'd accepted his explanation or not.

I forced a smile I didn't quite feel as I walked up to the hostess desk and requested a quiet table for three. She sat me near the floor-to-ceiling windows to wait.

There were a few other patrons in the place, but overall it was still too early for the dinner crowd. I ordered white wine, thinking it would give them permission to order whatever they wanted. But I didn't drink it.

"Judge Carson?" a man's voice said, drawing my attention to the couple as they approached. Middle-aged and wearing twin expressions of grief, the Haydens looked pretty much as I'd expected. I'd seen a few photos of their son, courtesy of Ben, and

I could see immediately where he got his good looks.

Walter Hayden stood about five-ten, with broad shoulders and black hair sprinkled with silver. Brenda Hayden was shorter— maybe five-seven—with the same brown hair and blue eyes I'd seen in their son's photos. Both held the haunted look of parents who'd experienced recent heartbreak.

We shook hands, and I gestured toward their seats. We stared across the table at each other, and I suddenly wished I'd ordered gin, straight up. From the hard glint in their eyes, I could tell these parents held strong anger toward me, regardless of what Ben had told them.

Why had I thought this was a good idea? I swallowed around the lump of dread in my throat and met their gazes directly. "Let me start off by saying how sorry I am about your son."

Brenda Hayden's face slowly crumped into tears, while Walter blinked at me. He put an arm around his wife's shoulders and pulled her to his side. The waiter who'd been approaching gave me a startled glance, and I shook my head, indicating he should give us a moment.

Walter Hayden frowned and stared out the window beside him, the lines around his eyes and mouth tightening. "Our son is dead, Judge Carson. He was hit by a car and mangled. And no matter how we process that information, you're partially to blame."

His response hit me like a sledgehammer to the chest. The air temporarily evaporated around me, leaving me speechless. Which was when I realized I'd expected them to have some sympathy for me. Yet, my situation was nothing compared to theirs. I was in trouble, but their son was dead. He was never coming back. How were they supposed to cope with that?

I didn't wallow in self-pity. And I never let anyone see me

cry. Not George, not anyone. *Suck it up, Willa. This isn't about you. It's about them.*

So, I shoved my personal feelings aside and kept going. "I understand how you must feel. And I'm so sorry for your loss. The coroner's examination shows that your son wouldn't have survived, even if he hadn't lunged in front of my vehicle."

"Lunged?" Brenda Hayden's eyes widened. "My son lunged into traffic?"

"The police have not confirmed exactly what happened. But he didn't simply collapse at the curb. He landed in the middle of the travel lane in front of my car, mere moments before I reached that exact spot." I kept my voice even and calm.

"Was he running? Misjudged the traffic and didn't give himself enough time to get clear of traffic on his way across the street? That happens a lot in Pittsburgh," Walter Hayden said, with so much hope in his voice that I couldn't have shot down his theory even if I'd had more evidence against it. Which I didn't. Yet.

"That happens here, too. So it's possible. That's what we need to find out," I said sympathetically. "I'd like to ask you a few questions about your son, if you don't mind. It might help us learn more about the circumstances surrounding his death."

Walter Hayden shook his head, still staring out at the riverfront. "The police chief spoke with us about Evan. We told him everything we know. Evan was a good kid. Never got into any trouble. Worked hard. Saved his money. I can't imagine why he would want to…"

"We don't know that Evan did this to himself. He might have made a mistake," I replied softly.

These parents seemed like good people who had loved their son. They were bewildered by his sudden death. I didn't have it in me to cause them more pain. Especially without concrete facts to back me up.

Still, the Haydens were misinformed about their son. While it might be kind to leave them with their illusions, and ordinarily I probably would have, I needed to know the circumstances leading to my part in this tragedy. We couldn't help their son now, but so much of my future, and George's future, depended on the outcome here.

Parents never wanted to believe their children had done anything wrong, and parents of a deceased child doubly so. Which was understandable. In most cases, no harm was caused by believing the best of a deceased loved one.

But Evan Hayden's coworkers claimed he was a jerk of the worst kind, and probably guilty of tax fraud.

Beyond that, he'd died from a toxic heroin overdose. Which meant he'd acquired the drugs from somewhere. He didn't make them himself. As a matter of public safety, police needed to find the source of that toxic heroin and shut it down.

And somehow, Haden had darted into the roadway in front of my moving vehicle, which had the potential to wreck my life, too.

Not to be too harsh, but none of his behavior was the kind likely to win Hayden a "son of the year" award.

CHAPTER TWENTY

Sunday, November 13
5:00 p.m.

I TOOK A DEEP breath and changed my approach. "So, your family is from Pittsburgh?"

Brenda Hayden sniffled, taking a Kleenex out of her purse to blow her nose before answering. "Yes. Laurel Heights area."

"And had you visited your son here in Tampa since he'd moved?"

"We'd planned a couple of trips at Christmas time," Mr. Hayden said, shaking his head. "But his schedule was always too busy."

"I see." Well, that was consistent with the workaholic personality Hayden's coworkers had painted. "And did you know any of his friends here in Tampa? Women he dated? Sports buddies? Anyone like that?"

"Since grad school, work was his life," Brenda Hayden said through her tears. "My son was dedicated to his job. He loved his work and gave up everything else for his career. He said he had years and years to date women and play golf, once his career was established."

She broke off as sobs overtook her again, and her husband pulled her into his arms.

I sipped my water and did my best to ignore the ache in my chest. I missed George. He was my husband, best friend, sounding board, and trusted confidant all in one. Maybe we could meet for a secret lunch. Yes. That sounded perfect. Someplace off the beaten path where we weren't as likely to be noticed.

"I'm sorry," Mrs. Hayden said after a few moments, pulling me back to the interview. "I just can't seem to grasp that Evan's gone. He had so much going for him in life. A full roster of successful clients. A new home he'd just bought. A girlfriend."

My attention snagged. "So he was seeing someone, then?"

"Nice gal," Mr. Hayden said, hailing the waiter and ordering iced tea for them. "We'd never met her in person, but we did a couple of video chats with her and Evan. Her name is Cindy Allen."

"Such a pretty girl." Brenda Hayden sniffed into her tissue. "Her family is from the Pittsburgh area, too. But Evan didn't meet her until they'd both moved here. A mutual friend introduced them."

"Do you have a photo of Cindy? Or do you know where she works or where she lives?" I asked.

Brenda Hayden shook her head. "You could check Evan's social media accounts. He might have some photos of the two of them."

Walter Hayden said, "I'm not sure what kind of work she did, even. I can't recall that Evan told us."

No romantic attachments had been mentioned before. Given the way Evan Hayden's colleagues felt about him, I wondered what kind of woman he'd be involved with.

I filed the information on my mental list of follow-up items and moved on. "What about other friends, male or female? Who was the friend who introduced Evan to Cindy?"

"He mainly spent time with his clients," Mr. Hayden said, stirring lemon and sugar into his tea. "Mitch Rogers was the one who introduced him to Cindy. He was Evan's client, but they were pretty close friends, too, I guess."

"The baseball player?" Even I'd heard of the Texas Sharks star pitcher, and I didn't watch sports.

George was an avid fan, though. From what little I'd heard, Mitch Rogers was an all-around nice guy—family man with a wife and kids in Dallas—and a golden arm that blew major-league records away like a Hayden Texas dust storm. Hell, even his nickname was squeaky clean. Sportscasters called him Mr. Family Friendly. The press constantly ran stories about him volunteering his time and money to children's hospitals and veterans' associations.

Evan Hayden's clients had included star athletes, but I guess I'd not expected him to appeal to such big superstars. Made a mental note of that, too.

"So, Mitch and Evan were good friends, then?"

"I'd say so." Mr. Hayden took a drink of his tea. "I mean, they spent a lot of time together recently. Every time I called to talk to Evan for the last month or so, he put me off, saying he had things going on with Mitch and that he'd call me back later."

"He had other clients he treated like friends, too," Mrs. Hayden said, still dabbing her eyes with her tissue every time her son's name was mentioned. "There was that basketball player, the one Evan had problems with recently."

Walter nodded. "Yeah, that's right."

Brenda balled up the tissue in her hand and met my gaze.

"Judge Carson, you don't think one of his clients had something to do with this, do you? What was that basketball player's name, honey? The one who accused Evan of some kind of financial problems?"

"Johnny Rae?" Mr. Hayden shook his head. "Nah. A misunderstanding, Evan said. They settled out of court. Rae never proved anything. Evan said the guy liked to gamble and drink. He probably didn't remember losing all that money in Vegas."

"Who is Johnny Rae?" I asked.

Walter looked at me like I had two heads. "*Johnny Rae.* Played four seasons for your local NBA team, the Tampa Brahmans."

The Brahmans were named after Florida's big cattle industry. Which was the sum total of my knowledge about the team, since George paid zero attention to basketball and I wasn't any kind of sports fan. So I nodded like I knew who the guy was, but I was thinking that maybe Evan was defrauding his clients as well as Uncle Sam. If Evan was skimming money from client accounts, that could be a solid reason to harm him. Maybe even a motive for murder.

The sun was starting to set, and the University of Tampa's skyline glittered through the restaurant windows. Walter Hayden fidgeted in his seat and glanced at his watch behind his wife's shoulder.

Time to wrap this up while they were still willing. I had another sensitive issue I wanted to discuss. "Did Chief Hathaway happen to mention the specific drugs found in Evan's system at the time of his death?"

"My son was *not* a heroin addict." Walter Hayden pounded a closed fist on the table that bounced the cutlery. A few diners turned to stare. His eyes glinted with anger.

Brenda Hayden took his hand to calm him. She said, "I'm telling you, Judge Carson, he was a health nut. Regular runner. A vegan, even. He would never have put that stuff into his body. No way."

Walter's gruff belligerence continued at a lower volume. "Someone had to have slipped it to him. In his food or a drink maybe. People do that. In bars and stuff. They think it's funny to see the clean guy falling all over the floor."

We sat in silence for a few moments. Walter was right. People did slip drugs into open containers in crowded bars. Usually roofies, so they could commit sexual assault or robbery and the like, without the victim fighting back.

"Please, Judge Carson, can't you help us?" Brenda Hayden said, imploring. "Someone killed my son. Please find out who did this. Please find out who poisoned him with that stuff. We really want to know."

There was no way I could promise any such thing.

I thanked the Haydens for talking to me, promised to keep in touch, said my condolences again, and then fled that restaurant like my butt was on fire. Outside, I released my pent-up breath and shook off the eerie feeling that Evan was standing close by, urging me to find his killer.

Mrs. Hayden's pleas chased me all the way back to Le Méridien. Along the way, I ran possible scenarios through my head.

Even the coworkers who seemed to despise him said Evan wasn't a drug user. If he hadn't injected the toxic heroin, then how was it administered?

Like Walter Hayden had said, someone could have slipped it into his food or laced his drink. My internet research said the drug was effective within thirty minutes if swallowed instead of injected. Plenty of time for a killer to get Hayden out to that dark and dreary stretch of sidewalk where no one would see them and then shove him in front of a passing vehicle.

My vehicle.

Inside my hotel room, I recorded the details of the interview while my conversation with the Haydens was still fresh in my mind.

When I'd finished, I ordered room service. Then I made a call to my judicial assistant's personal voicemail, asking Augustus to set up a lunch date for me with George and Ben Hathaway the next day. We had a lot to discuss.

CHAPTER TWENTY-ONE

Monday, November 14
2:00 p.m.

AUGUSTUS SET UP MY secret rendezvous lunch with George and Ben at a brewpub over in the Centro Ybor shopping and entertainment complex over on Fifteenth Street. I'd been there before and remembered the place had been quiet, dark, and—best of all—discreet. Plus, they'd had some of the best burgers in Tampa. The only problem was it was too far to walk.

I parked in the parking garage, collected my bag, and headed over to the brewpub. The short walk north on Fifteenth Street, across Seventh Avenue, then the quick sprint up the stairs felt familiar.

A large neon-and-wood sign proclaiming "Barley Hopper's" greeted me. I'd asked Augustus to book us a table later in the day, hoping to avoid the lunch rush and the crowds of matinee moviegoers from the theatres attached to the complex. The strategy worked. The place was all but deserted.

The pub wasn't ancient, but it was decorated with typical sports-bar atmosphere. Lots of dark wood, kitschy memorabilia, and an array of pull handles sporting labels for various micro-brewed beers. Multiple screens in various parts of the rooms replayed games like football, baseball, basketball, soccer, horse racing, dog racing, and finally, the Victoria's Secret channel. I raised my brow at that, but didn't mention it to the hostess who showed me to the table. If I remembered right, that same giggle network had been on the last time I was here, too.

George and Ben were already seated in the cozy booth for four. George took my hand as I slid in beside him and kissed me fast on the lips. "Missed you, Mighty Mouse."

"Missed you, too," I said, smiling.

Ben ducked behind his menu.

A pink-and-blue-haired waitress appeared to take our orders. I ordered my regular—a sinful cheeseburger with fries, a side salad, and unsweetened iced tea—while George went for an Angus steak salad and water with lemon.

Ben got a huge basket of sliders with fries and a diet soda, which made it my turn to roll my eyes.

After the server brought our drinks, I disposed of the small talk. "I met with the Haydens last night."

George still held my hand under the table. His warm fingers felt reassuring laced with mine. "How did that go?"

"As well as could be expected. They're mourning their son." I swallowed hard against the surprising lump of sadness in my throat when I remembered his mother's tears. I cleared my throat. "Anyway, I've got a couple of new leads for you, Ben."

"Great." His flat tone suggested the exact opposite. "Don't know how we ever managed to do our jobs without you, Willa. I can't imagine what we'll do when you get back to work."

I nodded to acknowledge the sarcasm. "I know you guys are working hard on this case, but my job is on the line here. You know CJ's started impeachment proceedings against me, and I've got a special judiciary investigations committee breathing down my neck for answers. I need to find out what really happened fast before I lose my seat on the bench. And that's before we even get to the fact that I'd really like to get back to my own home as soon as possible."

As always, George was the voice of reason, calming me down. "No one's disputing you have a vested interest in seeing this case solved. Ben's just trying to tell you to be careful and don't jump to conclusions before all the evidence is gathered. Right, Ben?"

The police chief gave my husband the facial equivalent of a rude finger gesture, which made George chuckle.

Ben sat back and crossed his arms. "What've you got?"

"I texted you the name of Evan's girlfriend last night, remember?"

"I do. We're running that down."

"He had a girlfriend?" George asked.

"So they said," I nodded. "Her name is Cindy Allen."

"What else?" Ben prompted.

"His parents say their son was pretty chummy with some of his clients. Some of those relationships were positive, some weren't. One client in particular was described as a very good friend and spent a lot of time with Hayden recently." I paused to be sure they were both listening and lowered my voice to avoid the chance that we might be overheard. "Mitch Rogers."

"Wait a minute. *The* Mitch Rogers?" George asked, pausing mid-sip of his tea. "The greatest pitcher Texas baseball has ever known?"

"That's the one. Apparently, Hayden was his financial

planner." I sat back as the waitress brought my salad and a basket of crackers to the table. "According to the parents, Rogers and Hayden had become good friends of late. Rogers introduced Hayden to his girlfriend."

Ben tore open a packet of saltines with his teeth. "From the way everybody we've talked to *except* his parents described Hayden, I'm surprised anyone could stand him. Let alone a guy like Rogers. Or any decent female on the planet whose main hobby isn't full body contact roller derby."

"Does seem strange," I admitted, pouring raspberry vinaigrette over my greens before digging in. I hadn't realized how hungry I was until now. The food wasn't the same five-star gourmet cuisine George served, but it was tasty all the same.

"I spent some time with the databases this morning. Like a lot of other sports types, Rogers has a house here. He and his family live out in North Tampa during the off-season." After swallowing a few bites, I continued. "And there was another client, too…a basketball player with the local NBA team. The parents said he and Evan had a falling out a few months back. The guy accused Evan of financial hanky-panky. They settled the claims before a lawsuit was filed. Probably hushed it up with confidentiality agreements, too. Which is why it didn't come up when I searched the court records before."

"Now that sounds more like Hayden." Ben crumpled his empty cellophane and reached for a second packet of crackers. Our police chief came by his burly figure honestly. "And I remember that. Johnny Rae was the guy."

"Johnny Rae? Seriously?" George asked, like a fanboy waiting for an autograph.

Ben nodded. "Yeah. He accused Hayden and his company of cheating him out of millions of dollars through bad investments in a bar one night. Hayden said Rae had lost the money gambling in Vegas. A fight ensued. We broke it up and didn't arrest either one of them. Probably should have."

George whistled. "Losing that kind of money could make a hothead like Rae homicidal, I guess."

"Hotheads like Rae don't need an excuse." Ben finished off another pack of saltines before sitting back and brushing the crumbs from his shirt. "But in the end, Hayden and the finance company settled it, like Willa said. No clue how much money got paid out."

"Maybe the guy held a grudge, though," I suggested as I finished my salad.

"Possible. But not likely. He got his money. He also got traded. Johnny Rae doesn't live here anymore." Ben took a swig of his soda. "We got another lead on a suspect, too. A guy that Hayden got into it with at a bar the same night he was killed."

The waitress cleared my salad bowl and refilled our drinks. The air in the pub filled with the aroma of grilling burgers and caramelized onions. My stomach growled loudly enough to be heard all the way over in Pinellas County.

"What did they fight about the night Hayden died?" I asked.

"We're still interviewing witnesses, but it sounds like there was a dispute of some kind. Over a woman or money or something else, we're not sure yet. As soon as I find out, I'll let you know."

Our food arrived, and we all dug in. Even connoisseur George, who tried a bite of my cheeseburger, raved about the deliciousness. I devoured my food like a starving woman. Sometimes you craved caviar and champagne. Sometimes you craved melted cheese and mustard and crunchy dill pickles.

Ben ate each of his sliders in one bite, like a hungry bear. No one spoke for a while as we enjoyed our food and our company.

Finally, stomach full and mind racing, I pushed my empty plate away.

"Oh, speaking of that girlfriend…" Ben wiped his hands and mouth on his napkin then reached into his shirt pocket and pulled out his phone. "I found these pictures of Cindy Allen in our database after you texted me her name. Seems she had a couple run-ins with the law back in Pittsburgh. And, wait for it…a past addiction problem with heroin."

He passed me his phone, and I stared at the images on the screen. She was pretty. A willowy body and bright green eyes. Her smile was sweet, but there was an aura of sadness there, as if she'd seen the darker side of life and it had left its mark. If she'd been a heroin addict, that could explain it.

I sent the photos to myself and then handed his device back and pulled her photo up on my phone. "Evan's parents said she and their son met after they'd moved to Tampa. She might have been the one who gave him the toxic heroin if she was using again."

"Could be," Ben said, swallowing his last slider. "We're checking it out."

The more I looked at the photos, the more familiar Cindy seemed, as if I'd seen her before. To my knowledge, she'd never appeared in my courtroom. I might have seen her almost anywhere, though. Tampa's population was well over 350,000, not including the metro areas. Chances were slim that I'd remember seeing her face in a crowd.

And yet…her eyes, her hair, the shape of her mouth. I felt almost certain that I'd seen her somewhere. I closed my eyes and let my mind float, trying to relax and not fight to remember.

It worked. Because I *had* seen her recently. Under emotional circumstances. The kind of memory that is most likely to stick in the brain. I remembered her and the place and a few more details, too.

The hospital. That night in the ER lobby. The couple in the corner.

Cindy Allen was the woman I'd noticed that night, the ringer for Sheryl Crow. Allen looked so much like Crow that they might have been sisters. They say we all have a doppelganger somewhere. An apparition or double of another living person. Cindy Allen was Sheryl Crow's doppelganger.

"She was at the hospital that night, Ben," I said, meeting his gaze over the top of my phone. "There was a couple in the lobby while I waited for George to get the car. They were off in the corner, consoling each other. I thought at the time that she looked so much like Sheryl Crow. I recognize her face plain as day. It was her, Ben. Cindy Allen."

"Interesting. But who's Sheryl Crow?" Ben tapped a few keys on his phone and found a couple of good photos of Sheryl Crow. He flipped back and forth between the two women, nodding. Then he clicked his phone off, shoving it back in his pocket as he slid out of his side of the booth. "Looks like I've got more leads to follow up on, then. See you guys later."

"Keep in touch," I said to him as he made his way to the door. He waved the back of his hand to show he'd heard me, but I didn't take that gesture as any kind of promise.

George settled the bill while my thoughts whirled. Was it pure chance Cindy Allen had ended up at the ER the same night Hayden died? Not likely. I didn't believe in chance. Which could have meant she'd been there because she knew Hayden was there. But how would she have known? She was already in the ER when I arrived. Which was before the accident story had appeared on the local news.

Was it possible that Cindy Allen had witnessed the accident? Had she been at the scene? Did that mean she was with Hayden before he died, too?

If all of my speculations were true, why hadn't she come forward once she knew Tampa PD was looking for help to identify Hayden's body?

But if she hadn't been present at the scene that night, how did she know Hayden was at the hospital? My questions were going around in circles.

Only one person knew the answers. Cindy Allen. She couldn't be that hard to find.

George and I walked toward the pub's exit hand in hand. It was too risky for us to be seen together outside. The vultures were still swarming over me, and there was no sign of it letting up anytime soon. But they'd stopped protesting at the entrance to Plant Key Bridge when I didn't show up for a couple of days. So our plan was working.

I pulled him over to a shadowed corner and kissed him sweetly on the lips. "Thank you for lunch."

"Thank you for setting this up. I meant it when I said I missed you."

"I know. I miss you, too." I patted his chest and smiled to make him feel better. "Don't worry. I'll be home soon. This thing feels like it's coming together."

We stood there, hugging like teenagers for a moment before leaving the pub separately and going in opposite directions, with a promise to talk again soon.

All the way back to my rental, I kept running through questions in my mind. How did Cindy Allen know what had happened to Hayden? Why had she arrived at the hospital so quickly? Who was that man with her? And on and on it went.

So many questions, so few answers.

But at least I had a new witness to locate, along with plenty of time on my hands to do it. Things were looking up.

CHAPTER TWENTY-TWO

Monday, November 14
5:45 p.m.

LOCATING CINDY ALLEN PROVED more difficult than I'd expected. I spent a couple of hours with my keyboard without any luck at all.

There were several different Cindy Allens on the various social-media sites, but none of them was the one I wanted to find.

She had no Florida driver's license, which was not too unusual, actually. When people relocated to Florida, they often kept their driver's license from their home state. Even though Florida law required them to change over, many new residents didn't know or didn't care, or simply didn't get around to it.

Florida has so-called "motor voter" laws, but in this case, she wasn't registered to vote, either. At least, according to the voter registration rolls I could access.

I checked the property records, but she didn't own a home in Hillsborough, Pasco, or Pinellas counties.

Florida doesn't have a state income tax, so there was no

reason for her employer to list her anywhere. If I'd had a social security number, I might have located a federal tax return or health insurance records, but I didn't have her social security number.

If she was licensed to do any kind of business in the state, I could find no evidence of it. I hadn't thought to ask the Haydens what kind of work Cindy did, but they didn't seem to know much about her. They probably had no idea. I wasn't going to bother them with the question until Ben Hathaway struck out, too.

He hadn't called yet, which could mean he was busy. Or it could mean he hadn't started looking for Cindy Allen yet. Who knew?

There was only one more thing I could think of to do. I'd seen Cindy Allen at Tampa Southern. Maybe someone working that night would remember her. With any luck at all, she'd have filled out information for a visitor badge or something.

Tampa Southern was within walking distance of Le Meridien, but with the November days so short, driving would be better than walking back in the dark. I pushed my chair back and closed my laptop. I slipped my feet into my shoes, dropped my phone into my purse, and picked up my keys.

If I couldn't find Cindy Allen, I'd have no choice but to leave it to Chief Hathaway, which was never my first choice. I crossed my fingers and hoped for the best as I made my way to the SUV.

Almost a week had passed since the incident. I planned to go back to work tomorrow. The vultures had stopped camping out at our bridge, but a few were still hanging around the courthouse, Augustus said when I last talked to him. Today might have been their last day. Surely they were tired of waiting for me to show up and had found something else to do. I hoped.

Thanksgiving was next week. I intended to be back in my own home by then. One way or another.

I'd forgotten that a Celine Dion concert was scheduled at Amalie Arena later tonight. It seemed everyone in three counties was attending. Which wasn't possible since the arena's seating capacity was only twenty thousand or so. But twenty thousand vehicles on our roads all at once, all going in the same direction, snarled traffic like a child's hair with bed head.

Bumper to bumper, vehicles were gridlocked all the way from the hotel on every surface street, all funneling into the arena. Vehicles barely moved an inch every five minutes. The drive would normally take five minutes. Tonight, I consumed forty-five minutes to simply reach the Kennedy Street Bridge and travel across the Hillsborough River.

Traffic didn't move any faster on the west side of the river, either. I navigated toward the Davis Islands Bridge only to see a ribbon of headlights stretched out along Bayshore all the way past our bridge to Plant Key. Poor George couldn't catch a break.

A helicopter overhead was broadcasting the traffic report. I turned on the radio. The reporter's observations were the same as mine. I'd make it to the hospital eventually, but the return trip to my hotel was destined to be a logistical nightmare, too. Which didn't make any difference at all because I couldn't simply turn around.

Nothing I could do now but grind it out. Going back was as impossible as going forward. Which was probably some sort of cosmic joke of a metaphor for my life at the moment, I figured. I didn't laugh.

Another forty minutes later, I'd finally parked at Tampa Southern and walked to the emergency room. As it had been last Tuesday night, the place was almost empty. Only one patient was seated. A young boy with a cut on his arm. His mother was holding a damp cloth on the cut for pressure.

"How long have you been waiting?" I asked the mom.

"Not too long. About an hour, I guess," she replied.

A frustrated curse almost crossed my lips, but I nodded and bit my tongue. I went through the doors into the ER and stopped at the registration desk. A form on a clipboard was perched on the counter next to a plastic sign that said, "Please sign in."

After ten minutes, a young man dressed in surgical scrubs returned to the clipboard. He glanced down to see that I hadn't written my name. He frowned and pursed his lips.

"How can I help you, ma'am?" he asked.

"I was a patient here last week. Tuesday night about midnight. I'd like to talk to whoever was working at the desk that night. Was that you?"

He shook his head. "Shift changes at ten o'clock. Joey Smithers works that shift. But he's off on Mondays. So he won't be in tonight."

I glanced up at the clock. It was already eight thirty. "I'm really trying to find a woman I met in the waiting room that night. I have something that belongs to her. I need to return it."

He frowned and cocked his head. "Was she admitted to the hospital? I might be able to look her up for you."

"I don't think so. I think she was…waiting for someone who came in on an ambulance that night," I replied. Which was apparently the wrong thing to say because his quotient of helpful attention instantly dried up.

"If she was waiting, not a patient, we would have no record of her," he said, putting some distance between us.

"How about surveillance video? You have cameras in the waiting room and posted around the parking lot, I noticed. Can I get someone to look at that video for me and help me find this woman?"

"You need to talk to security about that." He frowned and reached to pick up the phone. "Shall I call them over for you?"

What the hell. Why not? "Yes. That would be great. Thanks."

He punched about seven buttons into the phone and waited while it rang on the other end. When someone picked up, he said, "Yeah, this is the ER. Can you send a supervisor over here, please? I've got a woman looking for—well, I'm not sure what she's looking for. But she wants to talk to you…Okay…I see. I'll tell her. Maybe she can come back tomorrow. Right."

"Sorry." He hung up the phone. "They said they're short-staffed tonight because of the Celine Dion concert. They can't spare anyone to answer questions."

As he talked, he wrote a name and phone number on a Post-it and handed it to me. "You can call the supervisor in the morning. His name is Kevin Blake. If we have what you're looking for, this guy will be able to help you."

I took the Post-it and thanked him for the help through clenched teeth. Too busy to talk to me, indeed. I stomped out and started the long trip back to the hotel, empty-handed. No wonder it took Chief Hathaway so long to get anything accomplished if every call he made ended up this way.

Cindy Allen might as well have been living on the moon.

CHAPTER TWENTY-THREE

Wednesday, November 16
9:30 a.m.

CHIEF HATHAWAY CLAIMED HIS department was working on it, but he shared nothing new in the investigation into Hayden's death on Tuesday. By Wednesday, I'd fallen into a sort of routine—up before six to work out in the hotel gym, a light breakfast in my room, and then walk to the courthouse where I'd sort through boxes of paperwork that hadn't seen the light of day in years.

In a way, the *Stingy Dudes* trial being off my to-do list was helpful, even though I'd never admit that to CJ. He called at least four times a day, and I ignored the towering stack of pink slips with his name on them. The Special Judicial Review Committee had also called asking to interview me. But I still had no answers in the Hayden case, and until I knew what had happened to Evan Hayden, I wasn't speaking to them, on the record or off.

My luck at evasion would only last so long, though. If the Hayden investigation didn't break soon, I would have to seriously consider the possibility of giving up my job. CJ complained that I enjoyed making a spectacle of the courts, and he was wrong. It wasn't negative attention I sought. Not even remotely. What I wanted was justice. Every time.

If seeking justice sometimes came with a heaping side of unflattering attention…well, there was nothing I could do about that. I'd always been a crusader for justice in my own way, and I wasn't about to stop now. Even if it meant leaving the bench and returning to the practice of law when all this was said and done. I'd loved being a lawyer. Part of me wouldn't mind getting off the hot seat and back to the relative anonymity of working hard out of the spotlight.

Being a public servant wasn't all glitz and glamour. My life would be a lot simpler without CJ and all those disapproving power brokers constantly trying to keep me in the place they believed I belonged. Not to mention the pay cut when I took the bench. The money was certainly a lot better in private practice, as my colleagues often reminded me.

First, though, I had to get clear of the suspicion that I'd killed a man with my car. And avoid being charged with any kind of vehicular crime on that score.

Many people were shocked to learn that a convicted felon could hold a license to practice law. But only three states prohibited felons from practicing, and Florida was not one of them. Still, I meant to return to practicing, if it came to that end, with a clean record. Augustus and I worked through the morning, cleaning out storage boxes of records we'd moved over from the old chambers and either committing them to storage or filing them in the shiny new cabinets along the walls of our new chambers.

I'd wanted a paperless office for years. So far, it hadn't happened. But we were moving closer to the goal. Like everything else in government, the project marched ahead at the pace of a disabled snail.

After a nice lunch in my office—smoked turkey sandwiches on fresh-baked, cracked wheat bread from the deli across the street and iced tea to drink—we were ready to dig into another section of boxes when my desk phone rang. Augustus reached for it, but I stopped him when I saw the coroner's number pop up on my caller ID.

"Judge Carson," I said, answering on speakerphone.

"Willa," Dr. Martin Eberhard said, sounding slightly flustered as always. "The police chief requested a rush, so I've got the full autopsy results back on Charles Evan Hayden. I just spoke with Ben Hathaway, and he gave me the okay to call you."

I stood, knocked the dust off my jeans, and glanced over at Augustus who was unpacking yet more files from one of the storage boxes, somehow managing to keep his pristine suit flawlessly clean. How did he manage to stay so immaculate all the time? Once this horror show was over, I planned to find out all his secrets. Including that one.

I plopped into my chair and took a gulp of water. "Anything interesting turn up?"

"If you call a previously unseen mix of drugs interesting, then yes." Eberhard sounded downright gleeful. Scientists had a distinctly odd sense of excitement. "According to the toxicology reports, the particular blend of toxic heroin found in Hayden's system doesn't match anything we've previously seen in Tampa."

"I'm failing to see how that's a good thing, Martin. What about the rest of the state?" I frowned while I considered the possibilities.

Ben Hathaway had pulled Hayden's travel records. He'd flown a lot, often with his clients, but sometimes alone. If he'd died from a self-administered drug overdose, he might have bought the toxic heroin out of state.

Beyond that, Hayden's clientele consisted of sports stars and rich celebrities, all of whom traveled extensively, too.

We could reasonably assume the drugs were transported here by Hayden or one of his contacts, although that was a risky thing to do, what with drug-sniffing dogs at the airports these days. It made more sense that the drugs arrived in Tampa via ground transportation of some sort. Drug runners were more likely sellers.

But then, the toxic heroin would have shown up in Tampa before now.

"Nothing matches this drug in the FDLE databases, either," Eberhard said, drawing me back to the present. "Meaning nothing like this type of heroin has been seen in Florida at all."

"Were there matches elsewhere in the country?" I pulled out a pen and paper to jot down his answer. When I was actively working, I liked to document everything as it happened and then review it at the end of the day. But my whole routine had been thrown off by these events, and I'd resorted to scattered bits of paper and scratched notes on napkins until I could settle down at last and organize everything, preferably with a glass of gin and nice cigar by my side.

"This particular mix of fentanyl and heroin has entered law-enforcement databases in Maryland, Delaware, Rhode Island, Vermont, and New Jersey," Eberhard said. "The worst hit area, though, was Pennsylvania. They've had over a hundred deaths in the past three years from it."

As I scribbled, I noted this was yet another connection to Evan Hayden's past and another possible connection between him and his killer.

"Did the autopsy turn up anything else of interest?" I asked, keeping an eye on Augustus, who was still going through files across the room but was keeping an ear on my phone call, I was sure. Augustus, in addition to his excellent executive-assistant and paralegal skills, made for a terrific sounding board when I needed to bounce ideas off of someone. And yes, there was always a possibility that some of my information might make it into the hands of his powerful uncle, but that was a chance I was willing to take. Augustus was that good.

"The parents' DNA results came back a conclusive match to their son," Martin said. "We'll be releasing his body to them this afternoon. They plan to fly back to Pittsburgh tonight."

They'd been through so much. They'd be relieved to finally have their son returned to them. But with the body gone, I worried that the case would remain unsolved.

I thanked Eberhard and ended the call. For a while afterward, I simply stared into space as I worked things through.

It was quite a stretch to believe, but if this special, unique toxic heroin had been acquired for the purpose of killing Hayden or anyone else, that was some pretty cold premeditation. We'd been thinking lately that Hayden's drink might have been poisoned the night he died. But Hayden probably had a close connection to his killer, too.

Of the leads Ben had turned up, the two that stood out to me were Cindy Allen and Johnny Rae.

Domestic crimes were common. Perhaps Hayden and Cindy Allen had some sort of argument, and a nasty breakup. She might have harbored anger and resentment toward him. Maybe even enough to begin using drugs again. Under the influence and hurting, she could have slipped him the poison.

But could she have shoved him into the street, making sure he was killed? He was heavier than her. Unless they were standing at the accident site already, how would she have gotten him there? She couldn't possibly have done all that alone.

I thought back to the picture I'd seen of Cindy on Ben's phone and when I'd seen her in the ER. She'd looked too innocent to be a killer. But I wouldn't know a killer if I was sitting right next to one. I'd had it happen a few times. Trust me. Killers don't all look like Charles Manson and wear a neon sign over their heads flashing "Look Out! I'm here to kill you!"

Get a grip, Willa. I shook my head and took a deep breath.

Moving on to Johnny Rae.

Yesterday, I'd spent a couple of hours digging into Rae's falling-out with Hayden. Things had turned ugly fast after Rae accused Hayden of embezzlement and tax fraud. Hayden fought back. He was the suspected source of doping and steroid use rumors about Rae.

Rae was a favorite to be on the roster of US Olympic Basketball team at the time. The gossip ruined his chance to put his skills on display for a gold-medal team. He claimed millions of dollars in endorsement deals went down the tubes, too.

The whole dispute was at the top of every sports report everywhere for a couple of weeks. Since I never watched sports news, I'd missed the whole thing.

The dust-up ended as abruptly as it began.

There was no proof that Hayden was the one who had spread the malicious lies about Rae—and Rae's bloodwork had come back negative for any illegal substances—but the rumors of doping mysteriously stopped once the claims against Hayden and his firm were dropped. Didn't take a rocket scientist to put two and two together. Rae got paid. Problem solved.

Could bad blood between the men and a desire for revenge

have driven Johnny Rae to murder Evan Hayden with, ironically, an illegal substance? Of course it could have.

But in the six months since the nasty falling-out and its aftermath, Rae seemed to be getting his life back on track. He was engaged to the mother of his newborn son and had just bought a luxurious mansion on the exclusive Pointe of Harbour Island. Situated on Seddon Channel, his home had direct access to Tampa Bay and the Gulf of Mexico. Not exactly the type of property a man would buy and then commit a murder that would land him in prison.

Then again, killers rarely expected to get caught. Most imagined themselves smarter than your average law-enforcement officer or judge.

Most were wrong.

CHAPTER TWENTY-FOUR

Wednesday, November 16
4:30 p.m.

A COUPLE OF HOURS later, the phone buzzed again, but this time I let Augustus answer it. Good thing, too. The caller was the secretary for the special investigative committee trying to corral me into an interview again.

I couldn't hold them off forever, but I could postpone a bit longer. Something would break in the Hayden case. Until it did, I just had to stay out of CJ's reach and find Hayden's killer.

"How do you feel about the Haydens taking their son back home to Pittsburgh?" he asked after he'd taken a message.

"I don't know."

"Sounds like a good thing to me." Augustus added the pink message slip to the stack. "Let things die down a bit. Let those gawkers turn their spotlights elsewhere. Surely, there's something more exciting happening in the world for Rinaldo Gaines to focus on, right?"

He wiped his hands on a napkin and tossed it in the trash. All signs that he'd been digging through dusty files for hours disappeared.

I looked down and saw nothing but streaks of dust and smudges of dirt on my clothes. I looked a mess. I ran my fingers through my pixie-cut red hair and fluffed it out as best I could. "Maybe you're right."

"There's another good thing I don't think you've considered." He smiled, all white teeth and lilting Jamaican charm. "If the attention goes away, your life can get back to normal. No more living in a hotel. You can move back home, too. With George."

He might be the male version of Pollyanna, but he was also right. The hotel was luxuriously nice, no question, but I missed my husband and our dogs something fierce.

My smile widened into a full-blown grin. The knot of tension between my shoulder blades unfurled, and I straightened in my seat.

Things with my job might still be tenuous, but I'd faced worse. I'd get to the bottom of Evan Hayden's death from the comfort of my own home. "Augustus, can you call George and tell him that I'll be home for Thanksgiving, please?"

"I will." He cocked his head and looked at me quizzically. "But how are you going to get rid of those people who have been following you around?"

"My plan is to put them to sleep from boredom. And then hope something much juicier comes along to snag them," I said, grinning.

The legitimate news organizations had dropped off almost immediately when no further developments had turned up. Charles Evan Hayden wasn't a celebrity. He wasn't a local. He wasn't a power broker or a politician or even a particularly newsworthy businessman. There was nothing in particular to keep him in the news, so his story simply slipped away, replaced by new stories.

The number of gawkers, protesters, and vultures had slowly subsided over the days following Hayden's death. The paid protesters must have run through their budgets. For the gawkers, there was simply nothing much to look at. Watching me walk from the hotel to the courthouse every day was boring.

And the citizen journalists were still doing their best to keep the "Federal Judge Kills Pedestrian. Removed from Court" story alive, but with nothing new happening, they were running out of ways to say the same old, same old.

Except, of course, Rinaldo Gaines. I'd made a mistake by responding to him that first night. I'd watched his video channel, and he'd found about three dozen ways to slice that footage with images of me coming and going at home and at work. In short, he'd milked this thing for all he could get. Hits to his fake news channel had soared. His revenue was up, too.

He wouldn't give up his cash-cow story easily. He'd approached people who knew me and confronted them with offensive questions, which they didn't answer, of course. But he put the video online with his outrageous voice-overs. My colleagues were "covering" for me, he said. My friends were "hiding." I was "on the run" from him.

Not only was he one of the most offensive people I'd ever met, but he was also as tenacious as any junkyard dog on the planet.

"What we need to do is find something that's more interesting than I am so Gaines will move on," I murmured.

"Such as?" Augustus asked.

"We're almost at the end of hurricane season, so we can't count on one of those to rescue me." Flashing a big grin, I said, "Crazy things are always happening in Florida. Don't you read the papers? Entire neighborhoods falling into a sinkhole. Stupid kids doing illegal things and videotaping themselves while they do it. Something's bound to turn up."

"So your plan is to sit around and wait? Doesn't sound like you," he said.

"No, it doesn't. Which is why it's time for me to get out of town for a few days." I tapped my lips with a knuckle, thinking about where I might go to get out of sight and hopefully out of Rinaldo Gaines's mind.

I sat back in my chair and folded my hands to think. "While I'm gone, maybe the last stragglers will tire of waiting around if something doesn't draw their attention before I get back."

Augustus nodded. "When are you leaving and how can I help?"

"I've done everything I can to find Cindy Allen without success. I'm thinking she or some of her friends might attend Hayden's funeral in Pittsburgh." I held up my hand, palm out, when he gasped. "Hear me out. I won't be the cause of any more pain to his parents. Nothing of the kind. And I'm not going to cause a disturbance at his funeral."

"What are you planning to do, then?" Augustus asked, frowning.

"I'm not entirely sure yet. But if I buy a ticket to Pittsburgh and get on the plane, Rinaldo Gaines might come after me."

August frowned. "Won't that draw Gaines to the funeral? You know he'll cause even more heartache to Hayden's parents if he had the chance. You don't want that, do you?"

"No, I don't. So I'll have to figure out a way around him. He might have friends in Pittsburgh who could help him out, but I doubt it." I was thinking aloud, making a plan as the conversation progressed.

"There are other problems with your plan, too."

"Such as?"

"You want the vultures that are camped out in front of the judge's private entrance to the courthouse to see you go, don't you? And you want them to know where you're going. How are we going to make that happen?" Augustus asked, getting into the spirit of the plan.

I frowned. What I knew for sure was something I'd learned while practicing law. The only way to make anyone do anything was to incentivize them to do so. What would incentivize Rinaldo Gaines to get the hell out of my life?

The best answer was for me to get out from under the heavy weight of suspicion and get back to work. Gaines would leave me alone when I was no longer interesting. Or more specifically, when my life no longer served as click bait for his bottom-feeding audience.

What he was doing was harassment and stalking. I had not filed a complaint with Chief Hathaway because the extra publicity was exactly what Gaines wanted. CJ wouldn't have been unhappy about it, either.

But I'd decided to give Gaines a choice. Leave me alone, or go to jail. At the moment, I thought the odds were about fifty-fifty as to which he'd choose.

Decision made, I nodded once. "I'll go tomorrow. Between now and then, we'll figure it out."

"And what do you want me to tell CJ and the special committee? Besides go to hell, I mean," Augustus said with a grin.

"Just keep taking messages, unless they really press you. And then you can tell them that I was called out of town unexpectedly for a few days." I said, already checking online for plane and hotel reservations.

"What about George? He'll be worried," Augustus said,

continuing to tick off all the problems this impromptu travel presented.

"As soon as we figure everything out, we'll let him know." My attention was on the travel plans first. Which didn't take long.

A flight to Pittsburgh tomorrow morning with an open return date was both possible and pricey. I plunked down my credit-card information and paid extra for first-class seats with more legroom. No way could I fold my long legs into one of those standard coach seats. Besides, Gaines wasn't likely to have the money to buy a seat in the first-class cabin. I hoped.

I reserved a rental car and made a hotel reservation at the Pittsburgh airport. Then I checked the weather and shivered. The Pittsburgh forecast called for highs in the 50s and lows in the 30s for the rest of the week. At least it shouldn't snow. But I definitely needed warmer shoes and a coat. Gloves would be good, too. I'd brought none of that to Le Méridien.

"How long will you be gone?" Augustus wanted to know.

"A couple of days, more or less. But I'm going to be home for Thanksgiving, regardless. Which means I'll be gone for not more than five days." When the computer spit out all the confirmation numbers and I'd recorded everything where I could find it easily, I closed all the tabs and windows and turned to Augustus.

I waved to a chair, and he seated himself across from me. "I'm all ears," he said with a grin.

Which was when I explained my plans. He asked a few good questions but mainly agreed with everything I'd worked out.

We spent the rest of the afternoon collecting everything I'd need to make the trip to Pittsburgh worthwhile. Including Cindy Allen's last known address and Pittsburgh-area employers, and contact information for Charles Evan Hayden's college roommates.

Dr. Martin Eberhard, the medical examiner, returned my call. He provided the name and phone number for two Pittsburgh-area coroners who had identified instances of the same toxic heroin involved in Hayden's death. He said they'd be willing to speak with me Friday afternoon.

I collected photos of all witnesses Chief Hathaway had shared with me, along with their witness statements, and stored them on my phone.

I made two phone calls from my office to local media friends. Both went to voicemail, and I left messages requesting a return call. The favor I wanted was too sensitive to risk to a recording that could be subpoenaed and used against me at my impeachment hearing.

After that, I snuck out one of the side entrances and made my way back to Le Méridien to pack and prepare to check out in the morning. I wouldn't be returning to the hotel again.

CHAPTER TWENTY-FIVE

Thursday, November 17
9:30 a.m.

THURSDAY MORNING, I DROVE the rented SUV over to the
front entrance to the courthouse and waited for Augustus. He
made a big show of bringing a briefcase to my car. A few citizen
journalists stood on the sidewalk nearby and shouted questions
that Augustus, of course, didn't answer.

Rinaldo Gaines was there, front and center, just as he had been
every day since Hayden had died.

Augustus bent to open the passenger door and slipped inside
with me. Before I could ask why he was there, he said, "Let's
pretend that you need to tell me something on your way to the
airport on this impromptu trip, shall we?"

I grinned. "Nicely done. You have a future in covert ops."

Augustus frowned for the cameras, but he was enjoying
himself.

I pulled the SUV away from the curb and pulled into traffic
headed north on Florida Avenue. At the entrance to I-275, I

headed toward the airport. I drove slowly and made no effort to hide my intentions.

"I didn't see Gaines grab a cab back there," Augustus said. "Were you able to get your plans to him?"

"Yeah. I'm expecting to see him on my flight."

Getting word to Rinaldo Gaines that I was leaving town had been easier than I'd expected. The two legitimate reporters I contacted last night had zero respect for Gaines and were only too happy to help. They posted a couple of anonymous comments on his video channel about a certain federal judge who was on her way to Pittsburgh tomorrow.

His replies made it clear the chum we'd tossed in his waters had been too juicy to resist.

Traffic was heavier than expected. Once upon a time, I could leave the courthouse and be walking onto a plane in less than thirty minutes. Alas, those days were gone.

Augustus nodded. "I've been following his video channel since all this started. You should know I'm not the only one in the courthouse who is."

"CJ and the special committee are following it, too, you mean? How do you know?"

I flashed my left turn signal and moved around a slow truck in the right lane. The airport exit wasn't too far ahead, so I moved back to the right lane once I passed the truck.

"You and CJ don't talk to each other, but the judicial assistants and the law clerks do," Augustus said with a nod. "The gossip mill is alive and well among the courthouse employees."

I took a breath. Of course, they were talking about all this. How could they not be? It wasn't every day a federal judge was under suspicion for murder. "What have they been saying about my, uh, situation?"

"Well, they're annoyed about having so much more work dumped on them. They're all putting in extra hours and scrambling to reschedule their dockets. Our district is one of the busiest in the country. It's not a simple matter to absorb the workload of one of the judges. Especially one who works as hard as you do," Augustus said, finishing his sentence as I exited the expressway at the Tampa International Airport exit and headed north.

"What do you say in response to all that?"

"I say it wasn't your decision. That you'd be working, but CJ pulled the files." He paused. "Most of them are outraged about how you're being treated. You've got friends in the courthouse. More friends than CJ does."

I blinked back a spate of unexpected glassy tears. Augustus might have been an enigma, but his loyalty to me was absolute. "What about the *Stingy Dudes*? How's that going?"

"Okay, I guess. The trial resumed on Monday and witnesses have been traipsing on and off the witness stand pretty regularly, from what I hear."

I pulled into the lane marked "Rental Car Return," and drove to the drop-off location. We parked, and I handed the keys to the attendant. Augustus pulled my bag out of the trunk, handed me the briefcase, and we were on our way.

I'd already checked in and downloaded my electronic boarding pass. My flight was set to depart in an hour. I had time for coffee after I cleared security.

Augustus said, "I'll catch a cab back to the courthouse. When will I hear from you next?"

"I'm not sure. You have my itinerary. You can reach me by text. The flight time to Pittsburgh is slightly more than two hours. I'll be landing about lunchtime. And I'll call when I can."

"See you when I see you," he replied.

We exchanged smiles on the sidewalk at the entrance. Augustus turned left toward the taxi stand at the end of the building, and I walked through the glass doors.

Inside the terminal, I took the escalators up to the third floor and then the air slide over to the Jet Green terminal. My TSA PreCheck status gave me a shorter waiting line, but a long trail of travelers clogged the regular lanes. Passengers moved along slowly through winding lanes that were longer than the lines for the most popular attractions at Disney World.

I spotted Rinaldo Gaines three lanes away. He was standing behind a couple traveling with two kids and what seemed like everything they owned in the world. They might take a full ten minutes or more to get all that paraphernalia onto the screening belt and then get the kids through and repack on the other side.

I raised a hand to my mouth to cover the laugh. The guy was predictable. And he was also supremely annoyed. Perfect. With any luck, he'd give up soon. Or go broke first. Either outcome was fine with me.

By the time we passed through security, the gate agent had called my flight. My first-class cabin was the first to board. I settled into seat 2B on the aisle and stowed my bags. The seat next to me was occupied by a businessman, with two empty seats across the aisle. I breathed easier once those seats were filled by passengers who were not Gaines.

Several minutes later, I pretended not to notice him when he boarded. I turned my head to talk with my seatmate briefly. Gaines probably noticed me, but that was the whole point. So far, so good.

The flight to Pittsburgh was uneventful. I worked on the plane, spending time online to locate the neighborhoods where Cindy

Allen and Evan Hayden had grown up, and the nicer neighborhood where Hayden's parents now lived.

I knew a few lawyers and judges in Pittsburgh. I'd contacted them last night, just in case I needed help while I was in town. One of my theories is that we can get connected to just about anybody in the legal community with three phone calls. So far, I'd never lost that bet, and I didn't expect to lose it this trip, either.

We landed in Pittsburgh right on time. I was the fifth person off the plane. I stopped at the women's restroom to freshen up and give Gaines time to notice me before I rolled my luggage to the escalator and down to ground transportation.

On the main level, I walked to the garage, collected my key at the kiosk, found my rental, and drove away. Gaines was standing at the rental counter when I passed by. I half expected him to run for a taxi and yell, "Follow that car!" But he didn't.

The little twerp probably thought he knew where I was headed.

CHAPTER TWENTY-SIX

Thursday, November 17
3:30 p.m.

CHARLES EVAN HAYDEN'S FUNERAL service was
scheduled for Friday afternoon at 1:00 p.m. Visitation for friends
and family was tonight from seven to nine. I'd booked a room at a
nearby Hampton Inn, as if I'd planned to attend both.

My plan was to find Cindy Allen. I expected her to show up at
her boyfriend's funeral.

The drive from the Pittsburgh Airport east to Hayden's
neighborhood in Laurel Heights consumed fifty-three minutes of
roads winding through the hilly terrain. Colorful fall foliage
mingled with bare tree limbs, a few evergreens, and browned grass
along the roadway, already dormant.

Laurel Heights was a slice of homey Americana. A small
downtown area with the main street lined with sidewalks and old-
fashioned streetlights. There were storefronts on both sides,
already decorated for the holidays. Clusters of pedestrians wearing
coats, hats, and gloves walked along briskly in the cold.

The yellow-brick Butler Funeral Home was set back on a wide lawn at one end of Front Street. A spacious parking lot behind the house exited onto the back alley. There were no cars parked in the lot yet.

Across the street from the funeral home was a casual restaurant with a good view of the entrance, but no view of the parking lot. I circled around to the alley. The side entrance was covered to protect visitors from the elements. Most people would probably get dropped off under the cover or park in the lot and walk in through the side entrance tonight.

I'd hoped to stand outside and mingle with the guests tomorrow. But given the setup and the cold, people would be quick about coming and going. I'd be forced to go inside.

I drove through the alley and a few blocks north to my hotel. Once I'd established my bearings, I headed south to Bronsonville and the address on Cindy Allen's Pennsylvania driver's license. My lawyer friend had also pulled her credit report.

Her credit report looked about like I'd have expected for a heroin addict. She had trouble holding a job. Several long gaps in her employment history were listed. She didn't own a home or a car, but she'd filed for bankruptcy a few years ago.

Once upon a time, Cindy Allen had been a real estate agent in Bronsonville. After her last stint in rehab, she'd apparently moved to Florida—her credit report didn't show any further activity in Pennsylvania. She wasn't a licensed realtor in Florida, according to the state licensing records. But she might be working in a realtor's office.

I'd kept watch over my shoulder, but so far, I'd seen no sign of Rinaldo Gaines since I'd lost him back at the rental-car pickup. He wasn't an idiot. He would figure I was planning to attend the funeral and show up there.

But so far, Cindy Allen's name had not been out there. I hoped Gaines wouldn't know she existed. Or at the very least, that he hadn't been able to locate her, either.

The maps program on my phone led me straight to the offices of Bronsonville Realty, Cindy Allen's last employer in Pennsylvania. It was almost six o'clock, but the sign on the door said office hours ended at nine. Lights were on inside, and at least two of the desks were occupied. I parked the rental out front.

When I stepped out of the car, the full blast of wind that blew across the street made my teeth chatter. I snugged my summer-weight jacket closer around my body and hurried to the entrance. When I opened the door, an old-fashioned bell rang somewhere deeper in the building. A welcome blast of warmth surrounded me as I moved inside and closed the door.

The office was one large, open room in front of a divider wall. I guessed there were back rooms on the other side of the wall. Six smallish, modern desks were set out in no obvious pattern. Each desk had one chair on one side and two chairs opposite. As I'd noticed from outside, two of the desks were occupied.

"I'll be right with you," a man dressed in a casual sport coat, red hair, about thirty-five, called to me from one of the desks on the right side of the open floor plan.

"Thanks," I called back.

I studied the wall in the waiting area covered with photos of listings for local real estate for sale or lease. Next to the listings were photos of brokers and agents. None of them were Cindy Allen. Not that I expected her to be employed here now. Not really.

The carpet muffled his footsteps as he made his way toward me. "Larry Kent," he said, hand extended. "How can I help you?"

I didn't offer my name, but I did shake his hand. "I'm actually looking for a woman who works here. Cindy Allen. Is she around?"

Kent frowned and shook his head. "She moved out of state a few years ago. Florida, I think it was. If you're looking for a home, I'm sure I can help you."

"I'm really just looking for Cindy."

He narrowed his eyes and cocked his head, and I could see his welcoming openness morphing into closed and wary suspicion. Which made sense. I hadn't even offered my name, because it seemed smarter not to. Why would he trust me?

I put a warm smile on my face, hoping that would help. "Has anyone else been asking about her?"

"Not that I know of," he replied. His tone was decidedly frosty now.

He stood straighter and squared his shoulders, as if he might be preparing to toss me out the front door. I'd never been bounced from an establishment in my life. I wasn't keen for this to be the first time.

"I need to find her, and it's important. Someone close to her has died. We're trying to get word to her before the funeral." Judges don't lie. What I said was true, as far as it went, but I still crossed my fingers behind my back, just in case.

His stance and his face softened a little, which made me feel guilty. But I wasn't planning to harm Cindy Allen. All I wanted to do was find her.

"I don't know Cindy. She left the company before I started working here," he said.

"I see." I wasn't sure why I felt such disappointment. But I did. My shoulders slumped, and I stuffed my hands into the pockets of my jeans. "I'd really like to find her before the funeral. Do you have any suggestions? Someone else I could ask?"

He watched me and thought about things for a few seconds. Why this was such a tough question, I couldn't guess. But he was having some sort of internal decision-making issue about it, for sure.

Eventually, like after about a millennium or two, he said, "Wait here. I'll ask one of my colleagues for you."

"Okay," I said. He might have been headed to call the police, but I wasn't concerned about that. The Bronsonville police station was the next stop on my list, anyway.

While he was gone, I pulled out my phone and snapped a few photos of the smiling faces posted next to the real estate listings. At least one of them might know Cindy Allen. They were business people working in the community. They'd be fairly easy to find, if Larry Kent didn't give me anything useful.

A few minutes later, I'd ruled out three agents and identified another three as possibles based on biographical information, such as how long they'd worked here. A woman emerged from the back offices. She was older than Kent. I guessed her to be about forty-five. She was smartly dressed in a blue business suit and sported a fashionably trustworthy hairstyle.

"I'm Melody Menton," she said as she approached, extending her professionally manicured hand. "And you are?"

"Willa Carson," I said, giving her warm, dry hand a firm shake.

She crossed her arms in front of her. "I understand you're looking for Cindy Allen."

"That's right. Do you know where I can find her?"

"Cindy hasn't worked here for about five years. But we do keep in touch. I called her just now, in fact. She's in Florida," Melody said.

She seemed truthful enough. "She's not planning to attend the funeral, then?"

Menton shook her head. "Cindy and Evan Hayden broke up a while ago. She's moved on. She said he had, too. And they met in Florida, not here. She didn't really know his family or his local friends."

I watched her carefully. "Evan's parents told me they'd video-chatted with Cindy and Evan. I had the impression they liked her."

"I'm sure they did. Cindy's a very likable woman. But she'd never met them in person." Menton finished with a little shake of her head.

I could think of nothing more to say without causing offense. Questions like *where did Cindy buy her toxic heroin?* were too abrasive. Yet, that was precisely what I wanted to know.

"I'd really like to speak to Cindy. It's important. Would you ask her to call me?" I found a business card for Menton on the front desk and a pen to write with. I jotted my cell phone number on the back and handed it to her.

She took the card, glanced at it, and slipped it into her pocket. "I'll give her the message."

Although I didn't feel confident about Menton's promise, I thanked her and returned to my car. Now what?

CHAPTER TWENTY-SEVEN

Thursday, November 17
7:30 p.m.

I'D RETURNED TO LAUREL Heights and found a secluded vantage point to observe the Butler Funeral Home parking lot. Visitation had begun half an hour earlier, and several cars were already parked near the side entrance. If Rinaldo Gaines had located the funeral home and camped out here, I didn't see him. Yet.

A zoom lens on my digital camera was sufficient to snap photos of license plates and faces of the mourners as they arrived and departed. It was past sunset, but the lot was reasonably well lit, which meant the photos would be okay. None of Evan Hayden's Tampa friends and colleagues that I'd met had arrived. I recognized none of the people or the vehicles.

Visitation ended at nine o'clock. Mr. and Mrs. Hayden departed shortly afterward. Theirs was the last vehicle to leave the parking lot.

After they left, I moved my rental closer to the side entrance and parked. I hurried through the frigid wind and dashed inside. A middle-aged man was closing the door to one of the rooms, which was most likely where Evan Hayden's body rested in his casket.

"I'm sorry. Did I miss the visitation for Evan Hayden?" I asked.

He nodded. "The family just left."

"I came as fast as I could after work. Would it be all right if I just went in to pay my respects for a moment?"

He narrowed his eyes and sized me up.

"I can't make it to the funeral tomorrow. And I won't stay long. Five minutes at the most." I kept talking because I sensed he was weakening. "Please. This is the only chance I'll have to say goodbye."

He sighed and cocked his head toward the door. "Sign the guest book just inside the door so the family will know you were here. I'll finish locking up in the back."

I didn't promise, but he didn't seem to notice. He nodded and turned to the back hallway.

"I'll be quick," I assured him.

I went into the room where Evan Hayden was resting. The casket was one of the nicer ones. Mahogany outside and cream tufted interior. It was the first time I'd seen his face clearly.

I wasn't good with funerals. I skipped them whenever I could. George felt differently about them. To him, the funeral was a chance to say goodbye and to pay his respects to the deceased and the family. For me, funerals were a wrenching reminder of my mother's death. Which I truly did not need or want.

Somehow, though, seeing Evan Hayden lying there peacefully, not mauled by my car, was strangely comforting. My eyes watered, and I blinked away the tears. From the safe distance between us while we were in Florida, I'd begun to console myself with the knowledge that I hadn't killed Evan Hayden. But standing here as he lay in a coffin, his funeral set for tomorrow, the knowledge was cold comfort. Such a handsome man. His whole life ahead of him. Even if he and Cindy Allen had parted, there was another woman out there for Hayden. He might have married. He might have become a father.

I blinked a few more times, but the tears were welling faster than I could keep them at bay. I reached for a tissue from the box near the coffin and dabbed at the corners of my eyes.

"I'm sorry," I whispered quietly, as if he might hear me. If he did, he gave no outward sign.

Several sprays of flowers were displayed near the casket. The guest book rested on a podium off to one side. I approached the book and found a pen to write my name, as the attendant had instructed. There were three pages of visitors already listed. None were Cindy Allen. The visitors had probably been local friends and family. I didn't recognize any of them. But I pulled out my phone and photographed the three pages of names, just in case I might need them.

I didn't write in the guest book. But I closed it and put the pen down beside it. No one else would come tonight.

When I returned to the central foyer, the attendant was not there. I let myself out. I heard the door snug shut behind me and pulled on the handle to be sure it was locked. Then I kept my head down against the biting wind as I hurried back to my rental.

I'd let my guard down while I was inside. I didn't see Rinaldo Gaines leaning against my car.

"Good evening, Judge Carson," he said, almost politely.

I nearly jumped out of my skin. My heart pounded so hard in my chest it might have been auditioning for the drummer's stool in a rock band.

"What the hell?" I said as sternly as I could muster, given how breathless I was all of a sudden.

"Sorry. I didn't mean to startle you."

"Like hell you didn't. What is wrong with you? Don't you have anything better to do than slink around a man's funeral?" My heart was still pounding, but a few deep breaths would soon have it under control.

"I might ask you the same thing," Gaines replied. "You went inside. I had the decency to stay in the parking lot."

"Yeah, well you're a real prince," I said snidely. "What you're doing is criminal behavior. Stop harassing me, Mr. Gaines. Stop stalking me. And move away from my car."

He didn't budge. "I want an interview with you. One on one. You owe me that."

"I owe you nothing. Act like a human being and call my office. And move away from my car, or I'll call the police," I said as sternly as I could muster, given that my body was still shaking.

Truth was, I wished I wasn't standing here alone in this parking lot. I didn't own a gun, but I was sorry about that, too, right at the moment.

"You won't call the police. Know why? Because then you'd have to explain what the hell you're doing here. Which I'm pretty sure you don't want to do." He smirked like a Texas hold 'em poker master moments before he ran a table full of high rollers.

I frowned and stomped my feet, trying to stay warm. "Are you always so thoroughly disagreeable?"

"Pretty much." He shrugged. "What are you going to do about it? Kill me with your car?"

I gasped. Did he actually just say that to me? I should have simply walked away, of course. But I didn't. Where would I go?

Back to the building? Bang on the locked door until they let me in? And then what?

"Mr. Gaines—"

"Call me Ronnie. Everyone does." There was that smirk again.

"Mr. Gaines, I didn't kill Evan Hayden. You have incorrect information. Journalism 101 is: get your facts straight. Now move away from my car." I pressed the key fob to unlock the door. He didn't move.

"Why don't you give me the straight facts, then?" he said, placating me.

"Why don't you do your job? I won't tell you again. Move away from my car," I opened the door, slid behind the wheel, closed and locked the door. I started the engine, fastened my seatbelt, and flipped on the headlights.

He'd made no move to stop me, but he was standing directly in front of me so that I couldn't drive away. His body actually touched the vehicle. He'd placed himself right about the same spot where Greta had hit Hayden.

He held out both hands, palms up, and waved me forward.

I stared at him. The man was insane. When he was sure he had my attention, he leaned forward, fisted his hands, and pounded the hood of the car with all his body weight.

My visceral reaction was swift and frightening. Every nerve ending from toes to scalp was on fire. My muscles twitched.

When he saw my horrified expression, he laughed.

I had my foot on the brake, so I slammed the car into reverse and then punched the accelerator. The car bounced over the curb and onto the empty parking space behind me. I kept my foot down, and the front wheels followed the rear ones.

Now the vehicle was in the open parking lane. I kept going

in reverse. I watched the rearview mirror to be sure I didn't hit anything and glanced at him through the windshield.

He hadn't expected my move. When he realized my intention to get away, he chased me, waving his arms, yelling, "Stop! Stop!"

Instead, I drove backward through the parking lot, away from Gaines. When I'd put enough distance between us, I yanked the wheel around to the right. The front wheels followed the back ones, and the car twisted itself to a forward-facing position. Gaines was still running toward me, waving his arms, yelling, "Stop!"

I slowed, slammed the transmission into drive, and stomped on the accelerator. The tires screamed as they fought for traction. When they finally grabbed the pavement, the car jumped forward and kept going.

When I looked back, Gaines was standing in the middle of the parking lot, shaking his fists in my direction.

My chest continued to heave with ragged breaths for another couple of miles. Gaines made no attempt to follow me. Which probably meant he'd found the hotel where I'd planned to stay tonight. Not that I'd be heading there alone now. Not a chance.

When I could breathe evenly again, I found my phone and called the Pittsburgh police.

CHAPTER TWENTY-EIGHT

Saturday, November 18
1:30 p.m.

THE PAST COUPLE OF days had passed quickly enough, and the only thing I'd accomplished was getting Rinaldo Gaines out of my life for a while. He'd been waiting in the lobby of my hotel when I arrived Thursday night, as I'd suspected he would be.

But I didn't arrive alone. A local police officer was with me. He talked briefly to Gaines, who didn't deny following me here from Tampa as well as waiting for me outside the funeral home and in my hotel. Gaines didn't consider any of his behavior harassment or stalking, but I did. And the police officer agreed.

Gaines was arrested. Which solved the immediate problem and allowed me to spend a quiet night in my hotel on Thursday.

I did not go back to the funeral home or disrupt Evan Hayden's funeral. That would simply have been too cruel to Hayden's family, which I truly didn't want.

So I spent Friday talking to the local coroner and following up on the toxic-heroin leads. I learned more about toxic heroin than

I'd ever wanted to know, but none of it led me anywhere at all in the Hayden case.

A couple of lawyer friends invited me to dinner. Afterward, I returned to my hotel. Gaines was in jail, where the police officer assured me he would remain until Monday, at least. After that, I'd be out of the jurisdiction, and Gaines would probably make bail.

"We'll require him to return for trial, Mrs. Carson," the officer said. "But he seems like the kind of guy who isn't going to give up. He also seems a little unhinged. You should hire a bodyguard for a while after you return to Tampa."

I nodded, but I didn't promise. At the very least, Gaines was out of the way for now, and I could go home.

By Saturday morning, I was more than ready to leave. I'd accomplished nothing in Pittsburgh.

Or so I believed as I waited for my flight.

CHAPTER TWENTY-NINE

Sunday, November 20
8:30 p.m.

SUNDAY NIGHT, I SAT exactly where I wanted to be. A warm breeze drifted in from the Gulf, carrying with it the scent of salt, sea, and sand. My Partagas smoked lazily from the ashtray at my side, and a glass of Bombay Sapphire glimmered in the moonlight.

Open on my lap was my journal. I had finished writing down my notes about the Evan Hayden case a few minutes ago. It felt good to release them from my head and allow them to spill onto the pages. Something like a catharsis, I supposed.

Mainly, I was just happy to be home.

In this day and age of feminism and equal rights and diversity, some people still considered it strange for a woman to smoke cigars. I loved them. They were a delight to all my senses. Not to mention a fond memory of my past.

The smell of the rich and spicy tobacco. The feel of a pliable, well-rolled cigar in my fingers. All of it conjured sense memories.

Me sitting on my grandfather's knee while he puffed away. The happy times of my childhood. Before my mother's illness. Before my stepdad left. Years when I was young and happy and safe and secure.

Speaking of secure, in the background—over the gentle lap of waves against the shore in the distance—I could hear the murmur of conversations from the guests at George's Place wafting through the windows.

Rinaldo Gaines was sitting in a Pittsburgh jail, where he'd stay for a while. With any luck, he'd never come back to Tampa. It turned out that he didn't even live here. He actually lived in Colorado.

As for the other vultures, Augustus had been right. Once Hayden's body left the state for burial, they had moved on to other more profitable stories. The legitimate press had not been a bother, of course.

Business had steadily increased over the past three days for George's restaurant, and the numbers were nearly back to where they had been prior to my accident. At least one of us seemed to have a firm business footing ahead.

What was most precious to me, though, was that I had some of my life back again.

Well before six a.m. this morning, my eyes had popped open. George had still been fast asleep at my side, snoring softly. Harry and Bess were curled up at the foot of the bed.

I slid out carefully, pulled on my running clothes, and headed downstairs with the dogs in tow. They'd all but inhaled their food and then bounded down the steps to dash out toward the bay. I walked slowly, enjoying my first full day back by soaking in the rising sun. When the dogs circled back to join me, we took off into our morning run.

Pounding the sand, one foot in front of the other and breathing heavily, the stress that had plagued me for days cleared. CJ and his machinations to have me fired. The special committee and their constant hounding for interviews. Rinaldo Gaines and the rumors he'd been spreading for weeks. All of it slipped away, and I actually felt lighter.

One foot in front of the other, landing on the hard-packed sand, I'd focused on the Hayden case and the loose ends left to be tied up.

The truth was always in the details. Facts solved crimes. Emotions didn't. And in the Evan Hayden case, most of the important details were still missing.

There was a possible tie between the drugs found in Evan's system and his Pittsburgh hometown. But neither Hathaway nor I had located the actual seller of that toxic heroin, and we probably never would. Pittsburgh law-enforcement records didn't identify the seller, either.

Tampa PD did not have the time, resources, or authority to investigate out-of-state leads, even *if* they might have been fruitful. Big "if." Chief Hathaway had properly reported the case to FDLE, the FBI, and the DEA. There was nothing more he could do to locate the out-of-state seller.

The task was simply beyond his resources. Not to mention that Tampa PD had plenty of law-enforcement duties right here in Tampa.

We might never nail down the source of the drugs. But that wasn't the only problem.

Another big hole in the case was the timeline. Thirty minutes max, Dr. Eberhard had said, from ingestion of the drug to time of death.

Which meant Hayden's location prior to death could have

been anywhere within thirty minutes of the accident scene on Bayshore Boulevard at the time he'd been dosed. That was a pretty wide circle of possibilities, even if we only looked at commercial establishments.

Hathaway had followed up a lead about Hayden being involved in a fight with another man at a local bar that night. There were at least a dozen bars along Howard Avenue where the hipsters hung out after work these days. They wandered from bar to bar, stumbling into the streets with their open containers in their hands. Bar fights were common in that area, too.

But the spot where Hayden had hit my car was nowhere close to those bars. I'd clocked the distance between the last bar on the strip and the accident site at more than a mile.

If he had ingested the toxic heroin over on Howard Avenue, would he have gone for a stumbling, bumbling stroll alone in the dark and rainy night for half an hour before he keeled over and died?

Not likely.

My thoughts swerved to Johnny Rae as I took in the twinkling lights from the fancy mansions across the water in the distance. My gut still said it wasn't him. With his new family and his new start in life, I couldn't imagine him risking all that just to take out Hayden, no matter how heinous their quarrel. Especially after Hayden's firm settled the debts by paying Rae millions.

I shook my head. Nope.

Cindy Allen was still a viable suspect. There'd been something "off" in her eyes in the photo Ben had shown me that day in the pub. A haunted, hunted look that set off red flags in my mind.

She and Hayden had broken up, according to her friend and former colleague, Melody Menton. Allen didn't attend Hayden's funeral. She'd never met his parents. How invested could she have been in a past relationship at the time Hayden died? It didn't seem reasonable that she'd have tried to kill him.

Although I'd still like to find her and ask her myself. She hadn't called me yet, but that didn't mean she wouldn't.

If Cindy Allen had started using again, though, she might have hooked up with an old dealer from Pittsburgh. I had talked to a couple of dealers, but none admitted selling to her. Which didn't mean anything. Drug dealers didn't often come forward and admit they were responsible for killing their customers. No reason to believe anyone was about to fall on his sword here, either.

Until she was ruled out, the possibility existed that Cindy Allen administered the toxic heroin that killed Hayden. She might not have known the heroin was toxic. Maybe she didn't intend to kill him. Which would also explain why she'd shown up at the ER that night. Maybe she felt guilty. And maybe she was.

Regardless, Cindy Allen was still our best suspect.

The rest of my run was spent turning the facts over and over in my head until my brain felt like well-mashed potatoes long after we finished up and trotted home.

That had been several hours ago.

Laughter from downstairs drew me back to the present. I stretched my sore neck and shoulders before checking my watch. I'd been sitting out here writing for nearly two hours.

I yawned and stretched again, staring down at the notes I'd scribbled in my journal. My penmanship was much worse than my sixth-grade teacher would have allowed, but the mashed potatoes in my head were finally written down in one place, and I was sure I could decipher my chicken scratches eventually.

I closed the journal and set it aside. I went into the house and clicked on the TV while I searched the kitchen for a snack.

George had fed me handsomely before the dinner crowds descended, but that was hours ago. *Soupe a l'Oignon Gratinée*—onion soup topped with a slice of French bread and melted Swiss cheese—and *Salade Niçoise*—a traditional French salad of mixed greens tossed with potatoes, green beans, "Genova Tonna" tuna, boiled egg, olives, and topped with anchovies—only lasted so long.

As usual, the cupboards were devoid of everything except microwave popcorn. I snagged one of the packages, tore open the cellophane with my teeth, stuck the bag in the microwave, and pushed the popcorn button.

I wandered in front of the TV. A local breaking-news bulletin flashed across the screen. I grabbed the remote and turned up the volume while the popcorn went crazy in the bag.

The story itself was astonishing, although not the first of its kind in Florida.

"From preliminary reports on scene at the Aloft Apartments downtown, a local woman drowned in the swimming pool after being attacked by a giant Burmese python," the reporter read from the teleprompter. "The snake was found wrapped around her neck, constricting her airway and suffocating her."

The story was completely believable, as strange as it sounded.

Exotic snakes had become a real problem here in the Sunshine State. For the past decade or so, ecologists had been tracking the invasion of Burmese pythons. The species was an interloper from Southeast Asia. Pythons had taken up residence in the Everglades National Park and other areas of Florida.

At full maturity, the serpents reached lengths of twelve feet or more. The beasts were carnivorous. They killed by seizing prey first, using their large, rearward-facing teeth. And then they wrapped their bodies around the prey and constricted, effectively squeezing the victim to death.

Burmese pythons had caused major damage to the local
Florida ecosystems by eating their way through several indigenous
marsh mammals, like foxes and rabbits. They'd also decimated
populations of larger prey, such as raccoons, deer, opossums, and
bobcats.

The problem had started with people buying the cute little
foot-long baby pythons as pets. By the time the snakes grew to
lengths of eight feet or more, the owners could no longer handle
them and often dumped them in the Everglades.

Like many species, the Burmese python had multiplied and
adapted, reaching population numbers as high as a hundred
thousand, some estimated. Now, they were invading urban areas,
too, the reporter explained.

The camera cut away from the reporter to zoom in on the
EMTs fishing the woman's body from the pool. I stood
mesmerized by the live report. When the moonlight hit the
woman's face, the camera moved away quickly. The image
would be removed from the video when the story was replayed
later, but the image lasted long enough to burn itself into my
mind.

I punched the record button on the news report to save it, and
then pressed the reverse button.

When the video image returned to the woman's face, I pressed
pause.

She was willowy. Her blond hair lay limply against her head.
Her face was partially covered by her wet hair and distorted by
suffocation. But I recognized her.

The microwave beeped, and my heart jumped. I sagged down
onto the chair as my knees went wobbly.

I released the video with the play button just as the reporter
said, "The woman has been taken to Tampa Southern where her

family will be notified before her identity is confirmed to the public."

But I didn't need to wait. I knew who she was, without a shadow of a doubt. She'd looked so much like Sheryl Crow the night I'd first seen her. Pretty, and very much alive.

The woman who'd drowned in that pool was Cindy Allen.

CHAPTER THIRTY

Sunday, November 20
9:00 p.m.

IT WAS SUNDAY, BUT I didn't care. I called Ben Hathaway as soon as I could grab the phone from the kitchen. The only person I knew who worked longer hours than I did was Ben. Sure enough, he was in his office and answered on the second ring.

"It was her, wasn't it?" I asked without preamble. "Cindy Allen."

He cleared his throat. "This really isn't a good time to talk."

"Just tell me if it was her or not." I tapped my bare toes against the cold hardwood floor. "Please."

"It was Cindy Allen in the pool," he said at last. I exhaled my pent-up breath. "But she didn't kill Evan Hayden, deliberately or otherwise."

"How do you know?" I frowned when George walked into the room and met my gaze. He looked away fast, but not before I caught the hint of resignation in his eyes.

Deep down, he wished I would let Ben do his job. He wanted

me to be a great judge and a terrific wife and that's it. I knew how he felt because I wanted the same things. Nothing would have made me happier than to rewind the clock to that Tuesday night when I'd hit Evan Hayden with my car and change the facts.

I shook my head and turned to face the opposite direction, away from George. "It could have been her, Ben. The Pittsburgh coroner told me the same kind of toxic heroin found in Hayden's system had been implicated in several deaths there."

"And several other places outside of Pennsylvania." Ben's tone sounded cryptic, just like his expression, I imagined.

"What about their relationship? She and Hayden broke up. Cindy was devastated. Ex-girlfriends have done less rational things after a bad breakup than dose the guy with drugs. Especially if she didn't know the heroin was toxic," I said.

"It's a reasonable theory, but we haven't been able to prove it," he said, a touch of exhaustion creeping into his voice. I wondered if he'd even been home to sleep. With Cindy Allen's death tonight, I guessed not. "We don't even know for sure that they broke up. His parents said they were still together. If so, then she'd have no motive, either. Let it go. She didn't kill him. Trust me on that for a change."

I fisted my hand at my side and held my temper. It wasn't the words so much as the tone that rankled. Being a judge meant never having to stomach condescension from anybody. At least when I had the power to throw them in jail for contempt. This was not one of those times.

After a deep, calming breath, I leaned against the counter and forced a relaxed tone I didn't quite feel. "Fine. Tell me how you know Cindy Allen didn't kill Evan Hayden."

"Because I interviewed her yesterday. While you were gone. I planned to tell you, but we haven't had a chance to talk. You were out of town." He sighed, and I pictured him running thick fingers through his hair. "I also interviewed several of her friends and coworkers who corroborated her alibi for the time of Hayden's death."

"She wasn't using again?" I asked, unwilling to believe it.

"Just the opposite," Hathaway sighed as if he was demonstrating extreme patience. "She volunteered at a local addiction clinic, counseling other heroin addicts. She was required to submit to regular drug screens for the counseling gig. The most recent one was the morning after Hayden died. We checked the reports. She wasn't using."

My shoulders slumped as the truth hit home. Cindy Allen hadn't killed Hayden. Which meant that someone else had. And that person was still at large.

"Why did she go to the ER that night?" I asked quietly, not ready to let the matter go. "That's strange, isn't it?"

"She and Hayden were patching things up. They'd planned to have dinner the night he was killed. She went to the restaurant close to the scene of the accident. He didn't show up for dinner. She waited. She was there when she saw the breaking-news report." Ben took a deep breath that enabled him to continue. "As soon as she saw the report, she tried to reach Hayden. He didn't pick up her calls. She called Mitch Rogers, and he was worried, too."

I frowned. "Mitch Rogers?"

"The baseball player. One of Hayden's clients and friends, remember?" Ben said, as if I were the densest person on the planet. "Look, we can talk more later, but I really need to go. He's on his way here now to discuss the next steps."

"What kind of next steps are you discussing with a *baseball player*?" I asked, more than a little surprised.

"He was one of Hayden's clients. He's got connections. He's willing to help. Why wouldn't I work with him? We certainly aren't making much progress otherwise. Hang on." Muffled noises issued through the line as he excused himself. The sound of a closing door followed before Ben came back on the line. "You're right that asking for help from a civilian isn't my normal process, but this is *Mitch Rogers*."

His words held a level of awe most people reserved for moon landings. George had shown much the same reaction to the famous pitcher's name at lunch that day in the pub. My turn to sigh. Celebrities of all sorts were not the same as we mere mortals, I guessed.

Hathaway said, "He's agreed to help me get interviews with some of Hayden's other famous clients. People who have been ducking us and can have their attorneys give us the runaround for years. Anyone who can speed that process along and bring justice for Hayden and his family is good in my book."

That sounded more like the police chief I knew. And I had to admit the investigation had stalled. Broadening the list of witnesses could lead somewhere.

"What about the other two suspects you already have? Johnny Rae and the guy Hayden fought with at the bar?" I asked.

"The guy at the bar checked out. He didn't kill Hayden or anyone else. His alibi was tight," Ben said. "And Rae's clean, too. His attorneys negotiated a settlement with Foster & Barnes over the lost money. It was already done before Hayden died. Besides, Rae was out of town on vacation with his wife and baby that night."

A hand on my shoulder made me jump. It was George. He'd come up beside me, and I'd not even heard him move. He frowned, whispering, "What's going on?"

I relayed what Ben had told me. "You seem a little starstruck here, Ben. Have you questioned Rogers about the murder?"

"Contrary to what you seem to think, I do know how to do my job. I don't owe you any explanations, either." Ben's words were clipped, and I had the sense that I'd offended him and that he'd been holding out on me. But he gave in a little. "We interviewed Rogers by phone shortly after Hayden died. He wasn't ducking us. He went back to Texas for a team meeting that night. He was on the flight. He's got a plane ticket and witnesses who will back him up on that."

"Oh," I said, deflated.

Ben took a deep breath and let it out slowly, stalling, before he finally said, "I realize you've been through a lot here, but Rogers wants to help, and I plan to let him. Unless you have a better brilliant idea."

He paused. I said nothing because I had nothing.

Ben harrumphed. "I thought so. And like I said, he can open doors that are otherwise firmly closed to us."

"I haven't had a chance to brief you on my trip to Pittsburgh. And I know how much you love George's food." I looked up and met George's gaze, an idea forming slowly. "Bring Rogers to dinner tomorrow night at George's Place. We can put our heads together on these interviews he's offered to help with."

Ben didn't reply immediately. George's eyes widened.

"Say eight?"

George shook his head fervently, and I amended my statement. "No, let's do nine instead."

George nodded.

Another long-suffering sigh from Ben. "Fine. Sure. Why not. I'll invite him. We'll see what he says."

"Understood." I ended the call then crossed my arms. "Well, it looks like you're going to meet Mitch Rogers after all."

"Looks like it," George said, pulling me into his arms. "Want to go into town and have lunch at that new little French bistro on Gandy tomorrow morning? I hear they have the best crepes in town."

"Sounds good." I kissed him lightly on the lips before he gave me a quick squeeze and went back down to the restaurant to finish the evening.

I pulled my popcorn out of the microwave and went into the den to fire up the computer.

CHAPTER THIRTY-ONE

Monday, November 21
8:30 a.m.

I SLEPT SURPRISINGLY WELL, all things considered. After my run, I'd showered and changed.

This was a rare morning off for both of us, and I'd decided to take advantage of the laid-back attitude, choosing a pair of cream ankle pants and a yellow T-shirt paired with sandals. A quick blast of the blow dryer through my short hair, five minutes with my makeup, and I was ready to go.

George was waiting for me, dressed in a white polo shirt, khakis, and tasseled loafers without socks. I grabbed my tiny purse and Greta's key and headed for the door. "I'll drive today. We can put the top down."

"I need to stop off in the kitchen. I'll be right out," he said when we reached the first floor at the bottom of the curving staircase.

"Don't take long," I called back, setting my oversized sunglasses on my face and waving on my way through the front door.

When I'd first bought the Mercedes CLK convertible from the dealership, people complained the car was too flashy for a federal judge, but I hadn't cared. I ran my fingertips along her sleek black side to the door handle, then hesitated.

Greta was an old friend, had been with me for years, yet this would be our first ride since the accident. The dealership had delivered her here after the repairs were finished.

I walked around to the front of the car. The dent on the hood and the one on the bumper had been expertly repaired. Even the Mercedes hood ornament had been replaced. She was shined and polished to a high gloss. She looked every bit as good as she had the day she was born.

So, it was time to suck it up and get back onto that horse—or in this case, behind Greta's wheel again.

I clicked the button on my key fob and heard the familiar *snick* as her locks opened. When I opened the door, the smells of citrus cleaner and leather filled the air. The dealership had given her a complete detailing, too.

George met me in the driveway, his expression concerned. "Are you sure about this? After everything that happened, it's normal to feel nervous about getting back behind the wheel of your own car again."

"Hey, handsome." I grinned over Greta's black cloth-top roof as I pushed the key fob a second time to unlock the passenger door. "Hop in. I'm starving, and we need to hurry if we want to beat the after-turkey-day crowds."

I slid into my seat and closed the door and my eyes, just sitting there, hands shaking and pulse pounding. I could do this. I *would* do this. I'd faced down some of the worst criminals in Florida from my bench. I could drive a few blocks for lunch.

My key fob slid into the electronic ignition slick as ice and, holding my breath, I turned it. The engine roared to life, all Greta's power purring beneath me.

I lowered all four windows, reached up and pushed the release button and turned the handle to release the latches. Then I pushed the electronic button to lower Greta's top and just sat there for a moment, feeling the breeze.

Then, slowly, I fastened my seatbelt and shifted from Park into Drive, easing out into the driveway and across the Plant Key Bridge. Poised at the edge of the Bayshore, I squinted into the sunshine and waited for traffic to clear.

It was like I'd never driven Greta before, yet it all came rushing back at once. The thrill of driving her...and the terror of that night. I gripped the steering wheel, my knuckles white, and several times I nearly pulled over and parked along the side of the road, sure I'd never make it another yard.

Then, as we headed toward Gandy and made the turn, something changed. The tension inside me loosened as the wind whistled past. All those horrible, awful memories of the night I'd struck Evan Hayden melted in the bright, warm sunshine.

They didn't disappear completely. I doubted they ever would. But they faded enough so Greta and I could function as a team again. I eased the accelerator down and felt all Greta's glorious German engineering leap to my command.

It was healing. It was fortifying. It was exactly what I needed.

By the time I pulled into the parking lot at the restaurant, I felt more like my old self than I had since the accident.

"You look happy," George said after I'd leaned over and kissed him. He was beaming ear to ear.

"Never underestimate the power of a great car." I smiled back, giving his hand a quick squeeze. "Come on. I'm starving."

After we were seated and served, George asked, "So, why are

we dining with Ben Hathaway and Mitch Rogers tonight?"

I shook my head. "I'm not sure. Ben said Cindy Allen called Rogers the night Hayden died. When I looked Rogers up online, I realized he was actually the guy with Cindy Allen in the ER that night. I didn't recognize him then because I'd never seen nor heard of him before."

"Which confirms his story to Ben Hathaway, doesn't it?" George's eyebrows arched.

"It might." I nodded slowly as I chewed a dessert crepe filled with Nutella and topped with cinnamon. "But he was on his way to Texas later that night. I didn't hear any alibi for the actual time of Hayden's death. He could have been around when Hayden was being poisoned."

"If that's what happened," George said. "Keep in mind that Hayden could have overdosed himself. People say he wasn't into drugs, but most people addicted to illegal substances don't exactly go around shouting it to strangers on the street."

"Right. And Hayden worked in an industry that's pretty heavily regulated. Lots of money at stake every day. A drug addict wouldn't be the first guy I'd want handling my investments. How about you?" I cocked my head and nodded again.

George said, "Another thing. Hayden wasn't a small guy, and he was very near death before he fell in front of your car that night. Do you think a petite woman like Cindy Allen could have shoved him into traffic like that?"

I shook my head again. "Not without some help. When I was doing my research, I also noticed that baseball players are a lot bigger and stronger than they used to be."

"Meaning what? You think *Rogers* did it? Come on, Willa. That's absurd."

"I'm sure it is," I murmured, not sure at all.

CHAPTER THIRTY-TWO

Monday, November 21
7:00 p.m.

I'D SPENT THE AFTERNOON brushing up on Mitch Rogers trivia before getting ready for the big dinner that night so I could at least speak intelligently with the man. George, who was inordinately thrilled at the prospect of breaking bread with Rogers, had gone down earlier to check on lunch service then had returned to the restaurant at around four thirty to help the staff prep for dinner. His dedication went well beyond loving his career. It bordered on obsession.

Someone had once said to me at a party we were hosting that George had a "knack" for the culinary industry. After I'd squashed my inappropriate urge to smack her, I'd answered with as much cordiality as I could muster. Calling George's ability to build, manage, and maintain the five-star eatery a "knack" was absurd. His chefs had won the Golden Spoon Award multiple times, and *Florida Trend* magazine had voted George's Place the Best in Florida—twice.

I snorted and shook my head. *Knack, indeed.*

I had the doors to the veranda open, enjoying the sounds of seagulls cawing and the gentle swish of the waves against the shore. The weather was perfect, not too warm, not too cold. The setting sun cast the sky in shades of dusky pink and indigo.

Rogers had a beautiful, exotic wife and two gorgeous children. Genevieve Rogers was a lanky brunette who looked like a runway model. The boy was about twelve, Mitch Jr. The daughter was maybe ten, Melody Anne.

Ben had called to ask whether Genevieve Rogers might come to dinner with her husband tonight. Which meant I certainly wouldn't be the most attractive woman at the table.

I decided to pamper myself a bit and drew a hot bath in Aunt Minnie's old claw-foot tub. While I luxuriated in the bubbles, I ran through the information I'd gleaned about Mitch Rogers during my research, ignoring the baseball lingo, which I'd never memorize in time for dinner, anyway.

At just thirty-four, Rogers had racked up quite an impressive résumé. Already the recipient of three Cy Young awards and runner-up once, the worst he'd ever finished in a professional season for the prestigious pitching award was third overall. The crafty lefthander commanded at least four different pitches that relied on deception and changes in velocity, and he was coming off a season where he'd struck out 301 batters. Only once in the last seven seasons had he failed to make at least thirty starts.

Even for a person like me who knew nothing about major league baseball, his stats seemed amazing. Or maybe they'd just been presented that way by baseball types who were in awe of him. Either way, the guy was professionally impressive. Evan Hayden must have attracted some envy from his colleagues when he landed a client like Rogers.

On the personal side, Rogers had been born in Dallas. The family had moved frequently due to his father's job. He married Genevieve Walker, his college sweetheart. Her full-time job seemed to be charity work and raising their two children.

Like many celebrities, there was some tabloid gossip. His wife was rumored to be a bitch on wheels. And his son, Mitch Jr., had been arrested a couple of times for undisclosed boyhood stuff. The records were sealed because he was a juvenile.

The couple was applauded for humanitarian work in Africa, Cuba, and the Dominican Republic. His wife was the public face for that effort.

Rogers used substantial chunks of his multimillion-dollar-a-year-salary to build orphanages to treat HIV-positive children. He'd partnered with organizations who provided surgeries and medical equipment to the underprivileged. He even put his muscle where his wallet was, building homes for Habitat for Humanity.

He'd been dubbed "Mr. Family Friendly" by some awestruck fan. The moniker was oft-repeated and seemed well deserved.

All of which didn't pass the smell test. No one was that perfect, right?

After my bath, the air still held a hint of steam and the traces of George's Old Spice aftershave. I quickly styled my hair, then applied minimal makeup—a bit of mascara, powder, and my new favorite deep purple-red lipstick for drama.

I chose a simple ivory silk dress. George picked it out during a trip to Palm Beach several years earlier, along with the sandals that complemented it. With Aunt Minnie's platinum, diamond, and amber choker fastened around my neck and the matching earrings on my lobes, I felt her presence with me.

At a time when women were housewives and mothers, Aunt Minnie must've been viewed as radical and flamboyant. She

owned this property and these extravagant baubles and lived
precisely as she saw fit.

I loved her for it. When I had the time, I planned to delve
deeper into her history. Where had her early independent ideas
come from? What had made her into the woman she became? And
who, exactly, had given her all these expensive jewels?

If CJ's impeachment plans succeeded, I'd have plenty of free
time on my hands while I looked for a new job. Might as well
make good use of it.

I spritzed my wrists and neck with my signature scent, Cartier,
then turned to view myself in the full-length mirror. Not bad for a
woman my age. Despite all the stress I'd been through, I looked
relaxed and happy. Like a woman who mixed and mingled and
dined with celebrities on a regular basis. Which, thanks to
George's Place, I did.

I walked downstairs, greeting several guests milling about in
Aunt Minnie's tastefully decorated nineteenth-century foyer. Back
when she had lived there, all the antique secretaries, breakfronts,
and sideboards had been hers. Even the small butler's table
between the upholstered camelback sofas in the center.

Mildred Carson had been called Minnie all her life. A kind
soul with a more-than-colorful past, she'd left George her entire
home and the island it sat on, completely furnished, in her will. He
had been painstaking in its restoration. Tonight, it seemed as if
even the soft-blue *fleur-de-lis* wallpaper gleamed with its former
gilded excellence.

I wondered if Aunt Minnie would be pleased to have her
beautiful things returned to usefulness, or horrified at all these
strangers traipsing through her home seven days a week. Based on
what I knew about her, I figured it could go either way.

I made my way across the lobby, past the Sunset Bar, and

over toward the main dining room. I stopped to admire Aunt Minnie's Herend Zoo while I waited for George. The painted porcelain figures had reportedly been a gift from a Hungarian suitor.

Judging by the number of animals she had in the collection, the relationship must have continued for some time. All the creatures had been named by Aunt Minnie and had been part of the itemized inventory we'd received along with the house. George had since added to their numbers, in honor of his aunt, whenever a special occasion arose.

There was only one shop in the country that sold the figurines to George, a place in Beverly Hills owned by a remarkable woman who probably would've been great friends with Aunt Minnie had they known each other.

On the center shelf rested a pair of blue bunnies, joined at the hip, their heads leaning into each other as they shared a quiet moment together. Aunt Minnie's inventory list named these two "Willa" and "George" with a note that said, "Forever bonded, quietly a pair."

George greeted me a few moments later, looking extremely handsome in his tailored charcoal-gray suit, crisp white shirt, deep-burgundy tie, and Gucci dress shoes. He leaned over and kissed me, then stepped back to admire my outfit. "You look lovely tonight. Exquisite. I'm so glad you're home."

"Me, too," I replied.

He led the way to our favorite table and placed an order for two glasses of white wine. We enjoyed the cool, crisp taste of good chardonnay as we waited for our guests. Waterford crystal chandeliers sparkled from the ceiling, and Irish lace linens and vases of fresh flowers decorated the room. The whole picture was lovely and romantic.

"So, what were you up to while I was working this afternoon?" he asked me. I told him about my Mitch Rogers research.

George grinned, his expression skeptical. "You're an expert in sports now, eh?"

"Hardly." I chuckled. "I just wanted to know enough to avoid making a fool of myself during dinner."

"Hmm." George sipped his wine, watching me over the rim of his glass. "Please tell me you're not going to go Judge Judy on the man. He's offered to help the police. He was Hayden's friend."

"That doesn't mean he's done nothing wrong. I don't trust people who seem to be that pure."

"You don't trust most people at all."

"Touché." I had to smile at that, without apology. Skepticism was an admirable trait for a lawyer and for a judge.

A low murmur rippled through the restaurant, and I saw George's gaze widen slightly as he looked past me. I turned in my seat to glimpse Mitch Rogers enter the lobby with Ben Hathaway by his side—one tall and chiseled, one short and bulky. Genevieve Rogers was between them.

Every head in the place turned to stare as they walked toward us.

Rogers was lithe and handsome and clean shaven, unlike the bearded images I'd seen of him earlier that day online or that night in the ER. The articles I'd read suggested that the beard was one of his pre-game superstitions. Apparently, some players didn't shave for the duration of the off-season, thinking it brought them extra luck or something.

Ben had cleaned up pretty well, too, in a navy suit and red tie, brown hair neatly combed. I rarely saw him dressed so well, so it was a somewhat surreal experience.

But Genevieve Rogers was the stunner in that threesome. Almost as tall as her husband, her sleeveless gown revealed biceps to die for, and she had legs for miles. Her skin was more bronzed than a suntan commercial against the slinky white fabric. Long brown hair flowed down her back and swayed as she walked. She'd been a model once, so she might actually have posed for a statue of Athena, the Greek Goddess.

George walked over to escort them to the table. His admiration for the all-star pitcher was nearly palpable, and I had to bite back another smile. George traveled in some high-powered circles. Watching him starstruck was another surreal experience.

I began to think this evening might actually be fun, even though I'd had a different agenda in mind when I'd suggested Rogers come to dinner.

CHAPTER THIRTY-THREE

Monday, November 21
9:05 p.m.

"WE'RE HONORED TO HAVE you dine with us tonight, Mr. and Mrs. Rogers," George said as they approached the table. I stood for the introductions. "And let me introduce my wife, Wilhelmina Carson."

"Genevieve," she said as any goddess would, extending her hand. "Such a pleasure to meet you."

Rogers flashed me his camera-ready megawatter and gave my hand a firm shake. "Judge Carson, pleasure to meet you. Though I wish it were under different circumstances."

"Agreed." I took my seat again, and the others followed. "And please, call me Willa."

"Thank you," he said, oozing charm. "Please call me Mitch."

George sat to one side of me at our table for five, Ben on the other. Rogers was across from me. Genevieve sat between Rogers and Ben.

I leaned over and gave Hathaway a little tease, to show him

there were no hard feelings. "Nice to see you out of uniform tonight, Ben. I'd begun to wonder if you owned any clothing that wasn't tan."

"Same here, Willa." He flicked his napkin open across his lap. "Thought maybe you lived in those black judges' robes."

We gave each other uneasy smiles, and it seemed we were back to our usual places.

We all placed our orders with the waiter, then settled into polite small talk. Mostly we talked nicely about events. No politics, religion, sex, or anything at all that your grandmother would call impolite.

Once the topics of weather, the couple's charitable activities, and Rogers's illustrious last season had been discussed—during which I was able to hold my own, even citing stats from his games and scoring some additional points with George—we lapsed into an awkward silence. Rogers seemed uneasy, but I put it down to Hayden's death. I'd struck his friend with my car. His wariness around me was understandable.

"I'm so very sorry, Mitch, for what happened. I'm sorry for your loss." I watched his reaction to my words carefully, searching for any kind of odd vibe.

He gave a brief nod, gaze lowered, expression sad. "It wasn't your fault. The drugs in Evan's system made him do crazy things. I just can't believe he's gone."

I narrowed my gaze, feigning ignorance. "He was a regular drug user, then?"

"Evan?" Genevieve's surprise raised all the way to her perfectly arched eyebrows.

"No, not that I know of." Mitch shook his head and frowned. "That's why I'm volunteering to help the police interview some of his other clients. Someone had to have slipped that drug to Evan or convinced him to take it. That person is responsible for his death. Not you. I'll see justice done for my friend if it's the last thing I do."

While I appreciated his impassioned speech, there was something about Rogers that didn't ring true to me. Maybe it was because I'd spent so many years listening to guilty defendants spin lies and deceit in my courtroom. But this guy was off. I felt it.

Or maybe I just felt overshadowed by his amazingly beautiful wife. Who wouldn't be? The woman not only looked amazing, but we'd probably find her photo in the dictionary if we looked up "philanthropic." She was that active with her charity work, according to my research.

I glanced over at Hathaway, but he seemed to have no problem with Rogers's story. George, too, remained captivated by the baseball star in our midst. I sighed and tried a different approach.

Two of this guy's friends had died in the past two weeks, and he didn't seem very upset about that at all. Which was damned odd, if you ask me.

"I remember seeing you there in the ER the night of the accident. With Cindy Allen," I said, ignoring my husband's *be quiet* stare. "How well did you know her?"

"Oh, Cindy and I have been friends since I bought my home here in Tampa. She worked as an assistant at the real estate firm who sold me my property. She and Genevieve used to go to the same yoga class, too, I think, right?" He cleared his throat and glanced toward his wife.

"Yes. Cindy is a nice girl. Very good at yoga," Genevieve nodded.

"Right." Rogers placed his hand over hers and continued. "Ben said he mentioned to you that Cindy and Evan had a date scheduled that night. She was understandably upset. We both were. I offered to drive her to the ER. I was glad I was there to comfort her. We comforted each other."

Uh-huh. Smart of him to start acting like a bereaved friend. Finally.

The night I saw them in the ER, I'd thought they were a couple. They gave off that vibe at the time.

So were they? And if they were, had Hayden found out about it?

Jealousy was a strong motive for murder. I wondered if we'd been approaching this case all wrong. Had Rogers and Cindy Allen been having an affair behind Hayden's back? If so, then a reconciliation between the two would've been the last thing Rogers would've wanted.

Would he have killed Hayden to get him out of the way, though? Somehow, he didn't strike me as the kind of man who had trouble getting dates.

I cocked my head. "Perhaps you were offering Cindy more than comfort."

Rogers's eyes widened, and I wondered if I'd hit the mark.

Hathaway coughed loudly, and George's tanned face drained of color.

Genevieve's nostrils flared and her eyes flashed with anger in defense of her man. "That's absurd."

"It's a reasonable question. Cindy Allen is a beautiful woman. Those two were together that night when she needed comforting," I nodded toward Mitch.

She grabbed his hand. "Mitch's family means absolutely everything to him. You know nothing about us. Why would you suggest such a thing?"

Before I could follow up, the waiter arrived at our table again. Bad timing.

"Talk about saved by the food," Rogers said, his tone amicable. The hint of panic I'd glimpsed in his eyes had vanished, replaced by feigned interest as the waiter set out our appetizers.

I cocked my head and regarded them both. They were certainly a handsome pair. From everything I'd heard and read, they were an idyllic couple. Maybe his interest in Cindy Allen was purely platonic. But it hadn't seemed so that night in the ER.

I'd ordered the Venison *Carpaccio*, and George and Rogers had both ordered the Hot and Cold *Foie Gras*. Hathaway was staring at his plate of assorted mushrooms, fava beans, and summer truffles with morel sauce and watercress *coulis* like a hungry wolf that hadn't devoured any prey in weeks. Genevieve barely noticed the plate. Her willowy model's body suggested she rarely ate much of anything. What a shame.

As soon as he could politely do so, meaning right after the waiter had removed his hand from the plate to avoid being stabbed with a fork, Hathaway devoured his small portion in three bites. George and Rogers both attacked their *foie gras* with vigor. Genevieve moved the food around with a fork and then excused herself for a quick trip to the ladies' room.

I addressed my venison with deliberate restraint. I savored the green beans, celery root, pickled red onions, and Gaia apple topped with whole-grain mustard and rosemary-parmesan croutons served over the thinly sliced raw meat as if I had nothing better to do in the world.

This dish was one of my favorites. The combination of flavors wasn't anything I ever would have dreamed up myself, but they were exquisitely delicious.

Our friends who lived in Northern Michigan viewed deer as a nuisance. Like giant rabbits, they destroyed gardens and ate all the flowers with the same power as a high-speed lawn mower.

When no one spoke up, and while I had the chance, I repeated my question. "So, tell me about your relationship with Cindy Allen."

I continued to eat slowly, knowing the waiter would not return to remove the appetizer plates or serve our second courses until I'd finished and Genevieve had returned.

"You never give up, do you?" Ben growled under his breath. "Mitch is a happily married man. He's got kids. He and his wife work together in several Tampa-area charities."

"Yes, I read about all that. Quite impressive," I replied.

Rogers blushed. Actually blushed. I couldn't remember the last time I'd seen a grown man turn pink like that. "We've been so blessed in our lives, we feel like it's our duty to give back to those less fortunate."

"And we appreciate all the hard work you do," George added, giving me a look that screamed *hurry up and finish your damned venison.*

Savoring another bite, I set my fork on the side of my plate and took an appreciative sip of the 2012 Jean-Marc Brocard Chablis Grand Cru Bougros my husband had selected. The layered aromas of sun-ripened citrus, fruit, honey, brioche, and toasted hazelnut filled my nose, and the pure, fresh, crisp acidic structure tickled my taste buds. "And?"

"And what?" George and Ben repeated in unison.

"And what is it that you're not telling us, Mitch Rogers?" Holding out on my last bite of delicious venison was easier since I'd had such a nice lunch.

As it was, I could hold out all night, if necessary. Ben, on the other hand, must have skipped breakfast and lunch, expecting one of George's sumptuous dining experiences.

"How do you put up with her?" Ben asked my husband with mock exasperation.

George snorted and shook his head. "Mostly, I just try to stay out of her way."

From the twinkle in his eyes, I knew he was enjoying this play of wills between the three of us, but George always bets on the winner. In this case, me.

Finally, Ben had had enough and turned to me with a scowl. "This conversation is getting us exactly nowhere. Now, if you eat that last bite of venison, as soon as Mrs. Rogers returns, we can all get on with our meal. Mitch might be a bit more inclined to help us if he doesn't feel like you're about to break out the rubber hose."

Okay, then. We were all on the same page. No more bullshit. I ate the last of my food.

Moments later, the waiter appeared and removed our plates. I sipped more of my wine and waited.

"Look," Rogers said at last, as if he might say something helpful. He glanced quickly toward the back to be sure Genevieve wasn't on her way. "Evan wasn't the most popular guy. He rubbed people the wrong way. We had our share of arguments about it. But he didn't deserve to die. The drugs that killed him…the last thing I want is for that stuff to end up on the streets of Tampa. We need to get rid of it. I've got kids I love like crazy. And my kids have friends. I've got a responsibility to make sure they're safe. Right now, they're not. None of us are. What happened to Evan could happen to anybody."

"You think one of Hayden's clients is responsible?" I continued to watch him closely. Unable to put my finger on it. What was wrong with his little speech? "You really think you can get Hayden's clients, your teammates, people who are covered by layers and layers of protection, to talk to the police? Because my experience on the bench says otherwise. What I see, every day, is the more money people have, the less inclined they are to accept law enforcement poking into their lives."

"I've got nothing to hide." Rogers flashed me another one of those cover-worthy smiles.

Genevieve came back to the table, settling in next to her husband with a quick kiss on his cheek and a return to her previous calm. "I took a minute to check on the children. They made me promise to kiss you for them."

He smiled and squeezed her hand again as she placed her napkin onto her lap. She ignored me from that moment onward. Which might have been devastating to someone who wanted to be her friend, I supposed.

The waiter appeared again, this time with our salad course. Rogers and I had ordered the Asparagus and Vidalia Onion Salad while George and Ben and Genevieve had opted for the other choice, something the chef called a "Composed Salad." Honestly, to me it just looked like an ordinary tossed salad you could get at any fast-food place, but I supposed at these prices they had to make up a fancier name.

"You should probably talk to the people Evan worked with, too," Mitch said around a bite of asparagus. "If you haven't done so already. There was no love lost there when Evan died. Real cutthroat bunch in that industry."

Ben swallowed a bite of his salad then wiped his mouth with his linen napkin. "Already on it. Got a team over there again."

With that, Ben deftly turned the topic of conversation to Rogers's winning season and the chances of the Sharks making it to the World Series as we ate our salads and a basket of fresh-baked bread and rolls.

Finally, the waiter returned to clear our table then set out our principal dishes. We'd all ordered the same main course—roasted

Colorado lamb loin served with spring peas, chanterelles, and pearl onions with Dijon sauce. George's food was too good and deserved our full attention. All talking ceased while we appreciated the fine cuisine and shared a bottle of exquisite Brunello.

After dinner, Genevieve acquired a sudden headache and Rogers drove her home. I left George and Ben to discuss sports and returned upstairs for espresso and a cigar, wearing my sweats. I had plenty of new impressions about Rogers to record in my journal.

For starters, why wasn't he more upset about the death of two people he counted among his friends?

CHAPTER THIRTY-FOUR

Tuesday, November 22
9:00 a.m.

BRIGHT AND EARLY MONDAY morning, I was back in my chambers, ready to make an appointment at Foster & Barnes. There was something off about Mitch Rogers, but I wouldn't find out what it was by ruminating about him. I needed input from others who knew him.

At least until I could pinpoint exactly what was wrong with the story Rogers told.

I reached for the phone only to yank my hand back, startled when the intercom went off.

"Ben Hathaway on line two for you, Judge," Augustus said, chipper as ever.

I grabbed the receiver, then sat back in my office chair behind my desk. "This is Judge Carson."

"The autopsy reports came back on Cindy Allen," Ben said without greeting. "The python didn't kill her. She had an overdose of the same toxic heroin in her system that killed Evan Hayden."

Momentarily stunned, I blinked at the wall across from me. "I thought you said she wasn't using anymore."

"She wasn't." Ben's flat tone told me everything.

I sat forward and rubbed my forehead. "So, both she and Hayden were murdered?"

"*I've* got two murders to solve instead of one." Exhaustion leaked through Ben's tone. "You've got nothing more to do here."

I wondered how long the three men had stayed up last night. George's Place closed at midnight, but when I'd finally gone to bed after one in the morning, George hadn't come upstairs yet. He'd been beside me sawing logs this morning, though.

"Like hell I don't!" Indignation swelled inside me until I forced it to calm down. "I've got more at stake here than you do, Ben. You're doing your job. But I'm being *prevented* from doing mine. Ozgood Richardson and his special judicial review committee won't be satisfied until you've solved this case. I've got to prove I had nothing to do with Evan Hayden's death. The only way to do that to everyone's satisfaction is to prove who killed him. And it's highly likely the same person killed Cindy Allen, using the same murder weapon."

I paused, and a long silence filled the space between us. After a while, I said, "Now, what about the snake?"

Ben gave a long-suffering sigh, but he knew I was right. He might not love having me on the bench, but he didn't like seeing me railroaded, either.

"Same story. The python did cause asphyxiation, but Cindy Allen would have been dead within minutes anyway, given the amount of toxic heroin in her system," Ben said. "It's like the killer didn't learn anything the first time he tried to distract us when he killed Evan Hayden. He did it again with Cindy Allen."

"Your operating theory is that the same person is behind both crimes, then?"

"Most likely, since that particular mix of fentanyl and heroin has only been found once before in our jurisdiction. Namely, when it was used to kill Hayden."

"What about Rogers—" I started to ask, but Ben cut me off.

"Stop right there. It wasn't Rogers. Couldn't have been. I already confirmed his alibi. His wife swears he was at home with her both nights before the murders occurred. Which means he wasn't spending that time planning a couple of murders."

This got my attention. "Wait. You're still investigating Mitch Rogers? He's still a suspect? I thought you said he was working with you."

"I said he agreed to help get us connected to people we want to interview. I never said I trusted him." Another sigh traveled across the line before he gave in and stated the obvious. "Look, Willa, we're cut from the same cloth here, you and me. We've been around this game long enough to suspect everything people say and do. Mitch Rogers seems like a good guy on the surface, and maybe he is. I really don't care. All I care about is finding out who really killed Hayden."

I nodded as if he could see me. "And Cindy Allen."

"And Cindy Allen," Ben admitted. "If Mr. Family Friendly can help me do that? Great. Plus, working with him keeps him close so I can keep an eye on him."

I chuckled. "Aren't you just all practical all of a sudden."

"Yeah, yeah." Ben's weary tone belied the humor I felt coming through. "There's something else, too. They brought in one of Hayden's coworkers last night. Guy name John Cramer. While my officers were at Foster & Barnes, they took a look around and found a stash of heroin in the guy's desk."

"What? Tell me they had a warrant." I was on my feet now, too pumped with adrenaline to sit still any longer.

"Of course they had a warrant. His lawyer's here. He's cooperating, and we're still interviewing him, but I doubt he's the guy who poisoned Hayden and Allen."

"Why? He seems a likely candidate, doesn't he?"

"At first, he did. But he's a back-office guy. He's never traveled to any of the states where this toxic heroin was found. And the preliminary toxicology reports show his stash wasn't the same."

"So you're saying he's an addict, but nothing ties him to the murders," I said.

"We'll keep talking to him, but it doesn't look promising." Ben covered the receiver and said something to someone else. "I gotta go. I'll call you if anything useful turns up."

"Thanks, Ben." I ended the call then sank back into my chair.

Idly, I switched on my computer and typed Mitch Rogers's name into a search engine. Last night's dinner conversation ran through my mind. Nothing I recalled was particularly helpful.

Hathaway said Rogers had been home with his wife at the time of both Evan and Cindy's murders.

He might have planned an alibi and hired another person to poison his victims. But Rogers, with so much riding on his public image, wasn't likely to risk his own security like that. Two people couldn't really keep such a secret. More likely, Hathaway would find the accomplice and squeeze him until he confessed.

The bigger thing was what possible motive Rogers could have for murdering Hayden and Allen.

He and Hayden were best buds. Got along great, Rogers claimed. No one said otherwise.

Hayden was also his financial planner. Which meant Rogers

could stand to lose a lot of money if anything happened to Hayden. Men like Rogers held on to their money even tighter than to their wives and their jobs.

And Rogers was the one who originally introduced Cindy Allen to Hayden after she'd moved to Tampa. That ruled out jealousy as a motive, didn't it?

The Texas Sharks website posted last season's schedule. The season ended with a loss in the playoffs in mid-October. Which meant Rogers *could* have been in Tampa both nights, even though he declared that he had been in Texas the night of Evan Hayden's murder.

I scrolled a little further back in the season. Rogers had pitched three games in Pittsburgh earlier in the year when the Sharks played the Pirates. He might have acquired the toxic heroin while he was there.

In fact, Rogers had pitched games in several locations where this specific toxic heroin had been identified.

I reached for the phone to call Ben, then reconsidered. Hathaway had probably discovered Rogers's connections to those locations. And if he hadn't, I'd bring it up after I confirmed that Rogers had access to the toxic heroin. Hathaway had plenty to do without chasing down my theories, too.

Augustus knocked on my door, then stuck his head into my office. I looked up, eyebrows arched.

"The *Stingy Dudes* case just settled. Thought you'd want to know. Plea deals all around and full restitution of embezzled funds returned to the victims by the banks." He shook his head at me. "Smile, Judge. Things are looking up. CJ hasn't called once today."

I nodded. Silence from CJ seemed more ominous than his constant phone calls. I wished I could share his optimism, but at the moment, with no end to the Hayden case in sight, I didn't have an ounce of optimism left in me.

"Thanks for letting me know," I said, keeping my attention on the monitor as I worked.

He ducked his head out and closed the door.

I eyed the teetering stack of pink phone messages in my inbox. I'd put off both CJ and the special investigative committee for days now. They'd be coming for me in person soon. I had the feeling that my time was running out, and we were no closer to solving Hayden's murder than we'd ever been.

I needed to prepare myself to face the music and to prepare George for what might lie ahead.

CHAPTER THIRTY-FIVE

Tuesday, November 22
5:30 p.m.

THAT NIGHT WHEN I got home, I fed the dogs and let them out. I changed into comfy sweats and sat out on the veranda, enjoying a drink and a cigar while reading the newspaper until George finished up downstairs.

"Good evening, Mighty Mouse," he said, dropping a kiss on the top of my head before taking a seat in the chaise lounge beside mine. He set his drink on the table between us, and soon we both had dogs at our feet and contented smiles on our faces.

I wanted to hold on to this moment as long as I could, knowing our idyllic existence could all end without warning. After several moments of companionable silence, George looked over at me, his expression quizzical. "What's wrong? You look so serious."

"Sorry." I stared out at the now-dark water while George sipped his Glenfiddich. "Lot on my mind."

He laced his fingers with mine. "Hopefully all this will be

over soon and things can get back to normal. Though I won't lie. It's been nice having you around more. When you're working, we see each other so seldom."

"True. If there's been one good thing to come out of this, it's been having more free time." I sighed. "But that could all change soon. A lot of things could change."

"The impeachment, you mean?" He stroked his thumb over my skin. "Oz is pretty pissed I'd imagine. You've been avoiding his phone calls, too, haven't you?"

I bit my lip and nodded.

"Right. That means you've kind of stepped in it here." He considered that for a while. He's a fabulous strategist. I was hoping he'd come up with a brilliant solution. Instead, he said, "Hate to say it, but it sounds like a no-win scenario to me. It always has. This Evan Hayden case is nothing but an excuse. Oz would have found another reason to impeach you. He's been gunning for you from the beginning."

Although his words echoed my own thoughts, I didn't take it well.

George squeezed my hand and tried again. "What I mean is, you have a choice to make here. Give up and give in, or continue to fight. That accident was traumatic to you and to us. No matter how you slice it. Because of Hayden's death, even though you didn't kill him, you feel like you owe it to Hayden and his family to find out the truth, don't you?"

I nodded.

"But even if you manage to do that, you can't erase the tragedy. Things changed that night. You can't go back for a do-over, unfortunately." He paused and sipped and hummed a minute. "All you can do is move forward and decide how you want to live from this point on."

"I know," I said, still staring out at the horizon. He'd said nothing I didn't already know, hadn't already felt, a thousand times over. "It's just hard."

"It is. I wish I could fix it for you." George rose, taking the last sip of his single malt scotch as he did so. "I haven't eaten yet tonight. How about you come downstairs and we'll see what the chef's got left. Might take your mind off things for a bit."

Surprisingly, I was actually hungry. I looked down at my sweats. "Can you send me something up instead?"

"Sure thing, Mighty Mouse," he teased as he bent and kissed me again. "How about some gourmet cheese?"

I made gnawing motions with my mouth, and he grinned. Then I threw one of the pillows from my chair at his retreating back, missing by a mile.

CHAPTER THIRTY-SIX

Wednesday, November 23
9:00 a.m.

TOMORROW WAS THANKSGIVING. I walked into my chambers determined to get things done. I was tired of living under a black cloud of stress because of Hayden's unsolved murder and CJ's nonsense. I intended to get to the bottom of something today if it killed me.

Which it actually might.

Augustus was already at his desk, looking dapper as usual in a crisp black suit and lavender shirt that all but glowed against his dark skin. Instead of his normal smile, he gave me a concerned look. "Judge, wait. You might want to—"

But I was through waiting. I'd been waiting too long already. To have my cases returned to me. To get on with my life and career as best I could.

"No time, Augustus," I said, opening the door to my office. "Too much to get done today."

My steps halted as I nearly collided with two dour-faced suits who could only have been from some investigative committee somewhere. I'd seen that same resigned, barely resuscitated look on too many jurists before. My heart sank along with my hopes for the day. It seemed CJ and his proceedings had finally caught up with me.

Shoulders squared, I made my way around my desk, a polite smile plastered in place. Beneath my charcoal pantsuit and daffodil-yellow silk shirt, cold sweat prickled on my skin.

If I managed to get through this without suffering the metaphorical death of my career, it would be a miracle, considering we still had no proof that someone had deliberately shoved Evan Hayden in front of my car so fast that nothing I could have done would have mattered. Without that evidence, it seemed like normal people would always believe I could have— and should have—stopped before I hit him. Hell, even I thought so, and I'd been there.

Still, I wasn't a quitter. Never had been. I wasn't about to start now.

With as much grace as I could muster, I took my seat behind my desk and blinked up at my uninvited guests. "Judge Wilhelmina Carson. How may I assist you today?"

"You can start by answering some questions for us, Judge Carson," the short, stout woman with gray hair and pale skin said. She looked about sixty but was probably much younger. Hard government work had a tendency to prematurely age people. Just look at the presidents. Most went in as relatively virile men and came out wizened and haggard.

She took a seat in one of the chairs in front of my desk and set her somewhat tattered brown leather briefcase at her feet. Her male counterpart—silver hair, thin build, gaunt face—took the seat beside her.

"First, let me make proper introductions," the woman said. "My name is Miriam Gardner, and this is Frederick Burton. We've been appointed to conduct a preliminary investigation into the charges of misconduct filed against you."

"And what exactly are the charges? I haven't been told. And by whom were these claims made? No one has deigned to tell me that, either." I said, sitting back. My instinct was to cross my arms defensively, but that would only allow them to see my tension, and I didn't want that. Instead, I forced my muscles to relax and rested my hands lightly on the arms of my chair. "I should have the right to know."

Ms. Gardner gave me a flat look over the top of her black-rimmed glasses. "At this point, this is a preliminary investigation only. If Mr. Burton and I determine that the matter is sufficiently serious to warrant a hearing, then you will be provided with copies of all the information obtained during our investigation, including the name of the complainant."

It was probably CJ who'd filed this complaint. He'd all but told me as much that day in his office. I glanced at the teetering stack of pink message notes in my inbox. Of course, it was CJ. He was at the top of the list of people who wanted me gone.

But he wasn't the only one. Prescott Roberts and a few of his cronies weren't too happy with me, either. They were affected by the *Stingy Dudes* case. Roberts himself had made it clear that he'd expected me to dismiss all claims. Of course, I hadn't. He wasn't happy.

Any individual or group with knowledge of possible judicial misconduct or wrongdoing could file a complaint.

So, there was a remote chance it had been someone else. Still, I couldn't help feeling this thing was personal, not professional. CJ had been waiting a long time for an opportunity to replace me, and now he finally had a good shot.

Hell, maybe CJ was the one who killed Hayden and shoved him in front of my car, just so he could get rid of me. The very idea of the little man struggling to do such a thing would have been humorous if the situation weren't so serious.

Augustus appeared in the still-open door to my office, his gaze sympathetic beneath his raised brows. He was asking me if I wanted coffee. He had to know there was no way I was going through this nightmare without caffeine. Besides, maybe refreshments would help me with my tightlipped interrogators.

I gave him a curt nod, and he left, closing the door.

"Should I hire a lawyer?" I asked, only half-joking.

"You're always welcome to have a lawyer present at any time, of course. A lawyer would not be allowed to interfere at this point, however." Mr. Burton's droning monotone picked up the conversational thread. "The committee's investigations are confidential. If and when that changes, you'll be among the first to know. My advice, Judge Carson, is don't borrow trouble. If we have a problem here, we'll all have plenty of time to hash out the facts."

Augustus came in carrying a tray of coffee and miniature blueberry scones from the bakery around the corner. I had no idea how he'd known to go to the bakery this morning or bring the scones at just the right moment, but here he was.

He's Prescott Roberts's nephew, flashed in my brain, but I set it aside. If he'd been tipped off by his uncle as to this visit, that could explain why he had these treats ready.

But he'd looked as genuinely distressed as I felt when I'd walked in on the Black Suit Brigade, so I chose to believe he was as surprised as I was.

Once he'd played gracious host, poured coffee, and served up the scones, Augustus left the room. I settled back in my seat and girded my loins, metaphorically anyway. I resisted the urge to say, "Bring it on."

All I had to offer was the truth, and that would have to be enough. I took a deep breath and dove in. "Shall we start, then?"

"Please give us your recollection of the events of the evening of November eighth," Gardner said, setting aside her cup and plate to pull out a digital recorder from her briefcase. She placed the thing on my desk and clicked the button to start it. Its red light gleamed up at me like an evil eye.

As I relayed the factual details that were already contained in the police file, neither of my interrogators gave me any visible body language cues as to their feelings on the matter. No expressions. Not so much as a twitch.

I tried to deploy the same stoicism. I couldn't do it. The mental images of Hayden's body lying in the street and the dull, bone-crunching thud of his body hitting my car swirled in my head and heightened my senses. Still, I managed to finish without flinching or fumbling.

"Had you been drinking that night?" Burton asked.

"No. The police file contains my toxicology."

"You have a pretty close relationship with the local chief of police, don't you, Judge Carson?" Gardner again. Her gray eyes glinted like sharp steel.

"I try to maintain professional working relationships with all law-enforcement agencies, yes. It makes things much easier."

"Easier how?"

I straightened, my pulse quickening with anger. Just what exactly was she trying to imply? "If you're suggesting that I've received any kind of special consideration during the Tampa Police Department's investigation of this case, you're mistaken."

Gardner glanced over at Burton, who pulled out his phone and brought up several pictures. He passed the device over the desk to me with a bland look. "These were taken two nights ago at a restaurant. That establishment is owned by your husband, is it not?"

I stared at the photos of the five of us at dinner, drinking expensive wine and eating gourmet food. My chest squeezed with tension, seeing where this was heading. "Yes. What are you implying?"

"Strange, don't you think? That the police chief would be dining with the main suspect in a vehicular-homicide case. The only suspect, really. I'd say that's not standard operating procedure for his department, Judge Carson."

Heat prickled up from beneath the collar of my jacket while I struggled to keep my cool. "You've been misinformed, Ms. Gardner. I'm not a suspect at all. The information has not been released to the public, but Mr. Hayden died of a lethal dose of highly toxic heroin. According to the autopsy reports, he was already dead, or very close to it, at the time he lunged into the road. There was no way I could have stopped in time or avoided hitting him. But I didn't kill him."

"The officer investigating at the scene determined you were going at least five miles an hour over the posted speed limit in that area," Barton said. "Reckless driving is defined in this state as operating a vehicle with willful or wanton disregard for the safety of persons or property."

"You, too, have been misinformed. Check the records from my car's black box. I was driving the speed limit. No more."

"You hit a man, and he died, Judge Carson. Whether there were other contributing factors to his death makes no difference to our investigation. You've breached the public trust and undermined the public faith in the judiciary." She paused.

"Is that so?" My tone rose in anger before I choked it down to a normal level. "This was an accident, pure and simple. Unavoidable. No fault or malice on my part. If you think you can convict me based on what you have here, have at it."

Gardener exhaled slowly, as if I were getting on her last nerve. Which was only fair, since she'd long since burned through mine. "If only it were that simple, Judge Carson. You see, in serious matters such as these, we are required to not only take into account the complaint at hand, but to also look at the judge's career as a whole. And, unfortunately, I'm sorry to say this is not the first time you, or someone close to you, has run afoul of the law, is it? You tend to make a public spectacle of yourself all too frequently."

She didn't sound sorry at all. And I couldn't possibly respond to that without slapping that smug smirk off her face.

Barton stepped in to recite a list of my most egregious indiscretions—George's false arrest for murder at the top of a long list of highly public situations that made me look like a thrill seeker and publicity hound akin only to one of the Kardashians.

Taken separately, each of these cases could be explained away, justified as the right thing to do under those particular circumstances.

But taken as a whole, as much as I hated to admit it, I could see how my unorthodox approach to these activities while sitting on the bench might be construed as...*questionable.*

By the time Gardner and Barton were done, my situation seemed hopeless. It was clear to me now that they had already made up their minds against me before they'd even walked in the door. Truthfully, given what they knew and how they'd acquired their knowledge, the conclusions they'd reached weren't very surprising at all.

They showed themselves out of my office with a curt reminder that they'd get back to me as soon as possible, in no event more than seventy-two hours, and nary a look back at Augustus or me.

"That seemed brutal," Augustus said when he came into my office to clean up the remnants of our coffee and scones. "I tried to warn you before you walked in, but you didn't give me a chance."

"It's okay." I groaned and rubbed my eyes.

The whole experience had been just as painful as I'd imagined it would be. Perhaps they were right. Perhaps I had been living in a protected bubble too long, thinking my independence and my lifetime appointment made me invincible. Perhaps I should just throw in the towel and go quietly into that good night, as CJ wanted me to do.

My temples throbbed, and my stomach knotted.

"You look a little green, if you don't mind my saying." Augustus finished collecting the dishes onto his tray, then headed back for the door. "How about if I hold your calls and you have a bit of peace and quiet until you're feeling better?"

I nodded mutely, waiting until the door closed behind him before dropping my head on my desk, eyes closed. Seventy-two hours. That's how much time I had left to save my career. The only way I might be able to do that was to uncover Evan Hayden's real killer, the person who'd administered that toxic heroin and shoved him in front of a moving car. And even that might not help much. They seemed less focused on whether I'd killed Hayden. To them, Hayden's death was the last straw in a giant pile I'd been accumulating for a good long while.

Determination galvanized, I sat up and dialed Ben's number to see if he had anything new on the case.

I might have been down, but I hadn't lost this fight yet.

CHAPTER THIRTY-SEVEN

Wednesday, November 23
11:45 p.m.

GEORGE AND I WERE having a nightcap later that night. It was a quarter to midnight and the last round of patrons for the evening were wrapping up. I'd just finished relaying the day's events. My head throbbed from the stress.

"So, what are you going to do, then?" George asked after taking another swig of his scotch. "You don't have the proof you need, do you?"

"Not yet." I rolled my stiff neck and shoulders. Ben had given me exactly zero new information. Only a vague I'm-still-looking-into-a-few-things, which frankly didn't help me at all. Maybe by the time I was thrown off the bench, the case would be solved.

"I don't know. The fighter in me tells me to go on, to keep pushing forward, no matter how dire this all seems at the moment." Even I could hear the weariness in my voice.

"What about the rest of you?" George gave me one of his narrowed stares.

"The rest of me says to let it go. Let things play out. Pick up the pieces afterward."

"Hmm." He snorted. "My bet's on the first option."

"You know me too well." I grinned and leaned over to clink glasses with him. Being married as long as we had seemed to take the edge off everything, the good and the bad. Right now, I was more than grateful for such ordinary blessings.

George kissed me quickly, then glanced over toward the entrance of the restaurant, one brow raised. "Little late for dinner."

"Huh?" I tracked his gaze to a young woman who'd just entered. She was in her late-twenties, shoulder-length blond hair, conservative navy dress. I recognized her instantly, and my heart stumbled.

"George, that's Kelly Webb. She worked with Hayden at Foster & Barnes. The day I went to talk to them, Kelly took my card and said she'd be in touch if she remembered anything."

I pushed to my feet and hurried to the entrance to catch her before she turned tail and ran off. "Kelly?"

"Judge Carson," she said, her brown eyes wary. "I'm sorry to be here so late, but…"

"No, no. It's no problem at all." I ushered her back to the table where George and I were sitting and introduced them.

George offered her a drink, which she declined, then went to get her a glass of water from the bar.

Once we were alone, my curiosity got the better of me. "Why did you come here tonight, Kelly?"

"I think I might have seen something, the night Evan died." She kept her hands tightly clenched in her lap and her gaze lowered. "I didn't mention it to the police when they questioned me because, honestly, I wasn't sure it was important."

"But now you think it is important?"

She nodded. "I'm worried that I made a mistake. I thought you might be able to help me. Maybe tell me what I should do."

"I'll certainly try."

She didn't say anything else for a few moments, and I sensed she needed a bit of coaxing. "Is it about who might have given Evan Hayden the drugs?"

Another nod.

She said, "I wasn't a big Evan Hayden fan. Pretty much no one at the firm was. You probably got a sense of that. He was a racist, bigoted, misogynist who only cared about himself. He treated me and everyone else he came in contact with horribly." Kelly's voice broke. She dabbed her eyes with a tissue. "But he didn't deserve to die just because he was an asshole."

I reached over and laid a hand on Kelly's trembling forearm in a show of support. "But you think someone might have killed him because of his behavior?"

"No. Not entirely, anyway," she murmured.

"I don't understand."

"There was something else. Something I saw on his laptop the day he died, when I walked in unexpectedly." Kelly shuddered as if envisioning something disgusting. "Pictures. Videos, too. Of what looked like really young girls. They were doing…" She cringed. "Sexual things to adult men. I-I couldn't—"

She covered her face with her hands as George returned with her water. I met his gaze over Kelly's bowed head and gave him a warning look. He quickly made an excuse about checking on something in the kitchen and escaped.

I waited silently until Kelly gathered her composure and was ready to continue.

"Evan shut the screen fast once he knew I'd seen it. Then he gave me some baloney about the stuff belonging to one of his clients. He said the porn turned his stomach, and he was going to the police with it first thing the next morning."

"But he never made it," I said, piecing this new information together in my mind.

Hayden had discovered criminal activities involving one of his clients—child porn, from the sounds of it—and he'd decided to take it to the police.

Interesting, given that he'd been described as a lowlife villain by just about everyone I'd talked to.

It was possible he'd made up an excuse simply to get Kelly out of his office. What I knew about Hayden's personality suggested he'd have been more likely to take that evidence of criminal conduct and blackmail the owner with it.

"There was a party that night at Shannon's Irish Pub for all the firm's staff. Over on Howard. You know it?"

I nodded. "Everyone knows Shannon's."

"Right. Well, it was a year-end party. A celebration of all we'd accomplished this year." Kelly stopped for a sip of water, her fingers shaking as she picked up the glass. "We'd been there about an hour when Mitch arrived."

"Mitch Rogers?" I froze.

"Yep. All us girls thought he was so sweet. Always so nice and handsome and polite when he came into the office." Kelly shrugged, giving a little smile. "We knew he was married, of course, but a girl can have her fantasies."

"Right."

"Anyway, he came to the pub that night and pulled Evan aside. They were across the room from where I was standing, so I couldn't hear what they were talking about, but they both looked sort of upset. Which was odd, because I'd never seen Mitch angry. Even the time the stock market in Japan crashed and he lost a boatload, he just let it all roll off his back. He'd say, 'It's only money. I'll make more.'" Kelly's face scrunched up like a child's immediately before she began to cry.

"And then what happened?" I handed her a tissue.

Kelly wiped her tears. "Some guy sitting at the bar must've been drunk or something. He turned around and said something to Mitch that I couldn't hear. Evan took a swing at the guy and connected with his shoulder. The guy swung back and missed. Mitch dragged Evan away, and the fight ended."

The picture was coming together in my head. When witnesses said there was a bar fight, they must have meant the guy on the barstool at Shannon's. Hathaway interviewed that guy and concluded the fight wasn't relevant to Hayden's death. Which was probably true.

But Hathaway's team had missed the *other* bar fight. The verbal argument between Hayden and Rogers.

I nodded. "Is that all?"

"Mitch and Evan left maybe ten minutes after that, still pissed from what I could see. Arguing all the way outside." Kelly wound up her story. "And that was it. No one saw Evan again until he turned up on that news tip line asking people to call in if they knew who he was. That's when we called the police."

"I see," I said, although I didn't quite yet. Not completely.

Knowingly possessing, controlling, or even viewing child porn was a sex crime in Florida. A felony. Any image that depicted any child under the age of eighteen engaging in sexual conduct of any kind was a third-degree felony. Each image counted as a separate felony. Ten images, ten felonies, each with a possible sentence of up to five years in prison. Seizing the evidence and proving the crimes wasn't difficult because the internet services cooperated with police to shut down the purveyors of child porn.

I cocked my head. "Why didn't you report the porn yourself, Kelly?"

If Kelly had reported what she saw, it would have been simple enough to get a warrant for Hayden's laptop, locate the child porn, and charge him with possession. Hayden, being the jerk everyone said he was, would have implicated the client who owned the porn in exchange for a plea deal that would get Hayden a suspended sentence and a fine.

But it would have ended his career, most likely. He'd probably have lost his license. And even if he hadn't, who would trust him to manage their investments ever again after something like that?

Kelly's eyes widened. She sniffed and wiped her pert nose. "Evan said the porn belonged to one of the firm's clients. Which made the situation—sensitive. He asked me to keep it quiet and said he'd take care of it. With the party and all, I figured I had time to deal with it later if Evan didn't. I guess I was wrong."

I nodded, still thinking.

Even if Hayden had merely stored the child porn on his laptop, he was guilty of several felonies. If he'd used the porn to blackmail a client, he'd been playing with his own freedom, too. Blackmailers rarely stopped after one payment. And the target rarely let the blackmailer bleed him totally dry before he struck back.

Was the argument between Rogers and Hayden in the pub that night about the child porn?

Had Mitch Rogers, Mr. Family Friendly, been the client Hayden claimed was responsible for the child porn Kelly saw on Hayden's laptop?

If so, that would be the end of Rogers's life as he knew it. His baseball career would be over. He'd probably get hefty prison time. He'd lose his wife and kids. His whole life would've been ripped apart if Hayden disclosed that porn's mere existence to anyone.

"Kelly, were any other Foster & Barnes clients at the pub that night for the party?"

Kelly wiped her eyes again. "Oh, sure. It was a big crowd. At least a dozen clients were in and out before the night was over."

If Rogers wasn't the client who owned the porn, any one of Foster & Barnes's clients would be in the same situation when the porn was disclosed. The firm's clients were all powerful, wealthy people. Child porn could bring any one of them down in a hot Florida second.

According to the Texas Sharks website, during the past season, Rogers had been in several locations where the specific toxic heroin that killed Hayden was found. Rogers could have purchased it and brought it back to Tampa. So could several other Foster & Barnes clients and employees, probably.

The coroner had said that it could have taken up to thirty minutes for the toxic heroin to kill Hayden. Plenty of time for Rogers, or someone he paid, to dose Hayden and then shove him into the street.

The more I thought about it, the more it made sense for the killer to hire this out. The only problem would be the loose end. How could he be sure the killer wouldn't simply take Hayden's place and blackmail him, too?

"And you didn't tell the police any of this? Why?" Chief Hathaway would've had this whole thing wrapped up by now if he'd known about the porn. Once he'd found it, he'd have been able to trace it back to the owner.

"I didn't want to get Mitch in trouble. He's such a nice guy, and he's never gotten into some of the crap the other people in our circles do. With all that money lying around, most of our clients are always seeking the next big thrill. Heroin seems to be the most recent thrill they're all taking." She finished her water, then toyed with the glass. "Mitch was never like that, though. In fact, he took a lot of his profits and gave them away to charities and stuff."

It was the "and stuff" that was the problem. Guys like that were even worse than the quiet offenders because they tried to cover up their sins with cash and blarney. Too often, it worked.

I'd zoned out for a second there, but Kelly was still talking. "I'm sorry. What did you say?"

Kelly offered a weak smile. "There are actually a lot of people at our firm who've become heroin users recently."

"And the bosses are allowing that to happen?"

"Everybody denies it. The whole thing has caused a kind of 'don't ask/don't tell' situation."

"Meaning what?"

"Bosses might suspect, but no one says a word. As long as the profits keep rolling in and nothing goes horribly wrong, it's all fine. No one wants to get fired or worse," Kelly lowered her gaze to the table. "We're all hoping this stops soon. Before more people get hurt."

"What about Evan Hayden? Was he a heroin user?"

"No." Kelly gave a sad shake of her head. "Sometimes we wished he would. Might have improved his personality. But Evan kept his vices strictly to the job. All work, all the time. Money, money, money. In a lot of ways, I think money was his drug of choice."

Another thing that didn't make sense was Cindy Allen's role in all of this. Assuming she had one. Was her death unrelated?

That didn't seem likely, since the same toxic drug was found in her system and she had known both Hayden and Rogers.

Perhaps, she'd somehow seen the child porn. Maybe she knew

who owned it. Was the owner Rogers? Or Hayden? Or someone else?

I thought back to the night Mitch and Genevieve Rogers had dinner with us. I'd sensed something off about him. But I'd ignored my intuition because George was a fan and Hathaway recruited Rogers to work with the police.

After Cindy Allen died, Rogers had volunteered to help. Which kept him on the inside of the investigation. But Ben didn't trust him implicitly because he'd continued to run down leads involving Rogers right along with everyone else.

Hathaway was smarter than the average bear when it came to star athletes. We had dozens of professionals living and working in Tampa, including more than a few lawbreakers. Tampa PD had loads of practice dealing with entitled idiots acting as if fame and riches gave them a pass to do whatever they wanted, whether it was illegal or not.

"What happened to Evan's clients?" I asked Kelly. "Did they go to a different firm?"

She looked up at me, startled by the question. "Some did. But most were handed off to the other brokers. Why?"

"You wouldn't happen to know who's handling Mitch Rogers now, would you?"

"Uh, I think Max Fletcher took him on." Kelly arched her eyebrows as if she'd had to think about it. "The firm's having another party at Shannon's Irish Pub tonight to welcome a new crop of analysts aboard. That's where I was before I came over. Fletcher's there. Mitch, too. They seemed pretty chummy."

"Would you mind going back?" I asked impulsively. "And taking me with you?"

Kelly looked at me quizzically. "Yeah, sure, I guess."

"Hang on. I'll be right back." I made a beeline for George,

who stood at the entrance to the kitchen discussing tomorrow's menu with the chef. Placing my hand on his shoulder, I rose to whisper in his ear, "Call Ben Hathaway and tell him to get over to Shannon's Irish Pub. I'll meet him there."

I took a couple of steps toward the table where Kelly was waiting, but George stopped me with a hand on my arm. "What's going on?"

"Don't worry. I'll be fine. It looks like Mitch Rogers is into child porn. Hayden was blackmailing him. That's why Rogers killed Hayden."

George's eyes bulged like a cartoon character. "What?"

"Just call Ben and tell him to bring a couple of officers with him." I took a deep breath and let it out. "I think I might know what happened to Evan Hayden and Cindy Allen."

CHAPTER THIRTY-EIGHT

Thursday, November 24
12:25 a.m.

SHANNON'S IRISH PUB WAS still packed with patrons by the time I arrived with Kelly. It was going on twelve thirty now, and from the raucous noises and booming music, the party was just getting started.

We weaved our way through the crowd, the floor sticky with spilled drinks and the air sharp with the scent of warm bodies. I glanced around to locate Mitch Rogers, but no luck.

Kelly cleared a path toward the bar, and I followed in her wake, always keeping an eye out for Rogers. I hadn't told Kelly, but Chief Hathaway should be arriving soon, too. As we stepped up to the large half-circle oak bar and squeezed in between two men I recognized from my earlier questioning of employees at Foster & Barnes, I leaned forward to see around the bar.

Sure enough, there sat Mitch Rogers, having dinner with Tom Bradford, the guy I'd interviewed along with Kelly Webb at Foster & Barnes.

Bradford looked disheveled this evening, dark circles punctuating his eyes, hair and clothing unkempt. Much different from the slick hipster who'd given me a heaping helping of snark the one and only time we'd met. He looked scared and strung out and…like Hollywood's depiction of an addict too far gone to save.

If Rogers had paid someone to administer Hayden's deadly drugs, could Bradford have been his patsy? Along with a few others, he'd been arrested for heroin possession by Ben, then released when the drug didn't match the kind found in the victims' systems, but perhaps Mitch was paying him off in more than just cash. Perhaps he was helping to feed Bradford's addiction as well as his bank account.

"There they are," Kelly said, indicating the two men. "What should we do now? Call the police or—"

At that moment, Mitch Rogers looked up and caught my eye. His camera-ready smile fell slightly, and I could tell from the flicker of fear in his eyes that he knew I knew.

My pulse raced as adrenaline rushed my system. Rogers slid off his stool and backed slowly toward the door to the bar's back room behind him.

It had been a long time since I'd been to a party here, but if I remembered correctly, there was a back exit that led to the alley at the rear of the building.

I had a choice to make. Ben Hathaway should be on his way, but if Mitch escaped now, chances were high we'd never find him again. He had the financial means to travel anywhere in the world at a moment's notice, and the contacts to make it happen. There'd be no justice for Evan Hayden or Cindy Allen.

No proof for me to show the committee along with my written response to save my job, either.

In the end, I had no choice at all.

"Stay here," I said to Kelly, taking her arm and forcing her attention back to me. "Help keep the others safe, if it comes to that. Got it?"

She swallowed hard and gave a quick nod.

By the time I turned around, the door to the back room was swinging shut. Rogers was gone. So was Bradford. Panic quickened my steps as I raced for that back door, shoving people out of my way as I went.

The first thing I noticed as I pushed into the back room was Bradford's body on the floor, convulsing and writhing. My breath hitched. His face was the same pale gray as Evan Hayden's had been the night I struck him with my car.

I barely noticed the door shutting behind me as I rushed toward Bradford and dropped to my knees. He'd gone deathly still, like Evan Hayden when I found him lying on the pavement.

Hands shaking, I checked Bradford's pulse. There it was, faint, but present. I sent up a silent prayer of thanks, then patted the pocket of my blazer for my phone.

"You should have stayed out of it, Carson." Rogers's voice was soft, resigned. "Why couldn't you just let it go?"

One fluorescent bulb flickered and hissed from the ceiling, casting the room in a dull, greenish glow. Over my shoulder, I spotted him in the darkened room standing between me and the doorway, his normally sunny expression now haggard.

Rogers watched me with wary, wild eyes. Something glinted in his hand when the fluorescent caught it through the shadows. A steak knife. He'd probably grabbed it off his dinner plate at the bar.

"It was done. Over. Bradford was the last one, and then we'd have been done."

My whirling thoughts snagged on that "we."

My gaze darted toward the door as it creaked open once more.

Kelly Webb slipped inside, and my heart plummeted to my toes. Her sweet smile was chilling now, given the circumstances. My heart was beating so loudly in my ears I could barely hear.

"Tom did some of the dirty work," Kelly said, joining Rogers near the door. "Then he went and got himself arrested, and his usefulness diminished because he was being watched."

Right. So, there'd been three villains in this story, not just the one. I got why Kelly would be Mitch's accomplice. If they were sleeping together, then she had a vested interest in keeping her lover out of jail. And she'd mentioned Evan's accounts being dispersed amongst the other brokers after his death. If she'd taken on Rogers's finances—and not Max Fletcher, as she'd said—that gave her another tie to protect between them.

Any breaking-news stories about child porn would tarnish the squeaky-clean pitching star's money-making capabilities, even if he didn't get arrested. Kelly Webb, like many financial planners, worked on commission. The more money their clients made, the more they made.

But what about Bradford?

He wasn't dead yet, but the coroner's words kept repeating in my head. Death within thirty minutes. When had the toxic heroin entered his system? No way to know for sure, but it was obvious that if he didn't get help soon, he wouldn't survive.

Chief Hathaway had not arrived, and I had no idea when he would. Secluded in this back room, with the noise from the party outside and my own raging pulse all but deafening in my ears, I couldn't detect the sound of approaching sirens, even if there were any.

I was on my own.

"Let me go, Mitch." To my surprise, my voice sounded much

stronger than I felt, steady and in command, even over the chest-thumping bass of the music vibrating the entire building.

My best bet was to pretend that Bradford was already dead. If they perceived his threat gone, they might be more inclined to let me go. Rogers wasn't a psychopath, as far as I knew. He'd killed because he'd seen no other escape.

Kelly Webb's psychology was unknown. I didn't have a read on her.

"Listen, Mitch. I know about the child pornography, too. I know how desperate you were to keep that information from going public. But killing me won't help you. Just the opposite. I'm a federal judge." *At least for the time being.* "Let me go, and I might be able to help you work all this out."

If I got out of this alive, I wouldn't help him work anything out, of course. I'd take what information I had and go straight to the police. And later, I'd share it with CJ and the special committee.

I struggled to stand, slowly, my legs unsteady.

"...do you?" Mitch asked, and I realized he'd been talking.

My mind stuttered, trying to catch up with whatever he'd said that I hadn't heard. "I'm sorry?"

He gave me a look that made me wonder if he'd already figured out my plan. "You think you're such an expert in doling out justice, don't you?"

"Yes."

"But what if you're not? I've given away millions to charity, done good deeds all over this world. I'm Mr. Family Friendly. People love me. How is erasing all that 'justice'? All over one stupid mistake."

"Not one mistake, Mitch," I said as calmly as I could. "The porn was just the beginning."

"Yeah?" He reached fast for Kelly's arm, yanking her in front of him and pressing the sharp knife blade to her throat.

At first, she laughed, seeming to think it was a joke, but I could tell from the stricken, desperate look on Rogers's face that his intentions were not funny at all. Kelly's good humor faded as he caressed her face with the blade, tracing the flat side of it down her cheek until the tip rested under her chin. A smear of ketchup from his dinner, or Kelly's blood, left a dark trail on her pale skin.

She whimpered, like the mewl of a kitten, and met my gaze, confused and scared now.

My throat constricted, and I forced words past tight vocal cords. "Don't. Please. Killing Kelly won't solve your problems. It will only make them worse."

"I can't go to prison," he said, pressing the knife tighter to her neck. Kelly clutched his forearm tight, digging her nails into Mitch's skin. He flinched but didn't let her go. "I won't."

"Let Kelly go," I pleaded, holding my hands up, palms out. "Let her go, and we can work a deal. Negotiate. You're used to that in baseball, right, Mitch? Bargaining. Maybe you could give us the name of the dealer you bought the toxic heroin from in Philadelphia. That would be a sign of cooperation. And if the child porn was your first offense, then you can negotiate that, too."

None of that was true. He'd either killed or conspired to kill two people. Three, if Tom Bradford didn't get help soon. Bradford was still lying at my feet, his eyes flickering behind his lids, his complexion growing more mottled by the second. Images of Evan Hayden from the night of the accident swirled through my overtaxed mind.

Rogers chuckled, a mirthless sound. "Just let Kelly go, huh? That's all I have to do?"

"Please."

Hardness descended over his features. "I can't do that. You are the last two people who know the truth. If I don't get rid of you, then I'll lose everything. There'll be no leniency, not for me. I'm not an idiot. I've seen what happens to people like me who go bad. They'll take it all from me." He tightened his grip on Kelly, and she scrabbled to keep her feet on the ground.

My options were draining fast. With the party in full swing, it was unlikely anyone knew we were back here. Rogers could kill us all and leave by the back exit to the alley before anyone knew what he'd done. He'd disappear forever.

Where the hell was Hathaway? Cops. Never around when you need them, but commit a minor traffic infraction and they were there to slap you with a ticket in a hot second.

"You never asked me how I got Hayden in front of your car that night," Rogers said.

His words stopped me cold. He was setting some sort of trap. I could hear it in the tone of his voice, the slight sneer of each word.

"Wouldn't you like to know before you die?" His countenance had shifted now, from relaxed and smiling to cold and cunning. Maybe I'd been wrong about that whole psychopath thing.

Still, I had to keep him occupied until he made a mistake I could exploit. Or until Hathaway showed up. Whichever came first. "Yes."

"Then ask."

It was a stupid game, one designed to give Rogers the satisfaction of being in control, however temporary. I'd had enough experience with bullheaded, arrogant people over the years to recognize it. Unfortunately, in this case, I had little choice but to play.

Fine.

I squared my shoulders and bit out the question. "How did you get Evan Hayden in front of my car that night?"

"I had old Tom here poison his drink at that office party. He dragged Evan out the back." Rogers cocked his head toward the other side of the room and the red glowing sign proclaiming *Exit*. "Tom drove him over to Bayshore and dragged him across the road. Shoved him out in front of your car. If you weren't such a workaholic, you would have been home hours earlier. Could have been anybody behind the wheel. You just got lucky."

Lucky was the farthest thing from how I felt. "So, you paid Bradford to kill Hayden. Why? What did Hayden ever do to you?"

"Didn't cost me anything, actually. Well, unless you count the heroin." Rogers grinned, a sinister affair. "Tom couldn't stand Evan. Said it was a pleasure to wipe him off the face of the earth. Honestly, I think I'm about the only person who could stomach Evan at all."

"What about Cindy Allen?" That was the one piece I'd never been able to connect. "I thought she was your friend."

"She was," Rogers said, a hint of remorse straining his tone. "But then she and Evan started dating, and things got more serious than I'd intended. I couldn't take the chance that he'd told her about the porn and that she'd go to the police with it. I never wanted to kill Cindy, but it had to be done. Tom took care of it while I was busy. Gave me a solid alibi."

"And Kelly, how did she get involved?"

Kelly's eyes met mine over the top of his tree-trunk-sized forearm. Tears welled in her eyes, along with remorse, but she'd made her bed—both with Rogers and his murders. Now she'd have to deal with the fallout from those decisions. I just prayed it wouldn't be fatal for either of us.

"Oh, she was all too happy to hop on board once she took over my account and saw how much I was worth to her." Rogers gave a derisive snort. "Funny, but they never tell you that part about being rich and famous. That the more you earn, the more people will want to take everything you've got. She hated Evan, too, of course, but the child porn was a bit trickier. She was willing to look the other way when I promised her I'd downloaded the porn by mistake. Potential million-dollar commissions in her pockets covered a multitude of sins."

I averted my eyes, tension and nausea making me lightheaded. "What about your wife? Your children?"

"They'll get everything when I'm gone. I've already got it set up through Kelly here." He squeezed her neck a little tighter, and her eyes bulged. "A contingency plan. I can't make them sit through a public trial. My wife can't sit there and listen to people list all my horrible sins. I can't go to prison and lose everything I love because of you and your precious judicial system. I can't."

"Mitch, please." I tried one last time to get through to him. "You can't do this."

"Sure I can. I'm a star. I can do whatever I want." He pressed the knife harder against Kelly's throat, and she whimpered again, louder this time.

My stomach clenched. I had to do something. Given his current state of mind, he'd kill Kelly right in front of my eyes if I failed. While I watched, the tip of the blade pricked Kelly's skin again, and another drop of crimson welled. Her struggles increased.

"Say it," Rogers growled, "Or I'll slit her throat. You know I will."

Through clenched teeth, I echoed, "You can do whatever you want."

As soon as the words left my lips, the music on the pub's sound system screeched to an ear-splitting halt. My breath rasped loudly in the suddenly quiet room, mixed with Kelly's crying.

I checked once more to be sure I had no means of escape. No portals had magically opened up in the past thirty seconds.

I returned my focus to Rogers, knowing that help had finally arrived. "The police are here now. It's over."

"No chance. They can't get back here in time to save you." He shook his head, and his macabre grin showed off his straight, white teeth. "Kelly here's a goner already."

He pressed the knife tip further into her skin, and more blood flowed.

Kelly screamed and struggled to get away, but his grip held her with no effort at all.

A knot clogged my throat. I forced myself to breathe, to think. Chief Hathaway was out there somewhere beyond the door. He had to be. Why else would the music have stopped?

"First Kelly, then you."

"I never did anything to you, Mitch," I said, somehow finding a remnant of strength to force into my voice.

"And you gave me a solid cover for the murder of Evan Hayden. Thank you for that, Judge Carson." He snorted. "I hope you enjoy your unemployment."

"So that's it, then?" I fisted and unfisted my hands.

"That's it."

"No, it isn't." I took a quick step toward the door, hoping to throw him off balance. Or at least stall him until I could think of something better. Anything. But my mind was racing.

The sound of a booming bullhorn came through. "This is Tampa Police. Put down your weapon. Step out, Mr. Rogers, with your hands up."

Rogers kept silent, the knife still poised at Kelly's throat, his attention drilling a hole through the closed door. The fluorescent light above us flickered—once, twice—then went out, leaving the room bathed only in the red light from the exit sign.

"It was one mistake," Rogers whispered. "I can't lose everything I've built over one stupid mistake."

He headed for the back exit, dragging Kelly along with him.

Rogers tripped over Bradford's legs.

Kelly bobbled and then fell to her knees.

I charged forward to cover her trembling body with my own.

"Rogers, the alley exit is blocked. You can't escape. I'm counting from ten. Then we're coming in," Ben's amplified voice shouted from inside the pub. "Ten. Nine. Eight."

Above me, Rogers raised the knife, his face bathed in crimson shadows.

"Don't move," he said.

"Seven. Six. Five." Numbers continued to boom from the other side of the door. "Four. Three."

"I can't go to prison." Rogers straightened, the knife clutched tightly in his hand as he raised the blade, this time toward his own abdomen. "I can't."

"Two. One."

All hell broke loose moments later. There was a pained grunt from Rogers as he drove the blade deep into his own gut. At the same time, the doors burst open, and officers raced in, poised to kill.

I kept low on the floor, protecting Kelly, as the cops swarmed. She clung to me like a scared child—trembling, her breath coming hard and fast. I couldn't really hear anything over the cacophony of screaming patrons inside the bar and police shouts for assistance outside.

Kelly's sobs wracked her body. I felt some strange, misguided protective instinct toward her after what we'd just been through together.

I bent to whisper close to her ear, "Come on, Kelly. We have to get up. The police are here now. You have to get up."

Blood streaked her neck and cheek as she raised her face to me. "I-I'm s-sorry. Mitch s-said h-he loved me. He s-said w-we'd run away together when this was done, and I'm such an idiot, I believed him."

"Willa, are you okay?" Ben asked, kneeling down beside me.

"I'm fine. But Kelly needs help. Bradford, too."

Medics arrived, and I directed them toward Bradford, saying, "He's ingested toxic heroin. Maybe fifteen to twenty minutes ago."

They rushed to get him on a gurney and into the ambulance. I hoped he'd make it. If the antidote was administered soon, he could. I crossed my fingers for him.

Another pair of medics moved to deal with a groaning, bleeding Mitch Rogers. Apparently, his aim was off. From what I could hear the medics saying, he'd plunged the steak knife where the wound wasn't fatal.

Guess he'd be spending that time in prison after all. Unless some well-paid lawyer worked a miracle. I'd seen it happen before and Rogers certainly had the money to hire the best.

I squinted in the bright light now streaming in through the smashed door. "Took you long enough to get in here, though."

"Everybody's a critic." Ben shook his head. But he smiled and gave my arm a solid squeeze.

CHAPTER THIRTY-NINE

Thursday, November 24
3:17 a.m.

HOURS LATER, AFTER I'D been checked by the medics and interviewed by the police, I found myself in the passenger seat of Ben Hathaway's sedan, heading home at last. The scent of his hot coffee in the cup holder between us filled the air, and the digital clock on his dashboard said it was well after three a.m.

The bay lapped gently at the shore as we turned onto the Plant Key Bridge. Ben kept his focus straight forward, his fingers tapping lightly against the wheel to a tune only he could hear.

Finally, he said, "Rogers struck out. The docs at Tampa Southern say he'll live."

"Too bad for him. He'll spend the rest of his life in prison."

Ben looked as exhausted as I felt, but he managed a tired smile. "Kelly's going to be fine, too. She's already got a good lawyer lined up. He'll agree that she'll testify against Rogers in exchange for a lighter sentence. Maybe even probation."

I wasn't sure how I felt about that, so I nodded.

"Rogers is lawyered up already, too. Naturally. He may get some leniency because of his motives. But he won't get away with murder." Ben lowered his window a bit, allowing the fresh breeze inside.

"What motives are you talking about?" I glanced at him to be sure he wasn't joking. "Rogers was into child porn. He killed three people to keep that quiet. Why should he get any leniency for that?"

I shivered, mostly from the cold breeze blowing through his open window. The temperatures were chillier than normal for this late in the autumn, but I imagined he needed all the help he could get to stay awake. I didn't complain.

"When George called tonight, he told me what you said about the porn, and we checked it out. Just got the final word about an hour ago." Ben shot me a meaningful look. "Mitch Rogers didn't download the porn. His son did."

I gasped. "How do you know?"

"We have a lot of tools trained on that filth these days. We found the IP address easily once we knew what we were looking for. The porn was downloaded to the son's laptop. His mother found it." Ben paused and took a deep breath. "It wasn't Mitch Rogers the baseball player that Hayden was blackmailing. It was Genevieve Rogers. She paid him off to protect her son."

I shook my head. "Wow. So you're saying Rogers killed three people to protect his family?"

"You're almost there, but not quite." Ben sighed.

"What do you mean?"

"It's complicated. But the short version is that Genevieve is the one who paid Bradford to kill Hayden. Mitch didn't know about it until after the fact. Cindy Allen told him. Remember Mitch said his wife and Allen went to yoga classes together?"

I thought about this new data for a few seconds while Ben made his way closer to Minaret. After he dropped me off, I wouldn't have another chance to talk to him for a few days, probably.

"So what will happen to all of them?"

"They've all been picked up. We'll sort out who did what to whom, but in the eyes of the law, they're all guilty. You know that," Ben said.

"Right." Not a very brilliant response, but it was the best I could do at the moment.

"And you'll be glad to know you've been officially cleared in the death of Charles Evan Hayden. Sorry we couldn't do it sooner, but now that we have, that should also wrap things up with Ozgood Richardson and that review board. Right?"

"Special investigative committee," I corrected with a grin. He was trying to make me feel better. It wasn't his fault that I didn't.

He shrugged. "Whatever they call it, you're gonna be okay?"

"That should go a long way toward helping me keep my job." I glanced over at him. "Thank you, Ben."

"You're welcome," he said, not meeting my gaze. But his words were sincere, and that was all I needed. "Just try to stay out of trouble from now on, okay? You keep sticking your neck out the way you have been, and one day someone's likely to come along and whack your head off."

"I'd really like to stay out of trouble." I sighed.

I never went looking for trouble. Even so, trouble seemed to find me. There'd be another case, another lost cause, and somehow I'd be drawn into trouble again. Which was exactly what irritated CJ.

For now, though, all I wanted was to see George and my dogs and enjoy a good night's sleep.

Ben yawned, then asked, "Whatever happened with that case, the *Stingy Dudes*?"

"Oh, last I heard, they settled."

He chuckled. "Just like Evan Hayden and Johnny Rae, eh?"

I exhaled, sinking down into my seat. "Yep. Except nobody died."

Ben pulled up in front of Minaret.

"Happy Thanksgiving, Ben," I said as I opened the door and stepped out.

"Happy Thanksgiving, Willa. Give my best to George." He added, "Oh. And Rinaldo Gaines is back in town. He was at Shannon's Irish Pub tonight. But he's more likely to stick like glue to the Rogers family than to bother you again."

"We can hope," I replied before I closed the door and trudged into the house.

CHAPTER FORTY

Sunday, November 27
7:00 p.m.

RAIN PATTERED GENTLY ON the roof of the veranda, competing with the sound of waves against the shore. On Thursday, after a few hours' sleep, we'd enjoyed a quiet Thanksgiving with Kate and Leo and the rest of our family. They had lots of questions, but at Kate's request, they held them all for another time. Which was something else to be thankful for. A loving family who knew when to butt out.

It had been three days since Mitch Rogers had been arrested at Shannon's Irish Pub, and things were settling into a regular routine again.

I still woke up at night sometimes, imagining I was trapped in that dark back room with Mitch Rogers, his knife pressed to Kelly's throat, Tom's body sprawled on the floor.

I jumped at the sound of George coming in the door of our flat. It was nearly midnight now, and I turned in my chaise lounge to peer over the back. Even after all these years, the sight of him in his sport coat and jeans, clean shaven and hair freshly trimmed, made my heart flutter. He smiled as he puttered around in the kitchen, knowing I was looking at him.

"How were things at the restaurant tonight?" I asked, facing forward again.

"Good." The sound of ice tinkling into a glass followed by the glug of liquor pouring gently from the bottle reached my ears. "Full house again."

"Excellent." I swirled my gin and smiled in the darkness. "Did you bring me a snack?"

"Well, if you consider this a snack." He leaned over my chair to kiss me. He'd shed his sport coat now, shirtsleeves rolled up to reveal tanned forearms, lightly dusted with dark hair.

He settled into the chair beside mine and sipped his scotch. "What did you do up here while I was working?"

"Let's see. I played with the dogs. Finished typing up my written response to the committee. And I took a nap."

"All good things." He toasted me with his tumbler. "Do you think the committee will side with you on this one?"

"No idea."

"But you're not worried about it tonight?" George reached over and took my hand.

Concern pinched the corners of his eyes, and there was a seriousness to his mouth that belied the casual tone of his question.

"No," I said. "Not tonight."

George tugged me closer. He rested his cheek against the top of my head and pressed a kiss into my hair.

We sat like that for a long time, with the dogs snuggled at our feet, and all was right with our little world.

"If I ask you a serious question," George murmured against my ear, "will you give me an honest answer?"

"Maybe."

I'm not sure what it is about my husband, but George can piss me off, turn me on, make me question my judgment, and, in general, provoke inconvenient emotions. Which was what his question did now. I didn't want to deal with tough questions tonight, honest or otherwise.

"What will you do if the impeachment investigation doesn't go your way?"

I wasn't ready to make this decision yet. I hoped I wouldn't have to make it at all. And I didn't want to say that, either.

"Be a lawyer, I suppose."

"Really? After all this time?"

"Unless we've won the lotto lately." I tipped my head back to look at him. He shook his head. I smiled. "Hey, I did it before; I can do it again."

"No doubts here." His smile had returned.

George was extremely protective of me. But would he kill to protect me, like Mitch Rogers did to protect his wife? The thought horrified me. I was responsible for myself. I didn't need or want a knight in shining armor racing to my rescue, with honorable intentions or evil ones.

George gave my hand a squeeze. "I just know if Oz loses this round, he'll try harder next time. He won't give up."

"Neither will I." I kissed him again, grinning. "Neither will I."

THE END

ABOUT THE AUTHOR

Diane Capri is an award-winning *New York Times*, *USA Today*, and world-wide bestselling author. She writes several series, including the Hunt for Justice, Hunt for Jack Reacher, and Heir Hunter series, and the Jess Kimball Thrillers. She's a recovering lawyer and snowbird who divides her time between Florida and Michigan. An active member of Mystery Writers of America, Author's Guild, International Thriller Writers, Alliance of Independent Authors, and Sisters in Crime, she loves to hear from readers and is hard at work on her next novel.

Please connect with her online:

Website: http://www.DianeCapri.com
Twitter: http://twitter.com/@DianeCapri
Facebook: http://www.facebook.com/Diane.Capri1
http://www.facebook.com/DianeCapriBooks

If you would like to be kept up to date with infrequent email including release dates for Diane Capri books, free offers, gifts, and general information for members only, please sign up for our Diane Capri mailing list. We don't want to leave you out! Sign up here:

http://dianecapri.com/get-involved/get-my-newsletter/

CPSIA information can be obtained
at www.ICGtesting.com
Printed in the USA
LVHW112158090821
694964LV00016B/382